THE GHOST
OF
CAPTAIN HINCHLIFFE

A NOVEL

BASED ON ACTUAL EVENTS

DAVID DENNINGTON

ALSO BY DAVID DENNINGTON

THE AIRSHIPMEN

*My deepest gratitude to my consulting editor Lauren Dennington
—the best.*

ISBN- 13: 978-1546638506
ISBN- 10: 1546638504

Website: http://www.daviddennington.com
Twitter: @ddennington1
Facebook:

This is a work of fiction with both real, historical figures and fictitious characters based on actual
events which occurred between 1920 and 1930. Some events, dates and locations have been
changed for dramatic purposes and artistic license has been taken throughout.

While *The Ghost of Captain Hinchliffe* is based on actual events, characters, characterizations,
incidents, locations, and dialogue have been invented and fictionalized in order to dramatize the
story and are products of the author's imagination. The fictionalization, or invention of events, or
relocation of events is for dramatic purposes and not intended to reflect on actual historical
characters, history, entities or organizations, past or present. This novel is not intended to right
any wrongs or 'set the record straight' regarding past events or actions, but is intended to
entertain. Readers are encouraged to research the vast array of books on this subject from which
the author has drawn facts as well as the essence of events and characters. In all other respects,
resemblance to persons living or dead must be construed as coincidental.

Printed by CreateSpace, an Amazon.com Company.

Available from Amazon.com and other retail outlets.

Available on Kindle and other retail outlets.

For Laurie & Lee

And

Richard & Katie

With Great Love

"Death gives you a whole new perspective on life."

The Ghost of Captain Hinchliffe. May, 1928

Elsie Mackay

1

CAXTON HALL

Saturday, December 20, 1930.

It was dark and it was cold when Millie arrived at Caxton Hall in a black Daimler sent by the organizers to collect her from Pickwick Cottage. Despite the weather, there were throngs of people under the canopy awaiting Millie's arrival at the front steps. Two festive Christmas trees, decorated with colored lights, stood each side of the entrance. An advertisement in a glass case announced coming events.

TONIGHT 8 p.m.

MRS. HINCHLIFFE SPEAKS

LIFE AFTER DEATH

Speed Graphics flashed as Millie elegantly eased herself out of the limousine onto the sidewalk. For a few moments she posed, beneath a striking, red cloche hat, wrapped in black furs, her face radiant. Photographers and reporters pushed forward excitedly around her, calling out their questions.

"Mrs. Hinchliffe, what've you come to tell us this evening?"

"I am overjoyed! And tonight I shall tell you why," Millie responded.

"Is it true you're writing a book ma'am?"

"How do you feel about airships now?"

Millie closed her eyes, pained. "I'm very sad—and extremely bitter, as you can imagine. I suppose hard lessons have been learned by our government—at least we can only hope so!"

She made her way to the doors and was escorted along a corridor to the rear of the stage in the Great Hall. Caxton Hall, a place of some notoriety, built of red brick and pink stone, had once been Westminster's town hall. It'd also been a meeting place for British suffragettes, who held a Women's Parliament there and then marched to the Houses of Parliament each year to present a petition to the prime minister. The hall was also used by occultist Aleister Crowley, where his Rites of Eleusis—which some considered blasphemous and immoral—were performed. This was where concerts were held and where the famous performed.

There was an excited buzz in the auditorium filled with mostly older ladies dressed in their Sunday best. At last, the house lights were dimmed and a voice came over the speakers.

"Ladies and gentlemen, welcome to Caxton Hall. It gives us great pleasure to bring you a lady who needs no introduction, a person whom the British people have taken to their hearts. A lady who has for the past two years issued dire warnings—warnings from the grave. Mrs. Emilie Hinchliffe will speak to you about her experiences and the subject of 'life after death'. Please give a big welcome to *Mrs. Emilie Hinchliffe!*"

Enthusiastic applause erupted. All eyes watched the dark blue stage curtains in anticipation. And then, to everyone's delight, came the lamentation of Beethoven's Moonlight Sonata in its own mournful, ghostly voice. The Great Hall fell silent. The curtains slowly opened to reveal Millie at a grand piano, dressed in cobalt blue, surrounded by her artwork displayed on easels, each bathed in its own beam of light.

When Millie had finished playing the first movement, she got up and came to the lectern amid cheers and more applause. She looked down into the front row seats into faces she knew well, especially her good friend, Mrs. East. As the applause died, Millie instinctively scanned the auditorium for Hinchliffe. She checked the end seat on the back row. It was the only empty one in the house. A wave of sadness washed over her and her heart almost stopped. He'd gone. She'd be on her own from now on. For solace, she put her hand to her neck, touching Elsie's gold crucifix, preparing herself to begin. But before she did, she thought of Doyle. How she missed him. He'd been so good to her—a protective father figure. She remembered his words, and did as he'd instructed. She lifted her head high and spoke boldly to those at the back of the auditorium.

"Good evening, my name is Emilie Hinchliffe—my friends call me Millie." More applause. "... I've come here tonight to tell you my

THE GHOST OF CAPTAIN HINCHLIFFE

story." She gestured to the relevant subject of artwork as she spoke. "It's about an heiress, an aeroplane, a ghost, and the *mightiest* airship the world has ever seen."

Five hundred ladies and a handful of men listened in rapt attention, eager for answers. Nearly three years ago, Mrs. East, whom Millie had come to know and love, had been as equally transfixed at her kitchen table, next to the fire-grate oven. The old woman had sat watching the planchette on her Ouija board move slowly from letter to letter. Keeping her left hand on the wheeled gadget, with her right, she'd written down an incoming message in wobbly block capitals with a thick, black pencil.

PLEASE HELP ME I AM A DROWNED PILOT

Later, when Millie read those words, they'd made her cry. She smiled at Mrs. East and went on, "I know you've read the story of what happened to me, and to my husband and to many of his friends recently. Tonight, I'm going to tell you the *whole* story. During and after that terrible war, Ouija boards became an obsession. How could they not, with so many of our husbands, sons, fathers and brothers lost —not to mention our sisters who went to nurse those very men at the Front in those fields of death, to comfort and to heal. and who were, themselves, killed. My husband always called them 'Angels of Mercy'. There wasn't a family that hadn't lost *someone*. First, I'm going to tell you about the man I love and why at this moment I'm so happy. No, it's not about the money, although that will help of course, and guarantee our family's future, which Raymond so desperately wanted."

At this, applause broke out again accompanied by cheers—they'd heard all about *that*.

"Life was perfect. Raymond was a vibrant man, full of life and energy—and still is, I want you to know! He was a decorated war pilot, having shot down six enemy planes. Then he, himself, was shot down in the dark of night, crash-landing in a tree in Nieppe Forest. He never spoke of the horrors of that night—even to me. He didn't like to think about it."

The audience was giving Millie its undivided attention.

"Getting shot down cost 'Hinch' his left eye, and caused a bad leg injury. But this horrendous event didn't stop him, or diminish his love of flying, nor did it reduce his great sense of humor. He spent six months in hospital and three months at a convalescent home. He continued flying, getting certified in just about every plane there was. After the war, Raymond joined the new Royal Dutch Airline KLM, becoming their chief pilot. It was there, in Holland, that we met. I was at art school and working for KLM part time as a shorthand typist. A year later, we were married at a lovely, little church here in England. Many of his friends were in attendance—some of whom sadly are no longer with us, due to recent tragic events.

"After six blissful years of marriage, we had two beautiful daughters. Most days, he was off flying passengers to the Continent, at first with KLM, and then later with Imperial Airways. They loved him, but he said some passengers were a little fearful being flown by a one-eyed pilot.

There were a few chuckles at this.

"He pioneered new routes for Imperial with his close friend, 'Johnny' Johnston 'the Navigator'. They'd flown to India, Ismailia and Baghdad.

"One year, Hinch was asked to go to an aerodrome in France to *discreetly* retrieve a German Fokker war plane, which many of the French had taken exception to. They didn't want it anywhere near their Paris Airshow—and who could blame them for *that?*"

2

THE FOKKER

Monday, June 15, 1925.

Water splashed into the hedgerows from the brown and khaki war limousine as it rushed along the country roads near Thiepval toward Hinchliffe's old aerodrome. He'd been based there during the war—one of several places. He sat in the back seat. Smoke swirled from a cigarette he held in his left hand. In his right, between his thumb and forefinger, he rolled a string of worry beads with its black cat lucky charm—something he'd picked up at the souk in Baghdad and carried with him always. At this moment, being alone, his rugged face was haunted, his jaw set, his piercing gray eye, searching. Memories were still vivid, especially in *this* place. He heard the rat-a-tat-tat of Fokkers on his tail; saw exploding Archie and black smoke around him, planes on fire, men in flames, friends leaping out in death agony.

He was jarred from his reverie as the car slowed to turn onto the aerodrome. He resumed his determined air, taking a last drag on his cigarette before throwing it out. At the airport building, the car came to a stop and Hinchliffe clambered out with a word of thanks to the driver. He drew up his six-foot-one frame, his back ram-rod straight, and marched across the gravel parking area, his slight limp just discernible. He entered the office building. Two young secretaries looked at him approvingly, and then at one another.

"Bonjour, mesdemoiselles," Hinchliffe said.

"Bonjour, monsieur," the girls said together.

"I'm Captain Hinchliffe. I'm here to pick up the Fokker for KLM." His English was tinged with a Scouse accent. He repeated it in French.

The girls' eyes met again knowingly. One licked her lips.

"Zee Fokker is 'ere, waiting for you, monsieur," one said. Hinchliffe smiled to himself. A small, balding man fluttered in from an adjoining office, a look of disdain, a permanent smell under a bulbous nose.

"So, you 'ave finally come to remove this piece of junk from French soil, monsieur!" he snapped.

Hinchliffe grinned, unfazed—prone to toy with such people.

"I understand your sentiments exactly. I've had my share of encounters with these lousy Fokkers. I've had them shooting at me on *many* occasions."

The little man was suddenly interested. "Ah, really, monsieur?"

"One thing I can tell you though, these Fokkers are *not* junk!"

"It is *junk*, I tell you! Pah!"

Hinchliffe winked at the secretaries. "Bon après-midi, mesdemoiselles," he said, as he turned and walked out the glazed doors.

"Good riddance to you, English pig, and to your damned Fokker!" the airport manager snapped as the door closed.

"Beautiful English pig!" one girl purred.

Hinchliffe walked round the building to the plane: a gleaming red Fokker DR1 triplane. Hinchliffe caught his breath when he saw the black German crosses emblazoned on the side and tailplane. He'd seen these things in the Red Baron's flying circus. They used to swarm in masses of thirty or forty. They'd been imposing, although not always ready to engage.

He was joined by a mechanic, who told him the plane was gassed up, checked and ready. They nodded to each other, and after Hinchliffe had physically made his own inspection, he climbed aboard, pulling on his leather flying cap and goggles. He checked the gauges and worked the rudders and ailerons. Everything appeared to be in order. He ritualistically pulled out his lucky black cat on its chain of worry beads and hung it on the instrument panel and then gave the signal for the mechanic to prime the engine. This was done with a couple of turns of the propeller. The mechanic stood back.

Hinchliffe shouted, "Clear!" After turning on the magnetos, he gave another shout, "Contact!"

The mechanic swung the propeller. It caught first time with a pop, and the chocks were pulled away from the wheels. Hinchliffe eased on the throttle and with a roar, the Fokker pulled away. With a wave to the man, he moved toward the grassy runway.

Hinchliffe gave it full throttle and the aeroplane charged forward. The mechanic stood watching; in moments, the shiny machine was airborne, tearing into low cloud. The manager, who was watching from the window, stood with his hands behind his back, relaxed, pleased to get that horrible reminder of the war removed from his aerodrome. He nodded in satisfaction. But this was short-lived. Suddenly, they heard the unmistakable screaming whine of a plane descending from a great height above their heads—the sound of a crashing plane.

A broad grin filled Hinchliffe's face in the inverted Fokker's cockpit as it sped toward the airport building. The little Frenchman rushed back to the window, where he saw the Fokker speeding toward him at an elevation of twenty feet. The girls threw themselves under their desks. After skidding across the polished parquet floor, the manager dived down to join them.

In the cockpit, Hinchliffe whooped with glee and then pulled the plane up at the last moment. The tail missed the roof by inches and the building shook violently. Hinchliffe rolled twice, turned right side up, and climbed away into the clouds.

"Well, so much for discretion!" he muttered. He banked the plane around and set course for Holland, leaving a glorious red sky in his wake.

3

PICKWICK COTTAGE

Tuesday, June 16, 1925.

The following afternoon, Hinchliffe made a return flight with a plane full of passengers from Amsterdam to Croydon Airport. On arrival, he climbed into his sporty, dark green Bentley Continental and sped home. He always loved to get home to Millie and their three-year-old daughter, Joan. They'd bought the cottage with a small inheritance from his aunt in Lancashire and they'd built a modern, glazed addition, complete with a stone fireplace, as a studio for Millie. The blend of old and new set off the ancient cottage exceedingly well. They'd also built an extension at the other end, adding a bedroom and bathroom for guests.

The cottage, mostly of brick, had been painted with red paint at one time and this grinned through the white stucco in some places, adding a patina. An old stable and barn served as a garage and workshop. Some parts of the house were clad with white clapboard. The roof was thatched. It'd become their dream house. They named it 'Pickwick Cottage'. Millie liked the sound of it.

The glass studio was Millie's domain, for her art, photography and piano. In that room, she kept an old Steinway grand—not much to look at, but it sounded beautiful. She kept it in tune herself. As well as being a fine artist, Millie was an accomplished pianist. She'd had lessons in Holland as a girl, and although they said she was 'exceptionally gifted', she refused to pursue a career in music. She never felt comfortable playing in front of people. Hinchliffe always thought her talent wasted, which was true. Millie only had to hear a piece of music once, and she could play it back note for note. Similarly, if she saw something or someone once, she could draw them, or paint them. With the piano, as with her art, Millie released her emotions through her expressive, beautifully shaped hands, stroking and caressing the keys with tenderness, or sometimes pounding them. The melody ebbed and flowed, becoming a rushing torrent of a tidal river at one moment, and then a cascading waterfall another, or the calmer waters of an estuary, running smooth and deep.

Hinchliffe sped through the Surrey lanes into Kent, crossing a farm to their small hamlet of Toys Hill. This location was handy for Croydon Aerodrome and they could still live in splendid isolation. The village boasted a tiny post office and combined general store, a pub—the Coach & Horses—a beautiful 16th century Gothic church—St. Saviour's, and one of the brand-new, red phone boxes, which were sprouting up all over the country. Presently, after climbing the hills overlooking the Weald, he spied the cottage over the fields in the distance, located across the lane from Barney, the Blacksmith's shop. The cottage sat cozily between green walnut trees and hedges. Beside it, he noticed sheets billowing on the washing line. Millie had been busy. He had an idea.

He knew Millie would be in the garden on such a fine, sunny afternoon. She called it her 'little piece of heaven on earth'. In addition to other things, she was an avid gardener. The cottage was set in a typical English garden, an explosion of color from spring through autumn—a haven for birds of every kind. Their favorite place was the secret garden, enclosed by high, ancient red brick walls and tall boxwood hedges. A heavy, arched door closed off the entry, which could be bolted from the inside. They liked to sit on the park bench in that peaceful setting and read, or meditate under the walnut tree, while taking in the fragrances of blooms around them. Hinchliffe had slung a hammock between the wall and a small oak tree in which Millie liked to snooze, or lie naked in the summer sun.

Hinchliffe was trying to give up cigarettes and would sometimes sit in the garden puffing his Sherlock Holmes calabash pipe, listening to birds and buzzing insects and the gurgling brook nearby. Things were going well in their lives. With Millie's backing, he was making a good living, flying full time, and once in a while, transporting some VIP or other on a long-distance journey. Such VIPs included Ramsay MacDonald, the previous prime minister, Lord Thomson of Cardington, the past minister of state for air, and Alfred Lowenstein, one of the richest men in Europe—not exactly a friend, but Hinchliffe was probably the closest thing to a friend Lowenstein actually had. Hinchliffe and Millie were a good couple, deliriously happy, supporting each other's needs. But all that was about to change.

Hinchliffe turned slowly into the long, gravel driveway, passing the white picket fence he'd started building months ago. He needed to get

on and finish that one of these days. He cut the engine and coasted
toward the washing lines. All was silent, except for tweeting birds and
the faint pounding of Barney's hammer at his forge across the lane. He
could see Millie, her back to him, standing at her easel under the
wooden pergola. She was working on an oil painting of the brook and
rustic outbuildings. Two magpies dominated the scene. She was
carefully brushing in reeds at the water's edge with a fine sable brush.

A large sunhat obscured her beautiful face and long, shiny locks. A
paint-spattered beige smock covered her ample bosom, slender waist
and slim hips, from her neck to her ankles. Their daughter, Joan, was
playing with a frog she'd snatched from the brook, watched by Butch,
a black Labrador who loved to splash around in that water. In all her
twenty-eight years, Millie had never been so happy. He'd be home
soon. Good. She listened for the Bentley's growl.

Hinchliffe stealthily slipped out of the car and up to the washing.
He unpegged one of the sheets, threw it over his head and crept toward
Millie and Joan, waving his arms and making spooky noises.
"Oooooooh! Oooooooooh! Oooooooooooooh!"

Suddenly, Butch spotted the ghost and went on the defense, rushing
at Hinchliffe, barking ferociously. Joan was frightened at first, until
she recognized the flying boots at the ends of the legs, under the sheet.
Millie turned from her painting, her big, blue eyes wide, mildly
surprised for a moment. She shook her head as she put down her
brushes and pallet. Joan ran to her daddy, arms spread-eagled like an
aeroplane. Hinchliffe swept her high into the air, making plane noises,
while she giggled. But the dog persisted.

"That's enough Butch! It's only daddy, silly," Millie scolded. She
gave Hinchliffe a big kiss. They came together in big unified hug and
Butch, finally calm, stood on his hind legs, paws on Hinchliffe's hip.

"Come on, Captain Hinchliffe, I'll make you a cup of tea," Millie
said brightly, plucking her painting from its easel.

Hinchliffe glanced at it. "Lovely picture! You just love them
magpies, don't you!"

"As long as there's more than one," Millie answered.

Hinchliffe patted her behind as they trooped into the kitchen. Jars
of freshly bottled jam stood on the table. They were followed in by
Whiskey the tabby-cat, who jumped up, purring and mewing like mad
at Hinchliffe. Millie opened the fireplace oven and took out one of her
fresh baked loaves and a batch of scones. Hinchliffe breathed in
deeply.

"You've been busy, I see. This place smells like heaven," he exclaimed, seizing the cat and nuzzling her.

"You've come to the right place," Millie said. She put the kettle on and got the cups out. "Perhaps you'd drop a loaf and a couple of jars of jam over to Barney later, Hinch."

"Anything for you and ol' Barney," Hinchliffe said, grabbing Millie. He danced her and the cat around the kitchen, bursting into song, "Just Millie and me, and Joanie makes three, I'm happy in my green heaven—it's a cozy place, with a fireplace and a studio ..." He continued with his adaption of the song, now popular on the radio. Joan was delighted to be included.

"You're a good dancer—but the singing—not so much. You'd better keep your job with Imperial Airways," Millie said with a laugh. Hinchliffe frowned. She'd struck a nerve.

With a tray of tea and scones, they moved to Millie's studio, the largest room in the house. Its French windows along the entire back wall overlooked the garden. Millie set the tray down on her work table. Paintings and photographs adorned the walls—one or two done by Hinchliffe (he wasn't a bad artist himself). Propped up on a display shelf were two almost identical portraits of Alfred Lowenstein, wearing a business suit and a shiny top hat. In the second version, he was rather bland—meek even. In the first, his face displayed cunning and ruthlessness.

"I see you like old Lowenstein so much you painted him twice." Hinchliffe said.

"No, I don't like the man much, but I like the painting—the first one, that is. I'll keep it to show. I'll send him the second one," Millie replied.

"Poor old Lowenstein—he's *all right!* Somehow, I don't think he'd like the first one, though."

"Probably not."

"Good luck getting paid," Hinchliffe said with a half-smile.

Lowenstein had asked Millie many times to paint his portrait and, in the end she did reluctantly. She hadn't liked the way the man's eyes wandered all over her body. But she did it for Hinchliffe's sake. Lowenstein had the reputation of being a bully and of his business practices not always on the up and up. But he'd treated her husband all right, so far. He had a bad aura about him—much of it dark, unlike her husband's which she found to be a thing of beauty.

Sun streamed through the roof skylights onto another painting—an unfinished one—on its own easel. They sat beside it and had their tea and scones, smothered with jam and cream. Joan worked on a crayon drawing on the oak floor boards. Millie took fresh flowers she'd cut from the garden and laid them on the table. She began arranging them in a vase.

"I suppose, since your little 'Fokking expedition', we're permanently banned from France now, are we Hinch?" she asked, one eyebrow raised.

Hinchliffe cracked up. He was studying the unfinished painting. It was of a man standing by his plane—obviously Hinchliffe. "When are you going to finish this? Well, I just wouldn't plan your holidays there, if I were you, sweet pea."

Millie stopped to peer at the unfinished work. "Oh, I don't know, I'm thinking about it—probably when you finish my fence!"

Hinchliffe chuckled and gave her one of his 'touché' looks.

"And I suppose Scotland Yard will be knocking on our door any time soon, will they?" Millie added.

Hinchliffe loved what she'd done with this room. Much of the wall space was taken up with pictures and professional quality photographs of the children, Hinchliffe, local scenes, flowers. In the far corner, next to her dark room, a plate camera stood on a tripod. A smaller camera lay on the piano. On another easel was an enlarged photo of Hinchliffe in his wartime army lieutenant's uniform. Hinchliffe admired himself.

"You know, I hadn't realized I was so good looking."

"You ought to—you know you're my favorite subject. ... Oh, we had a letter from Kate Sinclair this morning. She said Gordon has lost his job and they don't have a roof over their heads—at least they won't in week or so."

"Tell them they can stay here as long as they like—we've got plenty of room—providing you don't mind."

"Oh, I don't mind. But let's hope *you've* still got a job by the end of the week!"

Hinchliffe coughed. He peered at the picture again. "When did you say you'd finish this?"

"I'll get around to it sometime, maybe. I need some materials."

"This isn't bad. You must finish it. We'll get you some more materials at the end of the month. The aerodrome manager was rude about the plane. That's all. Don't worry, it'll blow over."

"You and your precious Fokker!"

Hinchliffe grinned. It tickled him when she said that in her sexy Dutch accent. "Hey, you watch your language, Emilie Hinchliffe!"

After dinner, they went to bed early. Joan was in the next room. After a passionate hour, they lay together, sharing a cigarette. Hinchliffe's eyes scanned the walls, which were also adorned with photos: Hinchliffe and Millie standing together in their courting days, two years between them, an inflated inner tube around their necks, Hinchliffe standing beside his Sopwith Camel in a leather flying coat, collar up, his flying goggles pushed up over his flying cap—the indomitable ace. On the side of the plane were the marks of his six kills and the plane's name: *Allo Lil Bird.*

At times like this, they liked to chat, sometimes for hours. They talked about many subjects. They spoke about God and religion. Millie had attended Catholic church as a girl, but over time her faith had fallen by the wayside. It had been the same with Hinchliffe who'd attended the Church of England as a boy. Both of them were not 'religious', although they believed in 'something'—a superior being. After his brush with death and miraculous escape during the war, Hinchliffe was more than a little open minded about these things. Millie though, had premonitions, usually small things that happened. She supposed everyone did. Hinchliffe teased her about it sometimes, wiggling his nose and calling her 'my beautiful white witch'.

Hinchliffe kissed her cheek and grimaced. "Millie, I love you and the children more than anything, but you know, if I can't fly, I'll go nuts."

"Why, what's up?"

"They're dreaming up new regulations for one-eyed pilots."

"Nervous passengers?"

"Yup, I've gotta find something else."

It was on this night that Millie had the first of a recurring dream she was to have over the next couple of years. After a long kiss goodnight, they put out the lantern and fell into a deep sleep. A little after 3:00 a.m., Millie awoke from a dream. She sensed the presence of a man standing over her. He was more of a dark shape than anything —a shape without a face. She didn't feel threatened or frightened. Quite the reverse. Strangely, she was comforted by it. She drifted back to sleep with a feeling of calmness and well-being.

4

A DRINK AT THE ROYAL AERO CLUB

Monday, June 13, 1927.

E ver since his talk with Millie about his flying future, Hinchliffe
had nurtured ideas about making an Atlantic bid. In 1927, two
men had vied to be the first Americans across the pond from
west to east. One was Charles Lindbergh, a successful pilot, the other,
Charles Levine, a business entrepreneur. Lindbergh wound up beating
Levine to the punch, whereby his name would be forever enshrined in
the record books. Shortly after Lindbergh's solo achievement, Charles
Levine flew as a passenger from New York to Berlin. Once there,
Levine negotiated with Hinchliffe to fly him back to New York, and
thereby claim the east to west record—a much tougher proposition.
However, when all seemed settled, Levine decided he wanted to bring
a woman along for the ride—American socialite, Mabel Boll.
Hinchliffe would have none of that, and backed out immediately.
Hinchliffe was stuck and needed to find another sponsor—quickly.
Millie had gone along with the plan originally, but was relieved when
the Levine deal fell through.

He pondered asking Lowenstein to finance the project, but thought
better of it—if Lowenstein was interested, he would've initiated it.
Besides, Hinchliffe sometimes wondered if Lowenstein was as rich as
he appeared and if his business was fully solvent. His lifestyle,
aeroplanes, limousines and splendid properties in England and
Belgium led everyone to believe he was fabulously wealthy.
Hinchliffe wondered if maybe old Lowenstein had built himself a
house of cards.

Hinchliffe discussed his looming employment problem with his
good friend Sir Sefton Brancker, the Director of Civil Aviation. After
telling Brancker about the debacle with Charles Levine, Brancker
suggested that they get together for a drink to talk about Hinchliffe's

options. On a sunny afternoon in June of '27, Hinchliffe parked the Bentley on Piccadilly. He waited for passing cars and horse-drawn carts and, after stepping around sweet-smelling piles of horse droppings, crossed the road to the Royal Aero Club.

The one-eyed pilot was well-known in aviation circles, especially in the Royal Air Force and the Royal Naval Air Service. He'd flown a number of VIP's to far-flung places including many from this club. Hinchliffe was a member of the Aero Club, being a well-respected war pilot and holder of the Distinguished Flying Cross. The gentlemen's bar was located on the second floor. Its ambiance bore out its name with highly polished wooden floors, brass foot rails and bar uprights, portraits of great airmen adorning the walls and stuffy old men ensconced in deep, studded leather armchairs, hidden behind *The Times* or the *Daily Telegraph.*

One such patron was Alfred Lowenstein, whom Hinchliffe spotted as he entered the bar. Lowenstein had his head in a newspaper, which he lowered slightly on hearing Hinchliffe's footsteps. The only sign of recognition Lowenstein offered was a bored grunt and a grimace from his haggard, red face. Hinchliffe gave him a nod accompanied by an amused grin. He was used to Lowenstein's rudeness. He was a strange man.

At the bar, Hinchliffe was greeted by Brancker in his usual boisterous manner, after he'd got down from his perch on a high bar stool. At times, Brancker's initial appearance was deceiving. He appeared slightly unkempt and ill-bred in his rough tweeds. He made everyone feel special. And men like Hinchliffe *were* very special to him. Brancker's own record was impressive, being the youngest brigadier general holding important positions with the Royal Flying Corps and the Royal Air Force when he directed wartime flying operations.

"My dear Hinchliffe, so lovely to see you," he said. "What'll it be, old man?" His voice was rich and deep, and he spoke the most beautiful King's English.

"Just a pale ale, thanks," Hinchliffe said, hoisting himself onto a bar stool.

"How's that lovely wife of yours?"

"Millie's very well, Branks, thank you—in all her bloom—with our second one on the way."

"*Congratulations!* How far along is she?"

"Three months," Hinchliffe answered.

Hinchliffe knew Brancker wore a toupee. He found it endearing and tried his best not to focus on it. The barman took a bottle of light ale from the shelf and poured it into a tall glass for Hinchliffe.

"I was hoping she'd paint my portrait—would she still be able?"

"Oh, absolutely. Please come. She'd be delighted to see you."

"I certainly shall. Seen anything of our good friends Irwin and Johnny lately?"

"Well, I haven't seen Johnny since we did our last India trip, and Bird—not for a while."

Captain Carmichael Irwin's nickname, the future captain of *Cardington R101*, was 'Blackbird' or 'Bird'.

"You really ought to go up and see them, you know. They'd put down the red carpet for you."

Hinchliffe took a swig of beer. He was thirsty. It tasted good.

"So, you're serious about breaking some world records?" Brancker continued.

"The £10,000 *Daily Mail* prize would set us up for life," Hinchliffe said.

"What happened to Levine? I thought you were all set to go roaring off."

"That all fell apart. I need to do something *immediately*."

Brancker gave a sideways nod toward Lowenstein over in the corner. "What about him over there?" he whispered.

Hinchliffe screwed up his face and shook his head as though it was a bad idea. "No. I don't think so."

Things were getting urgent if he was to have a go at the Atlantic record. The world had been abuzz since May 21st when Lindbergh had landed at Lebourget, near Paris. The French had gone wild with excitement. Now, everyone was hell-bent on being the first to fly the Atlantic from east to west. Atlantic fever was palpable in Europe. Time was running out.

"Yes, the new regs are coming into effect next year," said Brancker.

"My days with Imperial are numbered. Flight records or private flights are all I have left."

"They were only too glad of you when there were hardly any pilots left. I may be the Director of Civil Aviation, but I don't make the rules!"

"More's the pity."

"You're better with one eye than any of these new young pilots with two. Remember, dear boy, whatever you decide to do, I'm at your disposal. We pioneers must stick together. There are tons of girls out there looking for someone like you to help promote *'the cause'*. I have one such gal in mind. In fact, I spoke to her only yesterday—she's an heiress—'bout thirty, and she's loaded! They say she's the richest woman in Great Britain—certainly the best dressed—and undressed too, I shouldn't wonder! She's dying to get in on this whole thing. She's a wild one—and a *real* looker!"

"You think she's worth considering?"

"Oh, most definitely!" Brancker gave him a sly wink. "But seriously, she's been a disaster, I suppose, a bit of a tearaway, but she's not a bad gal. She was married for a bit. She's a well-known stage actress too—"

"I don't follow all that stuff," Hinchliffe said, his interest waning.

"No, she's accomplished in a lot of ways. She's an interior designer for her father's ships, she's an engineer of sorts—and she's a *pilot!*"

Hinchliffe's interest perked up again. "Hmm, maybe I should talk to her, then."

"As I said, I spoke to her yesterday, and mentioned you. And she got *very* excited."

Hinchliffe nodded.

"She's very determined—I'll say that for her," Brancker added.

Suddenly, they were interrupted by a woman's cough at the doorway. And then a silky voice.

"Captain Hinchliffe?"

There was a great rustling as whiskey-sodden, red-faced gentlemen lowered their newspapers in unison, to peer down their noses at this unwelcome obtrusion—a woman at the door of the gentlemen's bar no less!

"Captain Hinchliffe?" the voice repeated.

All conversation ceased. What they saw was an exotically dressed beauty. She stood with one patent leather, two-eyelet, polka-dotted shoe over the threshold—an intolerable, some would say, sacrilegious, act! This vision, this gorgeous feast for the eyes, after adjusting the chic kerchief collar of her black silk crêpe dress, ignored their hostility and loped purposefully toward Hinchliffe. They watched her hips and her swaying box skirt as she moved. Brancker adjusted his monocle, fascinated and full of admiration.

"Captain Hinchliffe, my name is Elsie Mackay." Her voice was public school, Cambridge perhaps, with maybe a hint of refined Western Scotland in there.

"Your father owns most of the ships in the Atlantic, I believe?" Hinchliffe answered coolly.

"Only those of the P&O Line," she corrected.

Brancker climbed down from his bar stool and Elsie kissed him on both cheeks and shook Hinchliffe's hand.

"Well, look you two, don't mind me. I have to get back to an airship budget meeting at the office," Brancker said. Hinchliffe gave him a sideways look, realizing her arrival at this moment was no accident.

Brancker slunk out of the bar like a man who'd just lit a fuse. Elsie leaned in closely toward Hinchliffe and whispered. He felt her warm breath on his cheek. Her long eyelashes fluttered.

"I hear you want to take a shot at the Atlantic?"

Hinchliffe glanced at the door where Brancker had exited. "I wonder where you heard that," he said.

"I also heard Charles Levine dropped you."

"No, I dropped him."

"Why?"

"He wanted to take some woman along. Some feminist dame!"

"You have something against women flying aeroplanes?"

"No, three's a crowd, that's all. We'd have all ended up in the drink, and I don't wanna be in the drink!"

"That's logical, I suppose."

"Besides, it all turned out to be just talk."

"Talk's cheap," Elsie said. Then her 1920's eyes opened wide and bore into him, seducing and imploring. "Have lunch with me. I have a *serious* proposition for you."

Hinchliffe hesitated. He scratched his chin.

"What harm could it do?" she whispered with a disarming smile.

"It could kill me, I suppose."

He could think of a million reasons. He caved.

"Tomorrow. 1 o'clock. The Ritz. I've booked a table," she said.

"You're pretty damned sure of yourself, aren't you?"

"I know what I want, Captain Hinchliffe. And I know how to make things happen," she purred.

They decided to leave the bar as the other patrons were getting restless and the barman was looking most uncomfortable. As they made for the door, Elsie turned and addressed them.

"Gentlemen, I'd like you all to know that I am the proud holder of a Royal Aero Club Pilot's license! Maybe one day, I'll buy you *all* a drink."

No one said a word.

5

LUNCH AT THE RITZ

Tuesday, June 14, 1927.

The following day, Hinchliffe arrived outside the Ritz a few minutes early. His car was spirited away by the hotel valet. Before entering the building, he noticed a Rolls Royce slowing at the curb. He thought as much—it was Elsie. Her chauffeur opened her door and she slipped out, smiling up at Hinchliffe on the steps. She was dressed from head to toe in another splendid outfit. She'd obviously spent a lot of time on her getup this morning. Hinchliffe wasn't used to this. Millie wasn't a fashion-crazed flapper who spent hours on her hair and nails. *She* was a natural beauty. At this moment, he appreciated his wife even more.

All heads turned as they made their way into the dining room, where the maître d' recognized Elsie. Judging by the fuss he made, she was a regular patron. He led them to a quiet table off to the side hidden away behind green ferns and palms, with views of the park.

"I thought we could use a little privacy," Elsie said.

Hinchliffe stood as a waiter pulled out a chair for Elsie. They sat down and the maitre d' gave them menus with recommendations for the fresh trout, which they both accepted, after a starter of vichyssoise.

Elsie studied the wine menu. "I'd like to order a bottle of champagne." She noticed Hinchliffe frown. "No, not a premature celebration. Let's drink to the possibilities." She gave him a disarming smile and raised her eyebrows. "And to a new friendship, perhaps?" she said, as she placed a napkin in her lap.

A champagne bucket was brought to the table and the cork popped. Frothy bubbles fizzed into flutes. Hinchliffe was relieved to see the fizz didn't run over. He knew that French superstition from his days on leave in the Paris estaminets. He noticed a fellow with a five-o'clock shadow across the room eyeing Elsie through the ferns. She'd seen him too, but refused to acknowledge the poor sap's presence.

"One of yours?" Hinchliffe enquired.

"God no! No one of importance to me, I assure you."

Hinchliffe didn't see why it mattered. "Just an admirer, then."

Elsie looked into Hinchliffe's face as they chinked glasses, "To the possibilities," she said. He could see she was studying his eye-patch and scar. "Care to tell me about it?" she asked.

"No." Was all he said. He saw a wave of sadness pass over her face and a glimmer of compassion in her eyes.

She left it alone.

The vichyssoise arrived. Before they took up their spoons, Elsie held the gold crucifix at her throat between her fingers and closed her eyes. Hinchliffe assumed she was saying grace to herself. "You'll need more than a few prayers, you know," he said. She knew what he meant. She exchanged glances with the waiter who'd obviously heard the remark. She ignored Hinchliffe's rudeness. He continued, "What experience have you had, Miss Mackay?"

Her eyelashes fluttered, barely noticeable, as though not sure if his question contained a hint sexual innuendo. He watched her slip her sensitive fingers up and down the stem of her glass feeling its smoothness. She must have decided after looking into his stern face, it did not. She looked slightly disappointed. He could tell she was taken by his rugged good looks. He now sensed hunger in those eyes.

"I do most of my flying around Europe—for my own amusement," she answered.

Hinchliffe visualized her flitting around from one hot playground of the rich to another. She certainly was a beautiful woman though, he had to admit.

"I see," he said blandly.

The waiter whisked away the soup bowls and Elsie continued. "I intend to be the first woman to make the crossing," she said firmly.

"Whatever for? You certainly don't need the money."

"It's my destiny." She struck an idealistic pose, her magnificent eyes looking heavenward. "It's time women came out into the twentieth century, is it not?"

This irritated Hinchliffe. He'd heard too much of this nonsense lately. It was all the rage and it bored him. "I hadn't thought of making this flight on behalf of the women's movement, Miss Mackay," he said dryly. He thought of Millie at that moment. He was sure she'd agree. As far as he was concerned Millie was an independent woman, who lived her life the way *she* chose. Not a bad life, either.

Elsie pulled back. "Oh, no, ... I ..."

They hesitated while their trout was served.

"If I *were* to do it, Miss Mackay, it would be for the sake of aviation ... not to mention the money!"

"I'm prepared to finance *everything!*" Elsie said.

"Miss Mackay, do you have the slightest idea how difficult it would be to fly to America? This isn't a hop skip and a jump to gay *Paree* or *Cannes,* you know."

"I'll pay you a salary of eighty pounds—paid directly into your bank account every month."

Hinchliffe tried not to think about her tempting words. "I don't think you have any concept of what you'd be getting yourself into."

"I'm not interested in the ten thousand pounds prize money," Elsie said. Hinchliffe sat stony-faced. This really was tempting. "*That* would be all yours," she said.

"Thirty or forty hours of sitting in a freezing-cold, ear-splitting, nerve-wracking, flying fuel tank, with no toilet—that's what you'd be looking at, Miss Mackay. I doubt a little rich girl could handle that."

"Listen mister, by that time, we'll have got to know one another pretty well. I can pee in a jar like the rest of 'em."

A hint of smile passed over Hinchliffe's face at the thought of that. "I'll need to go too, you know," he said.

"I was a nurse in the war. I've seen it all. So don't you worry yourself about that," she said.

He leaned back in his chair, reassessing her. This endeared her to Hinchliffe more than anything she'd said or offered. He had the greatest respect for wartime nurses. He wished Brancker had told him this earlier. But he decided he'd press her just a little more for the hell of it.

She continued. "I'll buy the plane of *your* choosing."

"I still doubt you have any notion of how rough the great north westerly winds can get. Flying from east to west isn't the same as flying this way—nothing like!" Hinchliffe jabbed again.

"You think I don't know all that! I suppose what Lindbergh did last month wasn't so special?"

"No, I wouldn't diminish what that man did at all. He did a marvelous thing."

"And so will we!"

"But he wasn't the first. We shouldn't forget Allcock and Brown or Major Scott in his airship," Hinchliffe reminded her.

Elsie nodded her acquiescence.

Hinchliffe peered across at the man behind the ferns. Judging by his furtive glances, his interest in Elsie had not diminished.

Must be one of her old boyfriends.

"The prize money will be all yours. As to the fame and glory, we'll share that. But I'll pay you a fee on top of all that," Elsie declared.

Hinchliffe stopped and stared at her. He had to hand it to her, she was pretty damned determined.

"How much do you want?" she asked flatly.

He decided to throw her off with a silly number. "Ten thousand."

"Anything else?" she asked, unfazed.

"A ten thousand-pound life insurance policy."

This did faze her slightly. "Whatever for?"

"Do you know how many people have—"

"Yes, yes, of course I do! I've read the list. I know all their names by heart. But let's be positive, shall we?"

"I'm married with another child on the way."

This Elsie didn't know. Another hint of disappointment registered in her face. "I'd expected a little confidence, but I don't have a problem with that, Captain Hinchliffe. Now, do you know another pilot who could work with you as a substitute copilot, in case something happens to me?"

"Indeed, I do," Hinchliffe answered.

"Good. I'll pay him sixty pounds a month."

"I'm sure he'd be happy with that."

"Now, about this plane—" she began.

"I had a Stinson Detroiter in mind. It's a six-seater. The passenger seats could be removed and replaced with fuel tanks. It's got a pretty good record and its performance would suit us well—if we do this."

"You'll need to rush over there and buy it then. We don't have much time. This whole thing is urgent now. Everyone wants to do it. We've got to beat them all to it," she said.

"I reckon if I get over there immediately, we could have it here by the end of next month."

"How do you know?"

"I've already talked to the factory on the phone in Detroit. They have a couple of planes ready to go, subject to a few modifications we'd need."

She gave him a knowing look. "You're pretty damned sure of *yourself*, aren't you?"

Hinchliffe grinned. Elsie looked excited.

"Oh, one thing, Captain Hinchliffe, please make sure it has a bloody heater."

"Yeah, I'd make sure it had heater *and* a starter," Hinchliffe told her.

She looked at him as if to say, 'You knew that all along. You've been toying with me, you swine!'

"How's your wife going to feel about all this?"

Uncertainty washed over Hinchliffe's face. "I'll need to talk to her," he replied.

"Maybe I should pay her a visit," Elsie said.

Hinchliffe looked even more uncertain at that. He looked across to check on Elsie's admirer between the ferns.

He'd vanished.

6

THE QUARREL

Tuesday, June 14, 1927.

Sinclair and his wife Kate had lived in the small cottage guest wing since Sinclair had lost his job two years earlier. Everyone got on well together, particularly due to Hinchliffe and Sinclair's war connection. It suited Hinchliffe. They didn't get under each other's feet, and he liked having them there when he was away. Kate and Millie got on famously and were best friends. Joan loved having her 'uncle and auntie' around, too. Sinclair had made a substantial area into a vegetable garden which helped out with the food bill. He grew cabbages, carrots, turnips, potatoes, runner beans, rhubarb, tomatoes, and many other things. At the back of the garden, he'd set up a number of beehives and harvested honey and beeswax at the end of summer. He was adept at catching rabbits too, and had set up a chicken coop behind the outbuildings for the production of eggs, and sometimes meat for chicken pies and roasts. They paid rent when Sinclair was working. He worked in the Coach & Horses in the evenings sometimes and on the local farm when needed. The economy wasn't exactly booming.

When Hinchliffe returned from the city after lunch with Elsie, Sinclair was tying up tomato plants in his garden and Millie was attending to her hanging plants under the pergola. She'd been quiet all morning. Hinchliffe had told her about his meeting with Brancker and his brief talk with Elsie, and how she'd invited him to lunch at the Ritz. This had got Millie's hackles up. In her condition, she felt vulnerable and the whole Atlantic thing had begun to drag her down. She'd been stewing about things and waiting for Hinchliffe's return from his lunch with the beautiful millionairess.

She and Hinchliffe had had discussions for the last year about an Atlantic attempt. He'd presented the positive side. He'd not played down the danger, but he clearly felt his back was against the wall with his eye problem and his flying career at the airline about to come to an end. Lindbergh's success the previous month had brought everything to a head. It was now or never. Hinchliffe thought that one successful venture like this could solve all their problems—for life!

By the time he got out into the garden to Millie, her mood had hardened. As he approached her, she threw a pile of weeds and old pots into a wheelbarrow with a thud, not looking at him.

"Millie, what's up, love?" Hinchliffe asked.

"I've gone along with you and all your flights, but this'll be suicide!" she snapped.

"Look Millie, I'll minimize the risk, you know that."

"You can't control the weather, Hinchliffe! You know you can't. I'm not happy—not happy at all!"

"Branks has offered me anything I want. I'll get up to the minute weather reports from the met office at Cardington—and not only that, I'll be heavily insured."

This only made her more angry. "To hell with insurance! It's you I care about. It's having a father to our children I care about! Not money!"

Then there was the issue of the lovely millionairess. "Who is this woman you're talking to?"

It wasn't as if she didn't know. Hinchliffe had carefully explained everything yesterday. He hadn't even made up his mind to pursue it one hundred percent, even at this moment. He was on the edge.

"I've told you, Millie. She's part of the P&O shipping family. She's a feminist. Wants to back the venture to highlight women's rights."

Millie rolled her eyes. "God help us! You can't take two and carry enough fuel for a flight like that. Lindbergh did it alone."

"I'll have a plane designed to carry enough fuel and two pilots. It'd be better with two pilots."

"So, she's a *pilot?* And she's *beautiful!* What about Lowenstein? Wouldn't he sponsor you?"

"I'd rather not ask *him.*"

Millie grimaced.

"Look, it's strictly business, Millie. We'll be set for life if I can pull this off."

"If! ... And if you *don't?"*

Millie turned away and went into the house and slammed the door behind her. Hinchliffe watched her. He understood perfectly. She had every reason to be worried. He decided to cut the lawn and let her cool down for a while. He went in and changed into casual clothes and then went to the vegetable garden to speak with Sinclair. He didn't divulge the details of his meeting with Elsie. He'd give it all more thought first. After chatting, he went to one of the outbuildings, grabbed the push mower and got started. While he worked, Millie sat sadly at her piano, playing Chopin's Prelude in E Minor op 28 No. 4.

The haunting melody drifted across the garden. This didn't make Hinchliffe feel any better. He stared toward the French windows guiltily. In the meantime, Sinclair continued working on his vegetable garden behind the hedge, staying out of the way. If they were going to do it, he'd need to speak to him about Elsie's offer. He was sure Sinclair would be up for it. They were always short of money and Sinclair thought the Atlantic record was worth a shot, especially if they got the best equipment and made meticulous preparations.

After an hour or so, the lawn was cut and the piano was silent. Only the sound of a cooing wood pigeon could be heard now. Hinchliffe returned the lawn mower to the outbuilding and went into the house, looking for Millie. He went to the kitchen sink and washed his hands and then to Millie's studio. She wasn't there. He presumed she was in her adjacent dark room. He knocked on the door and went in. The room was lit by a candle. Millie was rocking a tray of photographic chemicals back and forth. An image of Millie and Joan gradually appeared—a photo Hinchliffe had taken a couple days ago in the garden.

"What are you up to?" Hinchliffe asked.

"Just finishing those shots you took," she said.

He put his arms around her from behind and squeezed her tightly, pressing his face against her wet cheek. Millie closed her eyes. He gently slipped his hands down over the baby.

"Don't worry, my darling, nothing bad's gonna happen. I'll never let you and the children down, you know that, don't you."

He'd always managed to reassure her, he was invincible. Hinchliffe left Millie to calm down for a day or two. He told Sinclair about Elsie's proposal and Sinclair expressed keen interest. It'd be a wonderful deal as far as he was concerned—sixty pounds a month while he was on the payroll assembling the plane and conducting tests seemed too good to be true. And there was always the chance he'd wind up as Hinchliffe's copilot at the end of the day.

Hinchliffe broached the subject again, telling Millie that he understood her feelings and that it was only natural in her condition—and he genuinely felt that. At one point, after Joan was in bed, he and Millie sat down with the Sinclairs and talked it over. Sinclair's obvious enthusiasm, together with Hinchliffe's, was formidable. Even Kate was positive about it, but Millie knew it was not *her* husband that would be at risk, unless Elsie backed out. Hinchliffe recounted the long-distance journeys he'd made: his trip to Baghdad with Thomson, his journey to Ismailia with Johnston, and other trips he'd made to Egypt. He'd flown for years with KLM and Imperial Airways for thousands of miles to Holland, France and Germany, without mishap—equivalent to crossing the Atlantic scores of times.

Hinchliffe was convinced there'd be no *more* risk with this Atlantic flight. Preparation was key, and the right plane, of course. He'd make sure they had the best plane available. The Stinson Detroiter would be the right one. He'd studied the blueprints and technical data and was absolutely convinced that with some added modifications, the risk would be lower than flying to India and back. Millie was showing signs of relenting. Hinchliffe wisely decided not to push her. He thought she'd come around eventually.

That issue was brought to a head the following day. Millie was in studio feverishly playing the stormy third movement of Moonlight Sonata. Hinchliffe was in the yard hanging Millie's new bird feeder. She thought she heard a motorbike in the front driveway. The doorbell jangled, but Millie ignored it, playing until the end of the piece. The bell went again. When she'd finished, she went to the door. There, she found someone dressed in a brown leather jacket, pilot's cap and goggles—about her own height.

"You must be Millie!" the rider said in a husky voice, removing a pair of gloves.

"Er, yes?"

"Hello, I'm so pleased to meet you," the woman said, thrusting out a beautifully manicured hand. "I'm Elsie, I *hope* you've heard of me." She pushed up her goggles to reveal her exquisitely made up, gorgeous brown eyes.

"Elsie …?"

"Elsie Mackay …"

The penny dropped. "Oh, yes, Elsie Mackay," Millie said with a half-smile.

"My goodness what wonderful playing. Was that you? I've been standing here for ages, listening."

"Yes, it was, actually. I'm so sorry—" Millie replied.

"Oh, no, no. It was great! What was it?"

"The third movement."

"The third movement? Well, whatever it was, it was absolutely *bloody* marvelous, if I may say so! And I just *love* your accent."

"Yes, I like yours too," Millie countered.

Hinchliffe was just coming in from the garden, and after puzzling for a while, figured it could only be Elsie at the front door. He wasn't sure where this would lead. It might spoil everything.

"Elsie! What brings you here?" he asked.

"I'm so sorry, Raymond, to drop in on you like this, but I was out riding through the South Downs on the old Harley and I thought, well, why not drop in and introduce myself to your wife—and yes, she *is* just as lovely as you said, and her music, oh my God!" Elsie clapped her hands together and rambled on in her frightfully, frightfully upper class accent. "Me, I know nothing about music—planes and horses are my thing—and a spot of tennis, of course."

By now, Sinclair was also entering the kitchen, leaving his vegetable garden to wash his hands for lunch. Kate joined them.

"I suggest you take Elsie into the garden, Ray, and we'll bring tea and sandwiches," Millie said, gesturing for Elsie to enter.

"On no, I couldn't *possibly*—" Elsie began.

"No. Please. Come on Elsie we can chat. Heaven knows we've lots to talk about," said Hinchliffe.

It was finally agreed that Millie and Hinchliffe would go and sit in the secret garden with Elsie, while the Sinclairs brought out the tea and a snack lunch, keeping Joan in the kitchen. They went to the garden. Elsie was impressed. She pulled off her cap and goggles and put them on the garden table.

"This is enchanting!" she gushed, spinning around. "What a marvelous place. You could ... you could walk around naked—"

"Yes, I often do. It's my little piece of heaven," Millie said.

"And I can quite see why," Elsie replied.

"You're an actress, aren't you?" Millie said.

"Well, yes, I have worked on a few films, but now flying is my vocation It's what I absolutely live for."

"The Atlantic?"

"Yes. It's something I need to do. It's there crying out to be done, and I think your husband is the perfect pilot for me. I've been searching for someone of his caliber for ages."

"I see. Are you confident? Is it really worth the risk?" Millie was weighing up her own risk at the same time, as spouses do.

"Absolutely! With plenty of testing and real preparation, the risk will be minimal. And the rewards—will be out of this world. The contribution to aviation will be enormous. Oh yes, it would be a wonderful thing. Believe me, I do not take this lightly. I'll spend any amount of money to get the *right* plane and the *right* pilot. *Safety* is my main concern above all else."

Hinchliffe was pleased. Elsie's performance was dynamic. She was coming across as responsible and business-like. He could tell Millie was impressed. Elsie turning up on a motorbike in her leathers was a nice touch. Better than the ditsy flapper. The refreshments arrived and the Sinclairs made themselves scarce. Soon, Joan came out, dying to meet Elsie. "Are you a film star, miss?" she asked.

Everyone laughed, and soon Elsie and Joan were playing with Joan's toys on the grass together. Elsie was a big hit. Later, the Sinclairs joined in the informal chat and Gordon was introduced as the possible substitute pilot. Elsie was thrilled to meet him.

Finally, Elsie jumped up. "Well, I must be off," she said. "It's been a thrill to meet you Millie, and your darling little girl. I'm so impressed with the family and everything. So, please think things over." She turned toward the house and then hesitated. "And look, Millie, if you're not all for it—I will understand, truly I will."

They entered the house and as they were passing the French doors into Millie's studio, Elsie saw the artwork and the piano. "Oh, what's this? May I see?" They all went in and Elsie's eyes were everywhere. She breathed in the odor of oil paint and turps as if they were fresh cut roses. "Oh, I do love that smell. Good Lord, what marvelous stuff!" She scrutinized the half-finished painting of Hinchliffe and then a finished portrait of Joan. "Oh, you *must* do me! Will you, *please*?"

"Yes, of course," Millie said.

"Oh, *promise* me? I'll pay you, naturally." Elsie made for the door and hugged Millie. "And of course, I'll abide by whatever you decide, Millie. Lovely to meet you. But you know, I think it's all coming together. I think it's *meant* to be." With that, Elsie donned her cap and goggles and they watched her hop on and kick over her huge, gleaming Harley Davidson and cruise off down the driveway.

"That's one impressive woman," Sinclair said.

"No one could deny *that!*" Millie said.

Hinchliffe grinned and gave Sinclair a sly wink.

Millie began to relent. Maybe she *was* worrying unduly. He'd always come back. Why had she been worrying so much? Hinchliffe's, and now Elsie's, enthusiasm was infectious, and Sinclair backed their confidence. That confidence now permeated the whole house. Maybe this *was* their big chance—one that might only come along once. They'd be secure for life! That evening, Millie gave the project her blessing. Hinchliffe hugged her with glee. "Thank you my darling," he said. "Thank you for having faith in me."

They went to bed feeling things had been resolved. Millie once again had her recurring dream. The entity came to her in the dead of night and leaned over her. She felt its kiss upon her lips. She was sure it was a man, but could see no face, just its black form. Again, she felt nothing but comfort, kindness and love emanating from it. She fell back into a deep sleep.

7

THE PLANE

Sunday, June 19, 1927.

Within five days, Hinchliffe was on board the White Star Line's *Olympic,* sister ship to *Titanic*, bound for New York. By June 26, he was in the offices of the Stinson Aircraft Company in Detroit. He'd sent them a telegram stating his interest in a modified Stinson Detroiter. The company confirmed that a plane was available and could be shipped almost immediately with the required modifications.

Hinchliffe spent four days at the factory and made friends with the managers and staff, including Eddie Stinson himself—another enthusiastic aviation pioneer. Hinchliffe went over every part of the plane: the Wright Whirlwind nine-cylinder engine; the tubular steel structure, including its type of wood and fabric; the wheels, tires and unique braking system; and its all-important instrumentation. They talked about radio equipment, but it was decided to save that weight and carry a few more gallons of fuel—that was an agonizing choice. A cabin heater was ordered and an electric starter. Elsie would be pleased about that. On Hinchliffe's instructions, she wired half the money before he returned home. The balance would be sent a month after the plane had been delivered to England.

The factory managers had an idea what the plane would be used for and promised to keep it quiet. The rear seats were removed and two large fuel tanks installed. This hugely extended the range.

.After five enjoyable days, Hinchliffe was back in New York boarding the Cunard's RMS *Mauretania* bound for Southampton. It had been a pilot's dream. Most pilots would never get to order the plane of their choosing—not to this degree—built to their own specifications. He was back home at Pickwick Cottage by July 6th— the same day the plane was ready for shipping from Detroit.

While Hinchliffe was in the States, Brancker had visited Millie's studio and sat for his portrait. By the time Hinchliffe got back it was taking shape. Brancker had struck a wonderful pose in his military tunic with a sash and a chest full of medals, a glint of light on his monocle. Millie had captured his charisma—the intrepid leader—Air Vice Marshall Brancker, Director of Civil Aviation! Millie sensed he was a man who loved the ladies. She could easily see why they loved him and his rakish mustache. The monocle, toupee and mustache contributed to his persona, but it was his vibrant enthusiasm for life that captivated everyone. He attracted people into his orbit like a star attracts planets. Hinchliffe thought 'old Branks' would be well-pleased. Millie said Brancker had a wonderful aura, full of blues, reds, white and gold, and she'd depicted these colors around him.

The disassembled plane was delivered to Brooklands Aerodrome, owned by Vickers Aircraft, July 17th, where Hinchliffe, Sinclair and Elsie were eagerly waiting to uncrate it. Elsie had rented a hangar and the threesome got right to it. They worked long hours, sometimes well into the night, and within two weeks the plane was assembled.

They all submitted a name and finally *Endeavour*, Millie's, was chosen. A sign writer was hired and he came down and painted the name on both sides of the plane with a brightly colored Union Jack. The plane, jet black with gold wingtips, looked magnificent. They thought that by next year, the Americans would be admiring it. Maybe they'd put it in the Smithsonian or the British Museum.

For the next few months, Hinchliffe, Sinclair and Elsie took the plane up for test flights. She behaved beautifully. The Brooklands runway, however, was too short for takeoff with a full fuel load. They'd have to find another runway, and they'd need to pay a visit to Cardington soon to organize weather reports.

During August, Hinchliffe was surprised to learn that a good friend of his, Fred Minchin, had been preparing to make an Atlantic bid with Leslie Hamilton in a Fokker monoplane called the *St. Raphael*. Everything had been kept secret so as to steal a march on other contenders, including Hinchliffe and Elsie. But the thing that concerned Hinchliffe most was the fact that the project was being sponsored by Lady Anne Savile and that *she,* together with her extensive wardrobe, would be accompanying them. He'd told Charles Levine to go to hell for that very reason—three's a crowd. Hinchliffe reluctantly went down to RAF Upavon to see them off. He doubted that they'd make it. And they didn't. After leaving Ireland they were never heard of again. Though this left the field still open, Hinchliffe was sick about it, and Millie even more so—she'd secretly hoped that Minchin's flight would succeed. Thereafter, the subject was avoided.

At the beginning of September, on a rather damp, cool day, the man with the five-o'clock shadow stood at the edge of the woods at the edge of Brooklands Aerodrome. He blended in perfectly with the oaks and bracken, his binoculars trained on the sky. The droning of a single-engine plane carried down to him. He studied it for a few moments and then turned his attention toward the buildings. Millie and Elsie were standing at the doors, shielding their eyes, looking at the sky. Behind them, he spotted Hinchliffe and Sinclair emerging from the hangar, also looking up.

The observer's name was George Hunter, a reporter with the *Daily Express*. He watched the Gypsy Moth circle and then touch down on the short, grass landing strip. He removed his binoculars and smiled. "The Director of Civil Aviation no less! Very promising indeed!" he muttered.

Hunter patiently waited as the plane came to a standstill near their hangar. He witnessed the big fuss taking place as Hinchliffe's group welcomed Brancker and Miss Honeysuckle, his leggy blond pilot and chauffeur. There was a lot of handshaking and backslapping, with the monocled Brancker strutting around like a little turkey cock. The reporter thrust his binoculars into his scruffy gaberdine raincoat and moved to a new vantage point.

The group made its way toward the hangar, led by Hinchliffe. Brancker spoke from behind him as they paused outside. "I just heard those ruddy Germans are breathing down our necks!"

Millie looked hopeful. "Will they be ready soon?" she asked.

"My spies in Germany tell me their plane could be ready anytime for testing," Brancker replied.

"We're going to beat them to it!" Hinchliffe assured him.

Millie looked down at the ground sadly, thinking about Minchin. She'd met him on a few occasions at Croydon airport where he, like her husband, had operated from as a pilot.

But Elsie was chipper. "Let's go in and eat and christen this bird," she said. She led them inside the hangar. Elsie had set up a table in front of the plane with a white tablecloth laid out with caviar and champagne. The plane was shrouded with sheets.

Brancker glanced toward it. "So, how *is* the new kite?"

Hinchliffe responded. "She handles extraordinarily well. But this runway's much too short."

"Well, if the Director of Civil Aviation can't solve that problem, then no one can, what! Ha, ha!" Brancker said, winking at Miss Honeysuckle. "I'll find you another airstrip, don't worry about that."

Everyone gathered around the plane and Elsie yanked off the sheets with a flourish. "Voila!" she cried. The brand-new, high-wing, single-engine plane gleamed under the lights. In the hangar, it had the look of pure engineering genius, a mixture of steel, fabric and varnished hardwood. Brancker admired her name expertly written on each side. He rubbed his hands along the gleaming, black engine cowling, lustfully, as though she were a luscious woman. But Millie looked like someone had just walked over her grave—or possibly her husband's.

"Oh, she's magnificent! Endeavour! How marvelous!" Brancker gushed.

"It's darling!" echoed Miss Honeysuckle, clasping her hands together.

Elsie poured the champagne into cut glass flutes, and she and Sinclair handed them round on a tray.

"To the *Endeavour*!" Elsie shouted enthusiastically.

"The *Endeavour*!" the others repeated. Millie put on her bravest face, and though misty eyed, she took photographs from which she'd later make sketches and paintings back in her studio.

Hunter had been watching this little ceremony through a window at the end of the hangar and, though he couldn't hear everything, he understood every word. He chuckled as he made his way back to the woods, where he'd parked his car on the trail. He had the beginnings of a story. A pretty damned big story!

Surveillance of Elsie Mackay was paying off. He'd been keeping tabs on her for months.

8

A VISIT TO CARDINGTON

Tuesday, September 13, 1927.

On September 13th, Millie and Hinchliffe headed north in their Bentley Continental. They roared through London via Westminster Bridge, past Big Ben. Millie wore a headscarf and sunglasses. It felt good in the sunshine with the top down, the wind in her hair. They drove down Whitehall, past Brancker's office, and around Trafalgar Square, where the pigeons were out in force. Ten minutes later, they were on the road to Cardington. They had to shout to be heard above the wind and the mighty roar of the 4½ litre engine. Millie was still pondering the whole business. She had her ups and downs, especially since the loss of Minchin, Hamilton and Lady Anne Savile. Hinchliffe had told her he didn't think they'd make it, and he'd been right. That business had unsettled her, but she took comfort in the fact that there would be only two in *Endeavour.*

Hinchliffe was looking forward to seeing his old buddies. Like Hinchliffe, Captain Irwin was an ex-Royal Navy Air Serviceman, while Johnston was an ex-Royal Air Force man. They'd met at a machine gun course at Grantham during the war, when Hinchliffe had volunteered for the RNAS, having served as an artilleryman at the Front in 1916. After watching a few dog fights over the front lines, he'd decided he wanted to be a fighter pilot. He met Johnston again during the war, when they were both on a navigation course in London. Irwin had flown blimps during the war, coordinating with surface ships in surveillance of German submarines around the English coast. He was now being groomed to take over *Cardington R101,* and busy assisting in construction, filing as-built engineering drawings, and putting together operational user manuals.

For many, airships were the wave of the future. They would become the ocean liners of the sky. But for others, they were considered to be nothing but deathtraps, and judging by their record, that was a fair assessment. However, there were those in England who were determined that this mode of travel would be made safe, or at least as safe as ocean-going vessels. In 1920, the U.S. Navy had decided to purchase *Airship R38,* under construction at Cardington. Hundreds of young men were sent to England to monitor construction and get trained as airshipmen and support personnel. But then tragedy struck, when during its final test, that airship broke in two over Hull. It crashed into the River Humber, killing all but four of both the British and American crews. The industry languished for a time, until a certain Lord Thomson came along and revived the industry in 1924, putting thousands back to work. Under Thomson's new Airship Program, two airships would be constructed, one, the *Howden R100* by Vickers Aircraft at Howden, the other the *Cardington R101* by the Royal Airship Works at Cardington. Construction of both ships would be under the purview of the Royal Airship Works.

After three years of experimentation and design, they were finally taking shape. It'd been slow, but those in charge at Cardington were determined to make sure these airships were as safe as humanly possible. Hinchliffe, being the practical engineer that he was, and although no fan of 'lighter than air' contraptions, was looking forward to seeing what his friends had accomplished. He didn't expect to be impressed.

"Does it really *have* to be the *Atlantic,* Hinch?" Millie asked suddenly, holding on to her scarf.

"The Atlantic's the prize. They're talking about a ticker tape parade. It'll be big."

This was the first Millie had heard of that. The thought was daunting. She pictured Hinchliffe and Elsie in New York riding in a procession in a convertible Cadillac with thousands of adoring fans waving and screaming as confetti showered down upon them. "Oh, my Goodness!" she exclaimed.

"But remember, we've got to keep it quiet," Hinchliffe warned.

The car sped north and within thirty minutes the great Cardington sheds loomed in the distance. They raced up to the guardhouse and, after announcing themselves, the gate opened. Hinchliffe drove up the cherry tree-lined drive to Cardington House, the administration building. It resembled a stately home, having been built by a philanthropist. It was set in magnificent gardens, bursting with color most of the year, and inhabited by thousands of happy birds of all species. The wealthy former owner had donated the great house to the airship industry to encourage its goals. Near the foot of the entry steps, Hinchliffe got out and went around and helped Millie out of the car. He slung her camera over his shoulder.

"Is all this secrecy really necessary?" Millie asked.

"You know what Brancker said—the Germans are almost ready. We must *not* alert them."

Millie took Hinchliffe's arm and they made their way carefully up the steps to the entrance doors. At seven months, Millie was getting big and moved around carefully. They entered the grand, marble reception hall. The place was like a museum, with ornate columns at the foot of a sweeping stone staircase. Hinchliffe went to the reception desk. "We're here to see Captain Irwin and Squadron Leader Johnston. The name's Hinchliffe."

A few minutes later, Johnston, the navigator, appeared, a big grin on his face—enough to light up the grand entrance hall.

"Oh, my God. I don't believe it. I thought you were dead! Crashed and burned in some jungle," he cried.

Millie was shocked at first, but that's how these fellows talked. The two men gave one another a bear hug and Johnston kissed Millie's cheek. Then Captain Irwin entered. Johnston turned to him. "Look who's here!" he said.

"The Blackbird! How are you doing for Goodness sake?" Hinchliffe exclaimed, shaking the captain's hand warmly.

"Not bad for a dirigible pilot, I suppose," he answered.

"In your line of work, you have every reason to be dour, even for a fine-looking Irishman," Hinchliffe teased.

Millie assessed Irwin. He was indeed a handsome fellow—his black hair slicked back with a fine parting. He had a kind face. She'd do some sketches of him and Johnston. Johnston was more hard-edged, but interesting. Irwin, in contrast, was thoughtful—perhaps fatalistic. His warmth and Irish wit, nevertheless, shone through.

"Wanna come up and see the ship?" Irwin asked.

This excited Millie. "Oh yes, could we?" she said, eyeing her husband. "That would be wonderful."

"As long as you don't have the damned thing filled up with hydrogen," Hinchliffe said. "I don't fancy getting blown to kingdom come—not today."

"Oh no, we don't have any gas bags in her yet, you old scaredy-cat," said Johnston, a frown of scorn on his chiseled features.

"All right then, perhaps Millie can take some pictures?" Hinchliffe suggested. The others had no problem with that, as long as they weren't for publication. They took a five-minute ride in Johnston's little black Austin over to the enormous sheds.

"Now, what's this rumor we've all been hearing, Hinch?" Johnston asked over his shoulder, a glint in his blue eyes, an eyebrow raised.

"What rumor?" Hinchliffe said, startled.

"The Atlantic," Irwin answered. "We've heard all about it, you know." His manner was one of disapproval—as though it were a foolish stunt.

Hinchliffe knew he'd have to tell them anyway. "Okay, you know why we're here. I need accurate weather reports. Can you help me?"

"We'll get you anything you want. But you're not serious about this, are you?" Irwin said, giving Hinchliffe his most dour Irish look.

Millie glanced dubiously at Hinchliffe and then back to Irwin and Johnston from the backseat. "He is. But maybe you can talk some sense into him. I've tried."

They arrived outside the gigantic shed. Millie was awestruck. Hinchliffe looked up at the building with trepidation as Irwin led the foursome to a side door. They entered the eight hundred and sixty-foot building. It was like stepping into another world. Hundreds of men swarmed around on ladders and scaffolding like ants, working all over the mammoth silver framing. The structure practically filled every inch of space up to the nearly two hundred feet high roof. Millie looked amazed and filled with dread at the same time.

Johnston raised his voice above the din. "What do you think then, Hinch?"

"I think you're all crazy. I think you're building yourselves a bloody great hydrogen bomb that's gonna blow you all to hell, like you bloody-well deserve!"

"Hinch!" Millie shouted. She agreed, but he didn't have to be that blunt.

"I'm telling you, you're all *crazy*!" Hinch said again, shaking his head.

Millie had the three friends pose while she took photographs. As they were doing this, some of the construction crewmen stopped to watch. Two engineers were studying the small party from an engine car slung beneath the airship, the base of the car at about eye level. They watched Hinchliffe with suspicion, while admiring Millie in her comely state. One of them, Joe Binks, a young man always with a quip or gibe, taunted his mate as he wiped his oily hands on a cloth. "'Ere, I don't want to worry you, Arthur, but that's our new captain," he said, indicating with a nod toward Hinchliffe.

"That's all we need, a one-eyed bloody skipper. What use could he be to anyone?" his mate, Arthur Bell, answered, switching his gaze to Millie, "Now, *she* might be a different story!"

As if on cue, Millie marched up and stood below their engine car, intrigued. She called up to them. "What is this you're working on?"

"It's an engine car, missus. It don't 'ave no engine in it yet, though."

Hinchliffe joined them. "So where's your engine?" he asked, looking at Binks.

"We're waitin' for 'em," Joe Binks called down.

"It's what powers the airship?" Millie asked.

"Yes, ma'am this one's gonna be *our* baby."

"So how do you get into it then?" Millie asked.

"We climb down that ladder up there," Binks answered, pointing to the ladder above their heads.

"My God! Not when you're in the sky, surely?"

"I reckon we'll get used to it, ma'am. At least, we 'ope so! We'll 'ave to, won't we!"

Millie had them pose together with Hinchliffe, while she took a couple of shots. She decided she'd probably do a painting of these happy fellows at some point.

Later, word got around that Hinchliffe was at the aerodrome and Wing Commander Colmore, the exceedingly courteous Deputy Director of Airship Development, suggested that they all meet over at the local pub, the Kings Arms on the village green. As Hinchliffe and his companions entered, all faces turned in their direction. Colmore stood at the center of the lounge bar, surrounded by his airshipmen. He reached out to Hinchliffe and took his hand.

"My dear Hinchliffe, I'd heard the rumor that you were coming up to see us. So glad you brought your lovely bride with you."

"How's it all going, sir?" Hinchliffe said.

"It's like giving birth. Although, I can't exactly say *we're* expecting quite yet!" Colmore said, glancing at Millie. "When's that baby of *yours* due, Millie?"

"Early December," Millie answered. "And you'll all be invited to the christening."

After drinks were served all round, Colmore turned to a jolly chap at his side, his face a little flushed. "You know Major Scott, of course."

Major Scott, Colmore's right hand man, was officer in charge of flying operations. Hinchliffe, Irwin and Johnston towered over him. He was the unsung hero of British aviation, having made the return journey to America as pilot in command of *Airship R34*. His should have been a household name—but wasn't. Millie had heard this from Hinchliffe and thought it a pity. She decided she'd paint his portrait. He'd done an incredible thing. She studied him closely, noting his striking red aura, which she'd learned over the years denoted he was a leader of men, and a risk taker. Scott greeted the Hinchliffes warmly. He eyed Millie's midriff and beamed a knowing smile.

"Another pilot in the making, I shouldn't wonder," he said.

"Oh no. One in the family's quite enough," Millie replied.

"Given up on aeroplanes then, Hinch? Looking for a job here with us?" Scott chided.

"Lord no!"

"What's all this we've been hearing about you and a certain beautiful heiress then?" Scott asked.

"What!" Hinchliffe spluttered.

"Heard you and the lovely Elsie Mackay are planning a little trip. It all sounds very dangerous, if you ask me," Scott barked. He was formidable—a bulldog.

Millie frowned and put her hand to her head. The ever gracious Colmore intervened. "I don't think you've ever met Colonel Richmond, the designer of our soon-to-be great airship, have you?" Richmond stood like a mannequin in a banker's suit with Brylcreamed hair. He gave them a stiff nod, appearing aloof. Hinchliffe got the impression he was a theoretician—an office-wallah—not a flier like the others. An outsider.

Colmore continued, "And here, I must introduce you to our very good friend, Lieutenant Lou Remington. He's from across the pond."

"Nobody's perfect" someone quipped.

"He's working with us now," Colmore added.

Lou Remington smiled good-naturedly. Millie noticed his aura. It was perfectly balanced. He was a superb soul and gorgeous to look at —like an American movie star, and well mannered. Millie and Hinchliffe took a liking to him.

"Lou was aboard the *R38* when it crashed into the Humber in '21," Colmore said.

"Dangerous bloody things, these airships," Hinchliffe snapped.

"He thought he was done with airships, didn't you, lad?" Scott said, moping perspiration from his balding head. "But we dragged him back into the game—we wouldn't let him escape!"

"Particularly since he'd married one of our English girls," Johnston said with a chuckle. "Best looking girl in Yorkshire!"

The American grinned, while he twisted her gold ring, as was his habit. "Fair trade," he quipped. Millie thought she'd love to paint that face one day.

Colmore continued, looking at Irwin, "Did you give Hinch the grand tour?"

"Yes, sir. We didn't get to see the girls working on the goldbeater's skins, though."

"Goldbeaters! I've never heard of such an animal," Hinchliffe remarked. He was teasing. He knew exactly what goldbeater skins were, and where they came from.

Scott stepped in to explain, mainly for Millie's sake. "They're the skins from the bellies of oxen. They are used by goldbeaters to separate sheets of gold when they beat them into gold leaf. Our ladies clean 'em up and make 'em into gas bags for the ship."

"You mean to say the fate of the British Empire rests in the bellies of cows!" Hinch gibed.

"I wouldn't put it quite like that, dear boy," said Colmore.

"I'll stick to wings for lift, I think," said Hinchliffe.

Richmond smirked. "So, you think aeroplanes have much of a future, do you, Hinchliffe?"

"Definitely! Eventually, they'll carry lots of passengers and huge payloads of freight or bombs."

"Is that so? How many passengers in your estimation?"

Hinchliffe considered for a moment, while he took a sip of beer. "Five hundred, I guess."

"What! In your dreams, maybe," Richmond snapped.

As Richmond chortled, laughter broke out all round the bar. Hinchliffe bristled. "And they'll get *much* faster," he said.

Hinchliffe wasn't the only one getting rattled. Johnston was too— not one to suffer fools. He was clenching his jaw and grimacing. Millie sensed underlying tension between some of the personalities in the bar. She found differences between ranks, personalities and ego's intriguing.

Richmond grinned for the first time. "How fast?"

"Six hundred, seven hundred miles an hour. Maybe more."

Richmond resumed smugly. "I shouldn't wish to land in one of those things at those kinds of speeds, old man." He gestured grandly. "No, it'll all boil down to safety and luxury in the end. The airship is the wave of the future. They'll gently float down to their mooring towers with grace and style."

All eyes turned to Hinchliffe expectantly. "You mean, as long as the wind's not blowing!" he said.

"You're not telling us planes aren't affected by weather, are you?"

"Give me a full tank and I'll take my chances," Hinchliffe replied.

The atmosphere in the pub was getting uncomfortable. Scott chimed in to change the subject.

"Tell us about your Atlantic plans, old man. We'll never tell."

Hinchliffe glanced at Millie and then back to Scott. "There's nothing to tell, Scottie, but I promise, you'll be the first to know, my dear chap," he said.

Express reporter George Hunter stood quietly at the bar sipping a pint of Watneys. The story was all shaping up nicely, and he was the only journalist working on the Hinchliffe-Elsie Mackay story.

During the following weeks, when everyone was over in Brooklands working on *Endeavour,* Millie produced charcoal sketches of Captain Irwin and Johnston as well as other scenes in the shed, including engineers Binks and Bell in their incomplete engine car. She also painted *Endeavour* in the hangar, along with dramatic pictures of the Cardington sheds, under a threatening sky. Scott's portrait would be her next project.

9

THE CHRISTENING

Monday, December 26, 1927 (Boxing Day).

Millie was dealt another blow of sorts during October. A beautiful young actress from Alabama, Ruth Elder, had set off in *American Girl* from New York with pilot George Haldeman to conquer the Atlantic. She wanted to be the first woman to do it, and this would put her career into high gear. After traveling twenty-six hundred miles, their plane conked out due to a broken oil line. Hinchliffe kept a close eye on Miss Elder's progress, since she was using the exact same plane. Elder and Haldeman ditched three hundred miles off the Azores and were lucky to get picked up by a passing cargo ship.

Hinchliffe and Sinclair immediately checked on *Endeavour*'s oil lines, making sure they were securely wire-locked in place. Ruth Elder and George Haldeman were feted in New York with a ticker tape parade in December for their accomplishment—she being the first woman to have piloted a plane for that distance over the Atlantic. Naturally, this put Miss Elder's career on a fast track. The event did little to hurt Hinchliffe and Elsie; in fact, they knew it would enhance interest in their attempt. However, it sowed further doubt in Millie's mind. But she kept it hidden.

Much changed at Pickwick Cottage on the first day of December. Millie woke Hinchliffe during the night, telling him it was time. After warning the Sinclairs, Hinchliffe helped Millie down the stairs and into the car, where he wrapped her in blankets. While she groaned in discomfort, he drove carefully to Croydon Hospital, about thirty-five minutes away. At 10:05 a.m., a baby girl was born, weighing seven pounds four ounces.

Millie came home four days later, and after a day or two, Hinchliffe went back to work at Brooklands with Sinclair. Kate took care of Millie and Joan. It was decided that the baby would be christened at St. Saviour's immediately after Christmas. Arrangements were made for Boxing Day and invitations sent out.

Everyone gathered around the font in the little Gothic church, the Reverend Grey presiding. Hinchliffe's friends from Cardington, Captain Irwin and Johnston attended, standing proudly in uniform. Brancker was there too, along with a few people from the village, including Barney, the blacksmith. They were all smiles as the baby, held over the font by the pastor, cried bitterly while he sprinkled water on her forehead. Hinchliffe, holding Joan in his arms, grinned at Millie and she smiled back radiantly. She'd recovered well from her confinement and was back to her normal weight, though a little pale.

Half an hour later, everyone gathered at the cottage, where a buffet had been laid out in Millie's studio. People were naturally taken with the place and were poring over the art, as they stood nibbling on crackers and cheese or smoked salmon and salad. Millie's garden was visible through the French doors; it looked damp, bare and lifeless. The studio was warm and cozy, with a log fire blazing in the stone hearth. A Christmas tree sparkled with lights and decorations hung from ceiling beams. Elsie was not present, but expected.

Presently, the front door bell sounded and Hinchliffe answered it. Elsie stood on the front step, dressed to kill. Beyond her, Hinchliffe saw her black Rolls Royce parked with its chauffeur off to one side.

"No motorbike today, Miss Mackay?" Hinchliffe said, with a grin.

Elsie was bearing a christening gift wrapped in pink paper with a silver bow. After a sideways glance for his tease, she beamed at him and kissed his cheek. She'd never kissed him before.

Millie appeared behind Hinchliffe. "Ah, Elsie," she said, with a smile of welcome.

"Millie, you look absolutely marvelous!" Elsie said, handing her the gift.

"Oh, I'm very well, and thank you."

"Come in, Elsie. Good of you to come on Boxing Day," Hinchliffe said.

"It was a good excuse to get away from my family. Sorry I couldn't make the church," Elsie said. "Did everything go off all right?"

"She cried a little at the font, but she was fine after that," Millie said.

They moved into Millie's studio. Things seemed a little awkward at first and a buzz went around the room as Hinchliffe made introductions.

"What'll you have, Elsie? Hinchliffe asked.

"Oh, I don't know if I should ... Oh, all right then ... you've persuaded me. White wine, if you have it, would be nice."

"I'll leave you with the vicar and Barney, the blacksmith, Elsie," Hinchliffe said, winking at the two men who seemed delighted to make Elsie's acquaintance and breathe in her exquisite perfume, which contrasted favorably with Barney's shaving soap. Barney had been honored to view Millie's pictures of himself shoeing a shiny black mare. Now, he was becoming hot and bothered in Elsie's presence and kept smoothing down his ruffled hair. She was only too pleased to talk about horses, being an avid horsewoman. Elsie had always felt much more at home in a blacksmith's stable than at a debutante's ball.

Hinchliffe went to the kitchen and opened a bottle of Sauvignon Blanc and returned with an overly generous measure. Elsie was complimenting Millie, who'd joined them, on her art again. Hinchliffe held out her drink and then went off to attend to other guests, including Brancker. Although Elsie had seen Millie's artwork previously she was still bowled over. "These really are lovely, Millie —*especially* the horsey ones. Raymond did tell me originally that you were an artist, but I had no idea."

The vicar looked at the unfinished portrait of Hinchliffe and was about to mention it as he sipped his lemonade.

"Don't ask!" said Millie.

"Right," said the vicar.

Elsie admired Millie's dramatic painting of the Cardington sheds, shrouded in storm clouds. She was also taken with the charcoal sketches of Irwin and Johnston and the two engineers in their engine car in the shed. Elsie compared the life-like character studies of the two officers to the men themselves, who were across the room inspecting Millie's painting of Major Scott.

Elsie was especially pleased when she saw sketches of herself on her Harley Davidson. She admired Brancker's portrait on an easel next to the piano. This was a duplicate Millie had made, as she sometimes did. Brancker had been thrilled with his own copy. People glanced at Lowenstein's portrait on display on its wall shelf. He stared from under his shiny black top hat. Millie had painted an aura about him that she'd seen. Its colors were brown and black with streaks of red. No one commented. Some raised their eyebrows. Elsie, however, saw Millie's artistry in it.

"Marvelous!" Elsie said. "I just can't wait for you to do *my* portrait. Millie, could I ask you to do something?"

"What's that?"

"Would you play that piece of music for us, the one you were playing when I first came here?"

This made Millie uncomfortable. She never played in public. "Er, well, it's not something I normally do. Let me think about it. Are you looking forward to moving to Cranwell?" Millie asked.

"Yes, but you're coming up there for the first week, aren't you?"

"Yes, and Ray'll pop down a few times before you fly off, I'm sure."

At that moment, Joan came to Millie in need of attention. "Mummy."

"Excuse me, I must get Joan some more trifle."

Hinchliffe returned to Elsie's side, her glass empty. "Let me freshen your glass."

Her eyes lit up. "Yes, the wine was welcome. I get nervous in front of so many new people," Elsie said. Hinchliffe hardly believed that. He took her glass and went back to the kitchen. Elsie noticed Captain Irwin, now standing next to her. She introduced herself. "Have you known Raymond for long?" she inquired. He explained how they'd met during the war.

Another guest then arrived, though somewhat unexpected. It was Alfred Lowenstein. Hinchliffe had invited him when at the club recently, not really expecting him to show up. Lowenstein entered also bearing a gift. He looked awkward at first, but after greeting everyone and having a drink, he settled in and moved around. He gave a start on noticing his portrait and went to it. He looked put out and put his hand to his temple as if it were throbbing. Millie came up behind him. He turned to her with an accusing stare.

"Millie, this one's much different from mine," he said.

"A little, I suppose," Millie answered.

"You've made me look like a ruthless mongrel. I want this. I'll buy it," Lowenstein said.

"What will you do with it?" Millie asked.

"I'll destroy it. I must have it."

"Oh, Alfred, whatever for?" Millie said, and then, "It's not for sale."

Lowenstein turned away in a huff, not used to being rebuffed.

After that, the afternoon proceeded smoothly, with Elsie chatting freely with all the guests, including Brancker, whom she'd known a long time and adored. He'd always made a point of encouraging pilots, especially female pilots—more especially when they were beautiful. She did her best to avoid Lowenstein who seemed too attentive. When Joan took her hand offering to show her the snowdrops, she was glad to accept, although there was no sign of snow. Elsie, now a little flushed, was first shown around the garden and then to the gurgling brook, where snowdrops were in early bloom. When they returned, not only were Elsie's patent shoes spattered with mud, but also her knee. She'd slipped on the slimy moss and fallen. Joan led her back to the kitchen, where Hinchliffe carefully cleaned and dried her knee and her shoes. Elsie was charmed.

"You're such a gentleman, Raymond," she whispered.

Soon, they heard gentle tapping on a glass. Brancker, standing in front of the piano, next to his own portrait, was poised to make an announcement. He had a spoon in one hand, a glass in the other.

"Ladies and gentlemen, may I have your attention for a moment. We are here today, on this joyous occasion, for the christening of beautiful baby Pamela. Please lift your glasses. We all wish her a life of great joy, good health and life-long prosperity."

Everybody raised their glasses. "Hear, hear!"

Brancker wasn't finished. "Now, there's something else I have to tell you all. But first, you must promise—you're all sworn to secrecy. Absolute secrecy! Agreed?"

There were cries of, "Yes, yes!"

"Of course."

"Absolutely, old man!"

Everyone had heard the rumors and suspected something was coming. All eyes were fixed on Brancker. "As you all know, Captain Raymond Hinchliffe is one of our greatest pilots, having been a war ace shooting down six enemy planes. Since then, he's made many historic landmark flights. Now, it should be no surprise that this brave airman is about to embark on yet another great flight. Yes, in the interest of aviation development and promotion, an Atlantic attempt will be made soon by this hero. Serving as his copilot will be …" At this point Brancker glanced at Elsie and held up his hand ready to single out the individual. He swung round and pointed to Sinclair.

"… Captain Gordon Sinclair!"

Everyone did a double take, with furrowed brows.

"I should also mention, that this daring project is to be entirely financed by the Honorable Elsie Mackay." Brancker beamed at Elsie, who smiled coyly, as she received light applause.

"This journey will be a tough one, but we know if anyone can make it, Captain Hinchliffe can. We shall be in debt to these two very brave aviators for years to come, and of course to Miss Mackay. So, once again, let us raise our glasses to these gallant warriors of the air and wish them the best of luck and Godspeed!"

Excitement swept the room. "The best of luck!" everyone said in unison.

Millie did her best to look happy. She decided to grant Elsie her wish. She sat down to hushed whispers, opened the piano keyboard and began to play. The guests were enraptured. After about half an hour, Millie got up from the piano. She'd seen Lowenstein standing at the window, looking distraught.

"Alfred, what's the matter?" She sensed his distress.

"Look out there. There's a magpie. One magpie! I don't like magpies," he answered.

"There were three just now, and one flew away and then there were two. Three for a girl, two for joy—"

"And now there's *one!* I know the damned rhyme!" he snapped. "Only too well ..." his voice tapered off sadly.

Millie realized she'd misjudged him. A black aura did not only indicate evil or hatred, but could also indicate depression. Smothering, debilitating depression and self loathing. She felt for him.

Lowenstein went home.

10

ELSIE'S PORTRAIT

Tuesday, January 10, 1928.

Elsie, decked out in a burgundy cloche hat and mink stole, stood perfectly still beside the piano, her pose provocative and idealistic—the perfect suffragette. She stared heavenward, a diamond-encrusted crucifix at her throat, a look of longing in her eyes. She was obviously thoroughly enjoying the experience. Millie stood at her easel, squeezing more dabs of paint in a fan around her pallet in varying colors.

The portrait was taking shape—though certainly nothing to be viewed or admired yet. This was Elsie's second sitting. She was a good model, but impatient to see the finished result. There was a lot of red in her aura along with streaks of yellow, pink, green, orange and gold. Millie also saw hints of darkness, but no badness in her. She put it down to over-ambition, or sadness.

However, one dominant color she saw did strike her. Purple. Lost love or, bad luck in love—although such people were capable of giving unconditional love.

"When will I be able to see it?" Elsie asked.

Millie took a broad brush and laid a thick coat of Titanium White around the head and background.

"In a few months. Nothing to see yet. I'm just blocking you in. Don't move. Originals take a while—they have to percolate. Copies I can do in no time."

Millie went to the corner and retrieved a tripod and set up her plate camera. She took four shots to use in future weeks, when Elsie wouldn't be available, although in truth, she had Elsie's image set well enough in her photographic memory. After their session in the studio, and the portrait was shrouded, they moved to the living room, where

Elsie sat happily with the baby in her lap, while Joan played with her dolls on the couch. Millie watched Elsie. She'd obviously make a fine mother one day.

"There, there little one," Elsie cooed. "Should I put her down now, Millie?"

"Yes, she's probably ready for a nap."

Elsie carefully laid the infant on her stomach in her bassinet. A tray of tea waited on the table.

"You're *so* lucky, Millie," she said.

"There's nothing stopping you, Elsie. Just find the right man. The rest is pretty easy."

"It's the first part I'm having trouble with—as *always*. If he's out there somewhere, I haven't found him yet. After this flight, maybe. I'm one of these girls who falls in love easily. *Always* with the wrong man, though. And it *always* ends up in disaster!" Elsie said.

"Then you must be more careful and more selective, Elsie."

"You know Millie, I was a nurse during the war and when I think of the millions of our beautiful young boys lost, I think one of them might have been my Mr. Right—and now he's gone forever. I was married a couple of times. They didn't end well, much to the chagrin of my father," Elsie said.

At times, to Millie, Elsie possessed a haunted look. She would capture this in Elsie's portrait. She must've seen some dreadful things. Was it that or bad luck in love, or the relationship with her father? Maybe a combination of all those things.

"Do you get along well with your parents?"

"They annoy me more than I can tell you," Elsie snapped. "I'm the eldest, and it is *I* that should be groomed to take over the family business, but no. I'm *female*. And being *female* counts for nothing!"

Millie added thwarted ambition to the list.

"So, you have brothers?"

"My brother is a sweetheart. I love him dearly. But it's hard for him. He's not cut out for the rough and tumble of it all."

Elsie poured the tea into the cups on the tray.

"So, how does your family feel about all this, Elsie?"

Elsie looked startled.

She went to pick up the milk jug, but sent it flying. "Oh, damn! They don't know about it. And we must keep it that way. I've tried a lot of things—acting, modeling, my father even let me design some of the cabins on his ships. Nothing lasts. Now, I feel right about this—yes, this is what I'm meant to do. It's all going to work out fine, I just know it. Maybe father will take me seriously after this."

Millie looked at her dubiously.

11

GRANTHAM

Friday, March 2, 1928.

O n a sunny but chilly Friday morning in March, they packed up
the Bentley, ready for the big move. Hinchliffe kissed the
children. It'd be a few weeks before he saw them again. He'd
miss them. The plan was to test and practice with the plane at
Cranwell until the spring weather of April or May. Then they'd start
out. Things were going according to plan and Hinchliffe was
confident. It was a pity the Brooklands airstrip was too short. That
place had been closer to home. But he was familiar with Cranwell.
He'd trained many fresh, young pilots there during the war.

Hinchliffe picked up Joan in his arms and kissed her tenderly. He
then delved into one of the large patch-pockets in his leather greatcoat
and produced a silver music box with a silver Sopwith Camel biplane
on the lid. It had a cherry colored nose, just like his own warplane. He
turned the key and the music box started, while the plane turned. An
inscription on the lid read,

TO DARLING JOAN, LOVE ALWAYS – DADDY

Joan was enthralled. She opened the box. Inside, Hinchliffe had
placed a photo of himself along with his golden military wings and a
few medals. Millie and Kate were tearful, but Joan took it in her stride.
She was used to Daddy going away on trips—but she'd soon miss her
mother.

"You be a good girl for Auntie Kate and help her look after your
baby sister," Millie urged, as she gave Joan a hug and big kiss.

"All right, Mum. When are you coming back?" Joan asked,
clinging to Kate's hand.

"I'll be back in about a week," Millie answered. "Give your Daddy another kiss."

Hinchliffe and Millie climbed into the car. As they pulled away, everyone waved goodbye.

"I'll see you soon, little one, I promise," Hinchliffe shouted.

"Just a few days, darling. Be good. Take care," Millie called.

After a couple of hours, they stopped on a country road for a break, to eat sandwiches and drink coffee. After continuing for another hour or so, the landscape became snowy, beautiful in the winter sun. Hinchliffe put the top down and Millie put on her sunglasses. Bundled up, they kept warm and savored each other's company.

Millie was having serious thoughts again. She put it down to 'the jitters'. It was all becoming a reality. She looked over at Hinchliffe and he smiled, confident as ever. Anyway, there was plenty of time, they'd got three more months. They'd get well prepared. He'd be successful; he always was. She relaxed and enjoyed the rest of the journey.

They soon arrived at RAF Cranwell, where they'd arranged to meet Sinclair. He'd expected to arrive around 1 o'clock. After checking at the gate, Hinchliffe pulled the car along a side road, parallel to the grassy runway, which had been covered with a dusting of snow. It was 12:45 p.m. They drank the rest of their coffee and watched the sky. It was clear and flat calm, the orange windsock hanging limply on its post. Just after one, they heard the unmistakable drone. *Endeavour* circled the landing strip and then made a perfect landing.

While Sinclair was taxiing up to the parking area at Cranwell, fifteen miles away in Grantham, Elsie's two limousines were pulling up to the Hotel George, followed by their white van. Elsie excitedly jumped out and barked orders to her staff, who set to it, carrying suitcases, bags and boxes into the lobby. Once checked in, the hotel staff carried Elsie's stuff up to her suite on the first floor. Elsie's servants and chauffeurs were assigned rooms in the attic.

Thirty minutes later, Hinchliffe's Bentley drew up with Millie and Hinchliffe in front and Sinclair in the jump seat. They made their way to the front desk; Hinchliffe and Sinclair carried their bags.

"I believe you have rooms booked in the name of MacGregor?" Hinchliffe asked.

"Yes. Good afternoon, sir. My name's Claude. Miss MacGregor has already arrived. You're booked in for a minimum of two months with the possibility of extending to three," the clerk answered. He handed two room keys to a bellboy, who led them to the staircase. A porter followed with the luggage.

An hour later, George Hunter's blue AC 12 Royal drophead coupé drew up outside the hotel. His eyes were searching. He drove round to the rear, where he spotted Hinchliffe's dark green Bentley, a black Rolls Royce, a black Daimler and a white transport van—the same one he'd seen at Brooklands. He was very pleased with himself.

"Yes!" he exclaimed clapping his hands together. "This is the stuff scoops are made of!"

Later that evening, Hinchliffe's team sat together in the dining room. Hinchliffe thought it premature to celebrate, and probably bad luck, but they were upbeat. Millie concealed her apprehension.

It'd been Sinclair's task to put together all the equipment, tools, spares and supplies necessary for the undertaking. Elsie had been in charge of transport and shipping, and of course, paying the bills.

"So, what do you think about the schedule now, Ray? How much more testing do you need?" Millie asked.

"Where are we now—March 2nd. Depending on the Germans and the weather—eight weeks, or so, I guess."

Sinclair sat back in his chair. "We've completed most of her testing at Brooklands. She came out with flying colors. We've still got to check fuel consumption and handling with a full fuel load," he said.

"Okay, I'll get back up here to see you off in May then," Millie said.

"I'll come down again a couple of times before we leave and say goodbye to Joan and the baby. Then I'll bring you back here to wave us off—that's if you want to," Hinchliffe said.

"I definitely want to!" Millie said, feeling a fluttering in her stomach.

Sinclair got up to leave, "Excuse me, I need to get a few things sorted out for the morning."

"Right Gordon, bring those other spark plugs. We'll try them first thing," Hinchliffe told him.

When Sinclair had gone, Hinchliffe turned to Elsie. "Have you taken out the insurance, Elsie?"

Elsie's discomfort was obvious. "Er, no, not yet. I've arranged for my bank manager to send the premium as soon as I give him the word. He already has all the documentation."

"Why wait? It's *very* important."

Millie put her hand on her husband's arm, "Ray, Elsie will get to it."

"No, that's okay, Millie. I wanted to wait a while, in case it gets out, that's all," Elsie assured them.

Hinchliffe gave Elsie one of his looks. "I think you're being over-cautious, Elsie. I don't want things going awry. It's *much, much* too important."

She hated those looks. They sliced her like a knife.

It sounded like pandemonium in the street outside the hotel the following morning. The hunt had gathered, with hounds barking, horses neighing and nickering, people jabbering excitedly, their steamy breath in the sunlight. Although bitterly cold, it was a beautiful scene in vivid colors of red and black against another fresh dusting of snow.

Hinchliffe's team, including Elsie and Sinclair, had breakfasted early and piled into Elsie's limo to get to the aerodrome. Millie would spend some time at the field with them and take photos. The driver would bring her back to the hotel when she'd had enough. The limousine slowly moved off behind the hunt. Millie was taken with the dazzling scene—it'd make a nice painting.

"Don't they look magnificent, Ray?" she said.

"They're all nuts, if you ask me," Hinchliffe grumbled.

After a slow drive to the edge of town, the hunt turned into a field. The car accelerated. When they got to the aerodrome, Elsie removed the tie-down ropes, while Hinchliffe and Sinclair brushed snow off the wings and fuselage. After that, Sinclair changed the spark plugs and closed the cowling.

Prior to Hinchliffe and Elsie taking off, Millie had them pose in front of the plane in the piercing, blustery wind. Hinchliffe looked grim, but resolute. Elsie forced a smile. She would've been horrified to know that all the while her actions were being closely observed, as they had been for months.

The *Daily Express's* George Hunter was once again lurking at the edge of nearby woods, a quarter mile away. He watched Elsie climb into the plane and grinned. He noticed she was in the pilot's seat, but then, he'd never seen Hinchliffe in that seat. He presumed Hinchliffe preferred sitting on the right side, due to his lack of one eye. Before lowering his binoculars, his gaze settled on Millie. He was struck by her beauty, his heart skipped a beat. He admired her for a few moments before thrusting his binoculars back into this overcoat pocket. A rook circled above and settled on a branch above his head, cawing loudly. It dropped a sloppy, white deposit on his shoulder.

"Well, thanks a lot mate!" Hunter exclaimed in his refined London University accent, thinking maybe he was being rebuked for looking at such a fine married woman. He looked up at the bobbing black bird. "Some people would take that as an insult, but I'm going take it as a sign of good luck—so there!" He brushed off the bird droppings with his handkerchief, pulled down his homburg hat, and marched off to find a more advantageous spot from which to spy. The bird followed him. "Go away! You're going to give me away, you soppy bugger," Hunter growled.

The plane had dual controls. Elsie was already in the pilot's seat, her seat belt fastened. She was anxious to get up in the air. After kissing Millie, Hinchliffe clambered in. He gave her a wave and a smile and winked at Sinclair. He pulled out his black cat lucky charm and hung it on the instrument panel as usual.

"Okay, let's crank her up," Hinchliffe ordered.

Elsie pulled the starter and the engine burst into life. *Endeavour* taxied slowly down the strip to the takeoff position. Millie and Sinclair headed back to the car to sit in comfort, out of the miserable wind. The huntsman's horn sounded close by in the woods, accompanied by thundering hooves. Millie wished she could see them. In the snow, they'd looked magnificent, but she sensed fear in the air. She knew it was the fear of the *poor* fox. She shuddered. Nonetheless, she'd try and get some photos if possible—but not of anything horrible, like the fox being … no, she couldn't bear to think about that.

Endeavour was now standing at the top of the field. Elsie ran the engine up and tested the magnetos. She waggled the ailerons and checked the elevators. She pushed her feet back and forth, to check the rudder was free, then gunned the engine. The plane was hesitant in the snow at first, but gradually worked up speed. They lifted off. Nearby, the red fox was running scared for his life, pursued by the yelping hounds. It darted from the woods into the open fields, but was losing ground. Elsie climbed to about 2,000 feet and circled the aerodrome. They had a bird's eye view of the hunt. Elsie was like a little girl.

"Oh no, little fox! Run! Run! Don't let them catch you!"

Hinchliffe seized the controls. "Here, let me have her!"

He gave it more gas and wheeled the plane around, climbing as he did so. He kept his eye on the hunt, at right angles to their path. Suddenly, he pushed the plane's nose sharply down. *Endeavour* screamed toward the ground at a sharp angle, between the fox and the lead hounds, cutting them off. At about fifteen feet, Hinchliffe pulled the plane up sharply with a great WHOOSH. The canines stopped in their tracks, howling in terror, forgetting the fox.

The steaming horses coming up behind lost momentum and traction. The pristine hunt became a mass of confusion, hounds and horses slipping and sliding in all directions. Four or five riders lost their seats and ended up red-faced in the snow, two face down. They struggled to their feet and shook their fists at the plane, muttering curses. The fox made a clean getaway into the woods.

Elsie clapped her hands together with glee. She looked across at Hinchliffe, a hint of love in her eyes. "So, you are an old softie after all, Raymond! Bravo!"

"I thought it might be nice for the fox to win for a change," said Hinchliffe.

Millie with her camera in hand had witnessed it all, but decided not to take pictures. Better not to embarrass these people any further.

It wasn't a pretty sight.

12

A SURPRISE VISITOR

Monday, March 5, 1928.

Things had gone well every day since they arrived; the plane was proving to be everything Hinchliffe had hoped for. It hadn't snowed anymore, so they were able to use the runway without problems. They ran fuel consumption tests and took off with heavy loads as expected for their final take off from Cranwell. Landing with that load proved to be tricky and hard on the wheel struts, but they seemed to get away with it. They landed with the full load four times. After that, they flew with the auxiliary tanks empty.

Hinchliffe had purchased an expensive compass that proved to be a fine instrument, or at least it did on these tests. Throughout operations, Millie took photographs. The whole gang was upbeat and they often struck silly poses for her. She'd develop them and mount them when she got home.

Millie got on famously with Elsie. She felt the poor girl needed a real friend. Elsie asked her to come flying with her and she accepted. Millie had done a lot of flying with her husband over the years, so it wasn't a scary thing for her. In fact, Millie was a pretty good pilot, herself. She could land and take off like a pro. They flew around the countryside for an hour and then over Grantham. Millie offered to land and Elsie encouraged her, which she did without difficulty.

"That was a damned fine landing, Millie old girl!" Elsie exclaimed as they taxied along the runway. When Elsie opened her door to get out, Millie found that her seat belt was jammed. Panic rose in her chest for a moment, and she couldn't breathe.

"Don't worry, Millie, I'll get you out," Elsie said. She went round to Millie's side and opened the door. "This thing jams sometimes. It's a knack, you just have to jiggle it around a bit, that's all." Elsie pulled the metal clasp from side to side. "There, no problem. You're free."

"I had a sudden fear of being trapped," Millie said. "I can't explain."

"I'll let you into a secret, darling—I have fear of the water! I can't even swim," Elsie whispered.

Millie looked incredulous.

"I almost drowned in the sea near the castle, as a child. Don't whatever you do, tell your husband. I plan to stay up in the air—not to go swimming!"

Often Sinclair took control of the plane (and Elsie), while Hinchliffe and Millie spent time together. Once they spent the afternoon in bed. Another time, they walked in the snowy woods after a walk around town. They'd never been happier, although Hinchliffe's looming departure gave Millie a knot in her stomach.

Hunter continued to stalk them. Once or twice, he even stood near them in the hotel bar, listening to their conversation. Hinchliffe noticed him and tried to place him. He could swear he'd seen him somewhere before—somewhere down south, perhaps in London. Hunter had a pretty good story by now and decided to break it. His editor had been on his case. He'd been taking too long on this assignment. He called the *Daily Express*.

"You'll never guess. They're all here—including Elsie Mackay! That's the icing on the cake. I smell something really big," he told the editor.

The next day, in Glenapp Castle in Ayrshire, Scotland, Lord Inchcape sat in his medieval chamber, wrapped in his burgundy, silk dressing gown. His nostrils flared and his eyes blazed. He stared in fury at the *Scottish Sunday Express*. The headline screamed:

LORD'S DAUGHTER TO FLY THE ATLANTIC
– ANY DAY NOW

Underneath the headline was a glamorous photo of Elsie, from her movie *Nothing But the Truth*.

Inchcape turned to his butler, standing stiffly beside the lord's desk.

"Get Jonathan!"

Elsie had upset the old man many times over the years. She'd married men he'd disapproved of and forbidden her to marry. There was always something. Now this! Five minutes later, Elsie's brother stood in front of his father. The old Scot threw down the newspaper.

"That sister of yours is about to go off and make a fool of herself again—and her family!" he yelled.

Jonathan picked up the newspaper and read the headline. He screwed up his face in horror. "Oh, no!"

"Get down there and find out if this is true. And if it is—*then stop her!*"

Hinchliffe, Millie, Sinclair and Elsie entered the hotel lobby after another successful day of testing. They looked pleased with themselves. Claude, the front desk manager, caught Elsie's eye and leaned forward. "Miss MacGregor!"

He had a bemused look.

"Yes."

"There's a young man here to see a *Miss Mackay*. I told him we have no one here by that name—"

"What's *his* name?"

"Jonathan Mackay, madam—"

"Oh, my God! Where is he?"

"Waiting in the lounge."

Hinchliffe stepped up to Elsie. "Who is he?" But Elsie was in too much of a hurry to answer. She disappeared along the corridor. Hinchliffe watched her uneasily.

When Elsie entered the lounge, Jonathan was sitting in an armchair staring into the flames of a log fire. Elsie flew to him and he jumped to his feet. "Jonathan, my darling, what on earth are you doing here?" she exclaimed, embracing him.

He stared into her eyes. "Oh, Sis, what's going on?"

"What are you talking about?" she demanded.

Her brother pulled out their father's folded newspaper from inside his jacket and held it up.

"Damn the newspapers!" Elsie shouted.

"Elsie, is it *true*?"

"I suppose father sent you?"

"He's in a fury!"

"He *would* be!"

The siblings said nothing for a few moments, breathing heavily, clinging to each other. Jonathan put his forehead against hers. "If there's any truth to it, I beg you to give it up. Leave it to others to pull these silly stunts. So *many* have been lost, Elsie."

"I'm financing the project, that's all. Come upstairs and freshen up and we'll have dinner with my two pilots. You'll see."

That seemed to allay Jonathan's fears. He followed Elsie to her suite and bathed. While he did this, Elsie scuttled off to Hinchliffe's room to inform him. Hinchliffe was none too pleased. He'd see how this all played out.

Hinchliffe, Millie and Sinclair were having their second cocktail in the bar when Elsie and her brother arrived. All were dressed for dinner. Initially, this meeting was strained. Hunter was sitting at the bar, his back to them. He soon realized he'd set the cat among the pigeons.

"Sorry we're a little late," Elsie said. "This is my brother, Jonathan. And this—" she said, singling out Sinclair, "—is Captain Gordon Sinclair, the *copilot*."

Hunter sat behind them, listening and smiling to himself. He lit a cigarette. Jonathan and Sinclair shook hands. Hinchliffe understood this order of introduction.

"And this is Captain Raymond Hinchliffe, the pilot, and his wife, Emilie."

Hands were shaken, accompanied by forced smiles. Hinchliffe was rather cool.

"Please call me Millie," Millie said pleasantly. "What brings you to Grantham?"

"I've come to visit my sister, Elsie, to see what she's up to. Our father has been reading the papers and—"

"I've told him that the newspapers have got the story all wrong, Gordon is the copilot, and I'm merely the financier of the project," Elsie interjected.

Jonathan looked from one to the other for confirmation. "Is it true?" the beleaguered boy asked. Millie took pity on him. Hinchliffe was debating with himself. He was uncomfortable. There was a lot at stake.

After a long pause, Sinclair jumped in. "I'm the copilot, as Elsie just told you. There'll be no room for three people on this flight, I can *absolutely* assure you of that," he said.

Jonathan scanned their faces. He seemed convinced, relief visibly showing in his face.

With this turn of affairs, Hinchliffe believed Sinclair could quite well turn out to be his copilot. "Captain Sinclair is an experienced veteran war pilot," he said.

Jonathan nodded. "I suppose that makes sense," he said.

"Let's go in and have dinner, shall we?" Elsie said, moving things along.

Hunter left the bar. He'd learned all he needed to know for one evening. He went to a small café in town where he had fish and chips.

Dinner went smoothly, with little alcohol consumed. A room was found for Jonathan and he stayed the night. The next morning, they took him to the station to return to Scotland. Once he'd gone, Hinchliffe's annoyance became apparent.

"It's my father," Elsie said. "He *mustn't* find out!"

"Look Elsie, if you're a liar, that's one thing, but I don't appreciate you making the rest of us liars!"

On the way to the aerodrome, Hinchliffe changed his mind.

"Gordon, take over for me today, will you, please? I'm going to spend the day with Millie."

"I'm leaving tomorrow," Millie said.

"Oh Millie, I'm sorry. I wish you could stay longer," Elsie said.

"I need to get back to the children."

"I got a couple of little gifts for them, for you to take back," Elsie said.

Hinchliffe and Millie spent a pleasant day together and after shopping in town, went back to the hotel room. It'd be a couple weeks before they'd be together again.

Back in Scotland, later that day, Jonathan explained the situation to his father, but the crusty laird remained skeptical. He took action, calling one of his cohorts in government, Sir Samuel Hoare, the present Minister of State for Air. The minister was sympathetic, having children of his own. He said he'd look into the matter immediately.

Later that night, Elsie sat unsteadily on a stool at the hotel bar. She was quite drunk. The necessity of having to lie to her brother had devastated her, and Hinchliffe's admonishment had upset her deeply. She wasn't sure if she could continue with this thing. The world was crumbling around her. She struck her lighter, its flame wavering under a cigarette. It wouldn't stay still. All eyes in the bar were upon her. Finally, another flame appeared under her cigarette from another lighter held by a steady hand—that of George Hunter. She drew hard on her cigarette and blew a smoke cloud across the bar. She nodded a dismissive thanks to Hunter, without batting a bleary eye.

"So, you're a pilot?" Hunter murmured.

"Who the hell are you?" she snapped and then, "Hey barman, give me another."

"Let me," Hunter offered.

Hinchliffe was standing at the door. He'd seen and heard enough, and finally placed Hunter. He pointed his finger at him.

"*The Ritz!*" he shouted.

Hinchliffe had seen him in the hotel bar and had his suspicions. The man seemed to have been taking too much of an interest in Elsie—as he'd done at the Ritz last June. Infuriated, he marched up the stairs to their room to find Millie. A few minutes later, Millie was in the bar assisting Elsie, and prising her away from Hunter.

"Elsie, what's wrong?" Millie asked, although it was obvious.

"I'm getting drunk, can't you see?"

Elsie knocked her drink over. It spilled over the bar and into her lap. She was about to fall off her bar stool, but Millie caught her, aided by Hunter. Millie studied the reporter for a second, and then with a nod of thanks, led Elsie out. Hunter found Millie even more attractive up close. He was smitten. He watched them leave.

"Come on Elsie, let me help you," Millie said.

As they went, people stared at Elsie in disgust.

"What you looking at?" Elsie yelled across the bar. But she was thankful Millie had shown up, welcoming her attention. They staggered together, arms about each other, toward the stairs. Once inside Elsie's room, Elsie flopped onto the bed.

"Oh, Elsie, what are we going to do with you?" Millie said.

"How I envy you," Elsie said.

"You're the one who has it all," Millie replied.

Elsie sat up. "If only you knew. That's where you're wrong. *You're* the one who has it all. I have *nothing*. My life means *nothing*. My looks are fading." She pulled at her hair, as though it belonged to a mangy dog. "Sure, I have money, my dear father's money. ... I'll never find a man like Hinch."

Millie put her arms around her and they hugged like sisters. "Don't be silly, Elsie, you're beautiful."

"I'm ugly!"

"Oh, come on! It's just the gin. You'll be fine in the morning, my dear," Millie said, turning out the oil lamp.

Elsie laid down her head and closed her eyes. "Oh, Jonathan, what have I done? Please forgive me ..." Her voice trailed off.

She was out cold.

13

BAD NEWS

Friday, March 9, 1928.

F riday morning was depressing, with sleet mixed with drizzle. Not a day for flying. Elsie arranged for one of her chauffeurs to take Millie and Hinchliffe to the station. As they were saying their good-byes in the lobby, Elsie put her hand on Hinchliffe's arm. "Ray, since it's lousy, I'd like to spend some time this morning studying the maps. Could I borrow them please?"

Hinchliffe dug his room key out of his pocket and handed it to Elsie. "Sure, they're on my table. Take care of them. Let me have them back when you're finished with them."

At Grantham Station, Millie and Hinchliffe walked along the platform arm in arm in silence, until they reached an empty carriage. Hinchliffe climbed aboard and stashed Millie's case in the overhead rack and came and stood with her on the platform. They wrapped their arms around one another and kissed. He pulled his watch from his pocket, its strap broken.

"You need to get a new strap, Ray. You'll need that on your wrist."

"I meant to buy one in town, yesterday. I'll get one, don't worry," he said.

There was a loud whistle and doors slammed down the platform. Millie climbed into the carriage and hung out the window. She reached into her handbag and pulled out the photo of her and Joan together Hinchliffe had taken in the garden.

"I meant to give you this earlier. Put it in your wallet," Millie said. He did so and they kissed again.

"It's been wonderful having you here, Millie. I'll always love you, you know."

"Take care, my darling. Please come down and see us soon."

"I will. I promise."

The train jerked forward. It traveled slowly, she from him, he from her. He became drowned in black smoke. It was then, in the blackness, she saw his aura—usually vibrant multicolors—now predominantly purple and mauve. As she moved away, the black smoke, too, turned into swirling clouds of purple. She didn't take her eyes from him until he was gone. She had an unbearable sinking feeling as he disappeared. What did it all mean? She sank into her seat. As she'd watched him, she'd felt his spirit slipping away, as though this iron monster was pulling them apart, clacking wheels measuring the distance, yard by yard. Millie felt terribly afraid.

While Hinchliffe and Millie were at the station, Elsie was letting herself into Hinchliffe's room. She locked the door behind her. The maps were on the table. She sorted through them: maps of England, Wales and Ireland; a large map of the Atlantic; and large-scale maps of Newfoundland, Canada and the northern states of the U.S.A. She returned them to their folder and put them back on the table. She looked around the room. Everything was neat and tidy. She went to the double bed and pulled back the covers and stared at the pillows. She wondered which side he slept. She rubbed her hand on one of the pillows.

After replacing the bed covers, Elsie went to the high chest of drawers, where Hinchliffe's black cat charm was lying in an ashtray. She picked it up and fingered the worry beads. Also resting there, beside his pocket knife, was his huge calabash pipe. She smiled and picked it up. She'd never seen him smoke it. She sniffed its bowl and then put the stem in her mouth and then, taking it out, she licked her lips and closed her eyes. She replaced the pipe and opened the top drawer, where she saw Hinchliffe's maroon sweater—the one he'd been wearing yesterday. She pulled it out and held it up. She buried her face in it, breathing in his manly odor, real or imagined. She hugged it tightly to her breast and closed her eyes again for a blissful moment. There was a knock on the door, startling her and bringing her back. She wondered if the Hinchliffes had returned. She wiped tears from her cheeks and hurriedly refolded the sweater, slipping it back in the drawer. She went back to the folder and opened one of the maps and spread it on the table, as though she'd been studying it. Then she opened the door to find one of the hotel maids with her trolley.

"Oh, come in," Elsie said with a flash of guilt and irritation.

"No, no. I'll come back later," the maid said.

"Please come in. I'm leaving," Elsie said. She returned to the table, gathered up the maps and left.

After putting Millie on the train, Hinchliffe returned to the hotel. He entered the lobby, where he was joined by Elsie who'd seen the car return from her window. Claude held up a telephone message. Hinchliffe read it:

Important you call me as soon as possible. Brancker.

Brancker had left his direct line number at the Air Ministry. Hinchliffe handed the note back to Claude.

"Please call this number."

He went straight to the wooden telephone booth at the end of the lobby to wait for the call. His mind went back to the hunt. He was about to receive a good bollocking, he was sure of that. He knew he deserved it. Presently, the phone rang. He picked it up.

"Hello, this is Hinchliffe."

"Ah, Raymond, thank you so much for calling back, old boy. How are things?"

"Excellent. Testing has been going very well. The plane is proving to be up to the task."

Brancker sounded hesitant, almost coy. "Good. I've just heard the Germans are almost ready."

"Damn!"

"Don't worry, they're heavily snowed in at the moment. Might be quite a while." Then he got ready to drop the bombshell. "Raymond there's something else. ..."

"What?"

"There's been a deuce of a lot of pressure here from somewhere."

"Why, what's happened?"

"I'm afraid I have to inform you that Cranwell will be off limits to you after Tuesday."

Hinchliffe was astounded. "*What!*"

"Deck's stacked against us, I'm afraid," Brancker said.

"Why? Who?"

"Someone is out to stop you."

Suddenly, it was obvious. He didn't need it spelling out.

"Hinch, promise me, you won't let this affect your judgment. Please, I beg you."

"It won't."

"Oh, and Raymond—"

"Yes."

"Don't cut up the hunt anymore, there's a good chap!"

Elsie was waiting outside the booth. She saw him downcast.

"What just happened, Ray?"

Millie's train sped through the countryside past Cardington. She sat alone with her thoughts. She glanced across at the great sheds. She thought of their good friends and their drink at the King's Arms. She wondered how they were getting on over there with the construction of their airship. Were they correct in thinking Hinch was crazy? Or was her husband right about their airship? She decided they were all crazy! She couldn't shake the feeling of doom that had descended over her like a clammy blanket. It was here, as she passed on her way by Cardington in the drizzle, that Emilie Hinchliffe made up her mind. He was *not* going! She knew her instincts were right. She would not stand idly by. She'd put a stop to it. *Whatever* it took. She'd write to him over the weekend. She had plenty of time. No need to panic. That was settled. As good as done!

Millie arrived home later that afternoon. Kate met her at the door with the baby in her arms. Joan was over the moon to see her and both Butch and Whiskey made a great fuss with tail-wagging and loud meowing. Millie knelt down beside Joan and embraced her. "My darling daughter, come here and give me a great big kiss. Oh, how I've missed you!" She picked up the baby and smothered her with kisses, too. Once inside the house, Millie fished out the stuffed, yellow elephant that 'Auntie' Elsie had sent and gave it to Joan. She was delighted. Millie put the second gift, a tiny pink teddy bear, alongside the baby in her bassinet.

Later that evening, after dinner, Hinchliffe, Sinclair and Elsie remained at their table studying a map of the Atlantic Ocean. Hinchliffe pointed at the coast of western Ireland with a steak knife. "From here, we'll head north-west toward Newfoundland. If the weather's favorable, we'll leave on Tuesday."

Elsie was shocked. This had all come so suddenly. "That's the thirteenth!"

"So?"

"Well, at least, it's not Friday!" Sinclair snapped.

Hinchliffe looked at her sternly. "Have you put that insurance in place, Elsie?"

"Er, yes, I'll check on that, don't worry," Elsie replied. Her response was evasive as the insurance was *not* in place. But the documentation was ready. She'd get it sorted out first thing in the morning. She knew her bank on the Strand was open on Saturday mornings. She'd jump right on it.

Hinchliffe asked Elsie to arrange to have the hotel kitchen prepare a generous food basket for 'a trip to the country— enough for six'— sandwiches, coffee, water, chocolate, hard boiled eggs and fruit.

"Rather a lot, isn't it?" Elsie asked.

"If we crash-land in *Newfoundland*, we might be glad of the extra rations," Hinchliffe told her with a crooked smile. Sinclair nodded in agreement. Elsie looked startled, then said she'd set that up for early Tuesday morning.

Elsie called the bank at 9 o'clock the next morning. She'd already filled in all the insurance forms and actually discussed the flight with her insurance company. Terms had been agreed. The premium demanded was extortionate. It was necessary and she was more than glad to pay for it, especially since she'd got to know Hinchliffe's family. Before leaving London, Elsie had lodged the documents with the bank and arranged for the manager to make sure all the documentation was taken by courier to the insurance company. The bank was happy to do it—the Mackays were a rich and powerful family, and the bank was willing to fulfill their every need.

"You have my signed check?" Elsie asked.

"Indeed, I do, Miss Mackay. I have it here in front of me," said the bank manager.

"Make sure the papers are in the insurance company's hands first thing Monday morning without fail!" Elsie demanded.

"'Absolutely, without fail. Yes, madam."

Whilst Elsie was giving her bank manager instructions from Grantham, Millie was sitting in her kitchen feeding the baby. Joan was eating porridge, Kate drinking tea. Millie had made her decision and had discussed her misgiving with Kate. Kate had been in full agreement, after putting herself in Millie's position. In fact, if Elsie decided not to go at the last moment, Kate knew she *would* be in Millie's position and she didn't like that feeling. The recent failed Atlantic attempts had completely changed everything for both women. They'd decided it would be better if the whole idea was dropped. *It just wasn't worth it!*

"I want you to know that you and Gordon can stay here as long as you like," Millie told Kate that morning. Millie thought that he and Gordon could work on something else together without this huge risk. Maybe a small European freight airline of their own, or something along those lines. They'd find investors. Maybe she'd go to work on Lowenstein herself on that score. She'd made a connection with him the last time she'd seen him. Elsie would just have to find another pilot.

In the afternoon, Millie went into her studio and began sketching out *The Grantham Hunt.* By evening, she had much of it blocked in: a snowy scene with colorful huntsmen and the hounds, set against the backdrop of the majestic Hotel George. It was going to be a beautiful piece of work—one of her best. While she worked, she thought of what she'd say in her letter to Hinchliffe.

Sunday morning, Millie sat at Hinchliffe's small desk in the living room and wrote the letter. It flowed straight from her heart.

My Own Dearest Darling Husband,

What I am about to write is hard in some ways, but very, very easy in others. I have agonized over this since leaving you on the platform in Grantham. As I saw you disappear in that horrible cloud of black smoke, I felt as if I'd never see you again—like a revelation. It was as if my heart was being ripped from my breast. And that is how it would be if anything happened to you. It's a risk I cannot live with, Ray. It's not worth ten thousand pounds, nor ten million, or all the money and jewels on God's earth. So, I am writing to you begging you to give up this Atlantic attempt, for my sake, and for the sake of our two wonderful children. Please, please, my beloved husband, don't leave us. Don't take this risk. Please understand I ask this of you only because I love you with all my heart and with all my soul.

Please come back home as soon as you can.

All my love, for always and forever, your Millie.

Millie read it through. She was satisfied. She stuffed it in an envelope.

Saturday and Sunday were perfect, sunny days spent carrying out the final testing of *Endeavour*, which performed admirably. Hinchliffe kept his eye on Elsie. She appeared to be upbeat and cheerful. He wasn't too worried about recent developments, it might have worked in their favor, what with the Germans ready to set off. As long as the weather held, they'd be all right. His biggest negative would be not getting down to see Millie and the kids before setting off. It felt almost like a betrayal. But on the bright side, it'd all be over in a matter of days. Done and dusted! Money in the bank—their future assured. Ten thousand in prize money. A ten thousand pound fee. You couldn't beat that for less than forty hours' work! That would be enough for him and Sinclair to start their own airline—or to retire and do absolutely nothing. He pictured himself and Millie lying in the hammock in their beloved secret garden with not a care in the world. It was all going to be worth it.

Life would be good.

On Monday morning, Millie and Kate wrapped up warm and went to the village post office. Hinchliffe would receive Millie's letter at the hotel the next morning, without fail. A great burden was lifted from Millie's shoulders. She believed, after careful consideration, Hinchliffe would give in to her wishes. He'd understand that it was out of love that she was asking it of him. Millie returned to her studio and continued painting *The Grantham Hunt.*

That afternoon, Elsie called her bank manager again to make sure everything had gone off without a hitch. He told her that the documentation, together with her signed check, had been taken by courier that morning and it was in the insurance company's hands. He'd personally called the manager of the insurance company who had confirmed this. Hinchliffe was relieved when she told him.

14

CONFESSION

Monday, March 12, 1928.

On Monday evening, Elsie's father was infuriated. Jonathan had been summoned and was once again, standing in front of the big desk, looking forlorn. Lord Inchcape flung down the *Edinburgh Evening News*. The headline came like a hammer blow.

MISS MACKAY READY TO MAKE
ATLANTIC BID

"I knew she was lying to you!" he snarled.

"This can't be true. She assured me," Jonathan stammered. "I met the pilot *and* his copilot, Gordon Sinclair."

"He's just a *shill*, you silly fool! Get down there and stop her. Take one of the cars and get on the road, *right now!*"

Jonathan rushed off. The butler organized the chauffeur. They drove off in the limousine as darkness was falling. They'd have to drive all night to reach Grantham to stop Elsie, if indeed, it was her intention to fly off the next morning.

Elsie had previously decided she'd go to church Tuesday morning at four-thirty, before they set off. After mass on Sunday, she'd arranged with the priest for a special confession and for him to give her holy Communion and a blessing. She'd promised a huge donation to the church. The priest was happy. The church needed a new roof. She left the dinner table early to check with the kitchen on the 'picnic basket' and get ready for the busy morning ahead. She needed to get to bed and get what sleep she could.

Hinchliffe and Sinclair also left to prepare for their early start. They climbed the stairs together. As they were entering their adjacent rooms, Hinchliffe said, "Gordon, be ready to fly tomorrow. There's a good chance she'll back out at the last minute." Hinchliffe came close to Sinclair and whispered. "If she bails, I doubt I'll get my fee, but you and I'll split the prize money."

"You bet, Hinch. I'll be ready, don't you worry," Sinclair replied, convinced Elsie would buckle.

"Oh, and Gordon, please change those plugs out again in the morning. I think we'll stick with the new ones. They might perform better," Hinchliffe said.

"Right you are, Ray. Consider it done."

Jonathan and his chauffeur were hampered by freezing fog when they reached Galloway Forest on the way to Dumfries. They crept along at twenty miles an hour to avoid ending up in a ditch. The fog got thicker the deeper they got into the woods and they had to reduce speed even more. At one point, a deer crossed in front of them. They hit the animal and skidded to a stop on the icy road. The injured creature got up and bounded off. One headlight was broken, spoiling their visibility even more. At this rate, Jonathan wasn't sure they'd make it in time.

Once inside his room, Hinchliffe took out his gear for the flight. He emptied the pockets of his flying coat onto the bed, removing unnecessary stuff—old receipts, coins, etc. He picked up his lucky black cat charm and placed it in the ashtray on the dresser, beside his passport, diary, wallet and heavy-duty pocket knife. He then contacted room service and ordered a bottle of whiskey. When asked what brand, he said it didn't matter. A bottle of Johnny Walker Black Label arrived ten minutes later. After tipping the boy, he placed it on the dresser.

Hinchliffe's beard now had a two-day growth. Before going on long trips he usually didn't shave. It was one of his idiosyncrasies. He shaved once his journey was completed—a good luck ritual. Next, he went down the corridor and jumped in the bath. He wouldn't get a bath for a couple of days. He looked forward to soaking in a big tub in New York in some swanky hotel, and then getting a luxurious shave in the hotel barbershop.

Jonathan and his driver had finally got clear of the fog in Galloway Forest, only to meet more of it when they reached Gretna Green. They'd limped on slowly to Penrith. And now later, whilst Elsie was on her knees in St. John the Divine Catholic Church, Jonathan and the chauffeur were crossing the Yorkshire Dales, stopping occasionally for the odd sheep, cow or deer on the glistening road.

Hunter eased the church door open and stepped inside noiselessly. From there, he heard the sound of whispering; first the voice of a woman, then of a man. He stealthily moved down the church. In the sea of darkness, flickering light spilled from a tiny open chapel between stone arches.

From behind a column, Hunter saw Elsie on her knees before a wizened priest, who sat in a stately chair in front of a tiny altar. They were surrounded by a mass of candles, Elsie's face wracked with guilt and sadness. She began her confession in a whisper. Hunter moved closer. He heard every word.

"Forgive me Father for I have sinned."

"How have you sinned, my child?"

"I have deceived my brother, I am going on a journey forbidden by my father. I have lied to them both. I *am* going Father, I *have to* go."

Hunter smiled to himself, shaking his head as if to say, *there you have it, Georgie Boy.*

"Why do you have to go?"

"It is my destiny, Father."

"Only you and God can know that, child."

"I feel such guilt, I cannot shake it. And there is something else, Father."

"What is it?"

"I am in love with someone."

"Love is a *good thing*—if it is wholesome."

"He is married, he has a lovely family and a wonderful wife."

"Then it is *not* wholesome. You must break with him!" the priest snapped.

"He does not know, Father. It is my secret."

"Nonetheless, you must break away from this man."

Elsie knew the old man was right. This might be the perfect opportunity to get away from Hinchliffe. Sever ties. She would consider this. She'd take this blessing and absorb strength from the holy Communion and see what transpired.

God help me, please!

Hunter had seen and heard enough. Feeling sorry for Elsie, he guiltily left the church without a sound. He returned to the Hotel George. Even for a reporter, he knew too much. He vowed he'd never disclose any of this to anyone.

Millie had gone to bed Monday night secure in the knowledge that Hinchliffe would have her letter in the morning. She slept soundly, that is until she had her recurring dream. Suddenly, she was aware of the amorphous, black entity entering her room. She could feel its love toward her. She was not afraid. She was much comforted by it, and welcomed its presence, as she usually did. But this time, as the entity got closer, it began to take shape. Detail and form became clearer. She could now make out a face and its apparel. It was a man in a great coat. She could hear the coat creaking and smell its leather.

As he leaned over her, his face came into focus. She saw the leather flying cap and the black eye patch. She realized with horror it was an apparition of her husband. She felt trapped, and couldn't move. She awoke in stark terror. She screamed, waking the baby in her crib. With shaking hands, Millie fumbled to take out a match from the box on her side table. She struck one. The hissing flame cast light over Hinchliffe's framed photo. She stared at it, before lighting the lamp. She struggled out of bed and went to the crib and took Pam in her arms. "There, there, little one. Mummy's here," she said, her voice trembling.

The Blessed Virgin stared down at Elsie with unseeing eyes. The priest placed his hands upon Elsie's head. "Your sins of deceit and foolish pride are forgiven. The sin you have not acted upon is also forgiven—you must make your break with this man. I'm sure you love your father and your brother very much—"

"I do Father, I do."

"For this deceit you must recite the Hail Mary fifty times every day for one month."

"I will Father, I will."

The old man made the sign of the cross and recited the prayer of absolution on behalf of the Holy Trinity.

"… Ego te absolvo a peccatis tuis in nomine Patris et Filii et Spiritus Sancti. Amen."

After saying prayers of the Eucharist, he held out the consecrated host to Elsie.

"Accepite, et manducate ex hoc omnes: hoc est enim corpus meum, quod pro vobis tradetur."

Hinchliffe was up at four thirty, after lying awake most of the night. He packed his suitcase ready for Sinclair to deal with later (or Elsie, if she decided she wasn't going). He put his leather flight bag on the bed. He pushed some items into the bag he'd need in New York; not much stuff, he'd buy clothing over there. He took the bottle of scotch and pushed it down the side of the bag. He picked up his passport and pocket knife from the chest of drawers and placed them in the side pocket of the bag. Millie had reminded him not to forget his passport. He would put the knife in his pocket later, when they got to Cranwell. He took his heavy flying coat and laid it over the wing-back chair beside the bed, together with his heavy trousers, woolen shirt and two sweaters. He took his padded flying boots from the closet and placed them beside the chair. He picked up his wallet and diary and stuffed them in his flying coat pocket. He stuffed his calabash pipe in the suitcase—he wouldn't be needing that.

The priest took a gleaming chalice and held it high in the air above Elsie.

"Accepite, et bibite ex eo omnes:"

He held it to her lips.

"Hic est enim calix sanguinis mei novi et aeterni testamenti, qui pro vobis et pro multis effundetur in remissionem peccatorum. Hoc facite in meam commemorationem."

Elsie swallowed the wine and the priest said,

"May the blessing of Almighty God be with you now and forever … in the name of the Father, the Son and the Holy Ghost, Amen."

Before Elsie's blessing was completed, Sinclair, dressed in his warm flying suit, had arrived at the aerodrome in the van. He went over the wings and fuselage removing snow that had fallen during the night. He lifted the cowling and changed the plugs as Hinchliffe had asked. They'd been debating about the plugs all week, and Hinchliffe had finally decided on these. Next, he went round the petrol tanks and bled off the sediment and any water accumulation. He then topped up all the petrol tanks from the storage tanks in the van. While he was there, one of the RAF men came over to check that everything was okay. Sinclair started the engine to make sure the plugs were functioning properly. They were.

Hinchliffe checked his bag and finished packing. He then went to the writing table and laid out a sheet of hotel stationery beside the lamp and sat down. He felt deeply troubled. This was going to be hard. He stared at the blank page trying to think what to say. He wished they had a phone in the cottage, but service wasn't available out in the country. A letter would have to do.

When Elsie left the church just after 5:30 a.m., she appeared to be at peace. Fortified. She'd made her decision. She climbed into the Rolls and headed back to the hotel. Once in her room, she sat down and composed a letter to Jonathan. Her tears fell on the paper as she wrote.

My Dearest Brother,

Forgive me for what I am about to do, and for lying to you. There just was no way out. I am sorry. I promise you though, soon, very soon, you will be very proud of your big sister. And I hope Father will be too. I pray for that.

My fondest love to you, and to Mother and Father.

Your ever-loving Sister,

E

Jonathan and his driver had picked up speed. They'd reached Doncaster and were making good time, heading south on the still dark A1.

Elsie's two limousines were waiting outside the hotel, their lights on, engines running. George Hunter was waiting around in the lobby, as he'd done this past few days. One of the hotel staff had kept him up-to-date with the latest developments, including the order for a 'picnic food basket for six'. Six! That'd be enough food for a long trip somewhere. Presently, Hinchliffe, dressed in flying coat and boots, came down the stairs carrying his flight bag. He waved to Claude, who wished him luck. It seemed by their knowing looks, that the hotel staff had figured out what Hinchliffe was about to do. They saw Elsie was involved, but not sure of her role. Hinchliffe knew Elsie had made arrangements to settle their hotel account through her bank. Elsie, dressed in her flying suit, soon followed, accompanied by her two maids and two chauffeurs carrying their luggage. She went to Claude at the front desk and handed him her letter to Jonathan. She instructed him to post it the following morning, Wednesday. Hunter stepped forward to Hinchliffe.

"Anything doing this morning, Captain?" he asked.

"You want the *big* story?" Hinchliffe asked tersely.

Hunter stared at him in disbelief. Something was definitely up.

"You bet, sir."

"You get the exclusive—on one condition!"

"Anything you say, Captain."

"You do *not* divulge who flies with me for twenty-four hours. Got that?"

"Oh yes. *Absolutely.* Yes, sir."

"Follow us," Hinchliffe replied.

Hunter rushed off to his car and jumped in. He popped a cigarette in his mouth and snapped his lighter.

"Today's your lucky day, Georgie me boy!" he exclaimed, rubbing his hands together. He inserted the ignition key and started the engine, then pulled round behind the big Daimler.

As Hinchliffe climbed into the Rolls with Elsie, the postman arrived at the hotel on his bicycle. He carried a stack of mail in his bag into the hotel and, with a nod to the desk clerk, left it at the end of the counter as usual. Millie's letter was at the bottom of the pile. The mail would be sorted out around 8:30 a.m. Elsie's servants climbed into the Daimler.

Elsie was no longer at peace. She was nervous. She sat with her head on the backrest, staring at the ceiling. Hinchliffe could see she was in a bad state. He decided to pounce. It was now or never.

"What is it to be then, Elsie?"

"I'm going," she said, looking out into the darkness.

"This is not a game, you know!"

"I've made up my mind," she said dully.

"The Atlantic's two thousand miles of unforgiving, cold, black water."

"Oh, do shut up, Raymond!"

"It's your brother, isn't it? He's messed up your head."

"I had no choice. I had to lie. Now just do what I'm *paying* you to do!" she snapped.

Hinchliffe saw the chauffeur glance at Elsie in his mirror as they slowly pulled away.

He said no more.

15

LEAVING CRANWELL

Tuesday, March 13, 1928.

Hinchliffe and Elsie, and Elsie's attentive chauffeur, traveled in silence through the sleeping town and out along the dark country lanes to Cranwell Aerodrome. The second limousine carried Elsie's two servants. The sun was breaking through scudding cloud as the procession, including Hunter's car, arrived. Sinclair was in the van keeping warm out of the cutting wind, having got the plane ready to go. He got out on seeing the limousines and came toward Hinchliffe. He looked hard at Elsie. She forced a polite smile, although he could see it was a strain. He gave Hinchliffe a questioning stare, but Hinchliffe's frown, and slight shake of the head, indicated that he'd tried to talk Elsie out of it without success.

"Did you change the plugs, Gordon," Hinchliffe asked.

"Yes, all done, and I ran her for a while. She's been purring like a cat."

"Good. I think I'll feel more comfortable with those plugs," Hinchliffe told him.

"I bled and topped up the tanks," Sinclair said.

"Thanks, Gordon. We'll need every drop."

Jonathan had made good time down the A1, and was nearing Grantham as dawn was breaking. He knew exactly where the Hotel George was, and they headed straight there. He jumped out, even before the wheels had stopped turning. He ran into the hotel lobby. His desperate expression alarmed Claude on the front desk. He was more concerned when Jonathan didn't stop, but sprinted up the stairs to the second floor.

"Sir! Sir!" Claude called after him.

Jonathan payed no attention, rushing straight up to Elsie's room. The door was ajar and a maid was cleaning and stripping the beds.

"Where's Miss Mackay?" he yelled."

"She be long gone, sir," the maid said, in her Lincolnshire accent.

Jonathan dashed next door into Hinchliffe's room. It was as Hinchliffe had left it. The bed had been straightened out. But all the decks were clear. Beside the bed was a suitcase. He lifted it and found it was packed and ready to go. He looked in the closet. Nothing. He went to the dresser. In the ashtray, he saw Hinchliffe's lucky black cat charm. He stood over it mesmerized, bewildered, full of dread.

Sinclair was wiping the plane over with paraffin again. It'd serve as a deicer, but who knew for how long. Elsie and her servants brought the food and drink supplies and laid them on the cockpit floor: four thermoses of coffee, eight bottles of water, many different types of sandwiches, hard boiled eggs and chocolate, as Hinchliffe had instructed.

Soon, an RAF man approached them from a nearby building. Sinclair came over to Hinchliffe as the man handed over a weather report from Cardington. Hinchliffe scanned it carefully. Elsie joined them.

"How's it looking, Ray?" Sinclair asked.

"Easterly winds to continue. Stiff breezes over the Atlantic. Not bad, right now," Hinchliffe replied.

"Is it a go?" Elsie asked.

"Yes, it is. What about you?"

"I'm coming with *you*."

"Are you absolutely sure about that?"

"Definitely!" she nodded her head vehemently.

Hinchliffe thanked the RAF man and put a finger to his lips. The young man gave him an understanding nod and a wink. Hinchliffe was a legendary figure on this aerodrome.

Elsie went to her servants and chauffeurs and they looked at her in alarm. She hugged them one by one. The two girls began to cry, the men looked downcast. Hinchliffe studied the scene for a second. Elsie could be a brat at times, but her servants were devoted to her. He and

Sinclair exchanged glances. Sinclair looked away, barely able to conceal his disappointment.

Jonathan came down the stairs into the lobby two at time. He bounded up to the front desk.

"What's happened to Miss Mackay?"

"She left about an hour ago," Claude replied.

"She's gone to Cranwell, right?" Jonathan asked.

"I suspect that's where they all went, sir, servants an' all."

"How far is it? How do we get there?"

"Out of here take the road to Ancaster and Sleaford. It's about fifteen miles. Look out for the RAF Cranwell sign. You can't miss it. It'll take you about 30 minutes."

"Where can we buy petrol, we're almost empty?"

"About a mile up the road on your way there, sir. Good luck!" Claude suddenly remembered the letter Elsie had given him to post. He read the name and address. "Oh sir, what was your name again?"

"Jonathan Mackay."

Claude squinted at the envelope. "Ah yes, the young lady left this letter for us to post, but you might as well take it now."

Jonathan took it, nodded his thanks and rushed out to the car, clutching the letter. He jumped in and they sped off. He ripped the letter open and gasped on reading the first line. They found the petrol station on the way, which was closed. They had to wait another agonizing ten minutes for it to open.

Elsie climbed aboard *Endeavour*. The smell of petrol in the cockpit was overpowering. Hunter grinned—*she* was definitely going!

"Okay, crank her up!" Hinchliffe shouted. Elsie pulled the starter. The engine now didn't want to start. It started on the third try. Smoke belched from the exhaust across the field. Hunter, who'd been keeping out of everyone's way, closed in on Hinchliffe for a quote.

"It's *America*, right Captain?" he shouted above the din.

"Yes, it's *America!*"

"Are you confident?"

"My confidence in this venture is one hundred percent!" Hinchliffe told him. He sounded wooden.

Hunter shook his hand. "The very best of luck to you both, Captain Hinchliffe," he said with sincerity.

"Go and see my wife. She'll give you photographs for your story," Hinchliffe said. He turned his back to the wind, pulled out his diary and scribbled inside. *My confidence in the venture is 100%.*

He then tore out a page and wrote a message.

To all at Cardington. I promised you'd be the first to know! WGRH

"Please send this telegram to Cardington," he said, giving it to Sinclair. He then handed his diary to Sinclair with ten ten-pound notes tucked inside. It was cash he'd brought to Grantham and would no longer need. "Hold on to this please, Gordon. And would you mind buying Millie two dozen red roses. Oh, and yes, give her this," he pulled out his letter to Millie. Sinclair put everything in his pocket.

Sinclair was almost in tears. "Sure, Ray." The two men embraced. "I wish I was coming with you," Sinclair whispered hoarsely.

"Take care of my family please, Gordon."

Hinchliffe climbed into the copilot's seat on the right side with a casual salute to Hunter. The group on the ground, including six more RAF men who'd come out from their building, watched as the plane made its way unsteadily in the snow, toward the end of the runway. The windsock stood out flapping from its mast pointing west. They heard the engine revs increase as Hinchliffe tested the magnetos. Then a roar, as it moved in their direction, bouncing and rolling for what seemed an eternity. The plane's right wooden strut cracked as it hit a drift of frozen snow. But for now, that didn't matter.

Endeavour pushed on against the wind, seeming not to want to leave the earth. Finally, the heavily laden plane lifted off with creaks and groans, alarming Elsie. This was the heaviest they'd ever been. There were sharp snaps as the undercarriage brushed low trees at the end of the runway. Hinchliffe weaved between the rest, gradually gaining height. The small band of mesmerized spectators, bundled in heavy coats and scarves, stood watching the sky in a daze as Hinchliffe wheeled the plane around. Jonathan's limousine came tearing along the aerodrome road at that moment. He got out and rushed to the edge of the airstrip as the black monoplane bearing his sister flew directly over his head.

"Oh, Elsie!" he cried. He put his head down on a fence post and wept.

Elsie spotted the limousine first and then her brother, his head down, watched by her father's chauffeur. When the plane had reached 500 feet, and was well on her way, Sinclair stalked off to Hinchliffe's Bentley in a fury. He pounded his fist on the trunk. Hunter started off toward Sinclair to get his story, but then thought better of it. He went towards Jonathan, but the chauffeur aggressively waved him away. He rushed to this own car and set off to find a phone. This was indeed the 'big story'! All kinds of drama!

Elsie didn't look at Hinchliffe, not sure he'd seen Jonathan. She took out her handkerchief, wiped away her tears, and blew her nose. He remained silent, keeping his thoughts to himself.

Millie was still shaken by her dream the night before. What did it mean? It seemed like a terrible omen. She'd felt the love and compassion surrounding the entity, but this was entirely different—this was her husband. She still couldn't shake the feeling of being trapped; that had unnerved her even more. She was relieved that the letter would be in his hands this morning.

Thank God I sent that letter!

It'd all turn out for the best, she was sure of that. Ray would be a bit cranky at first, but he'd come around, he'd come home and that would be the end of it. She went into the studio and after settling Joan down with some crayons and paper and laying Pam in her bassinet, she resumed work on Elsie's portrait. *The Grantham Hunt* was coming along well, too. She'd let it sit for a while. The thought of having lots of work ahead made her content. Hinchliffe's portrait still remained half-finished on another easel beside the piano. She's get around to that when he came home.

Jonathan was driven to nearby Sleaford in great haste. They found a phone booth and he put a call through to his father at the castle. Lord Inchcape's private secretary stood beside him while Jonathan gave him the bad news. His father was crushed. "Get back here now. And don't talk to any reporters," he said wearily. Jonathan replaced the phone in its cradle, beaten. Lord Inchcape turned to his private secretary. "All my daughter's bank accounts are to be frozen immediately."

Sinclair returned to the Hotel George for their suitcases. He packed them in the trunk of the Bentley and went back to the front desk to tell Claude the rooms had been vacated. Millie's letter remained at the front desk with the rest of the unsorted mail. On his way out of

Grantham, Sinclair stopped at the post office and sent Hinchliffe's telegram to Cardington.

While Sinclair sped south in the Bentley, and Jonathan and his driver traveled north in the Rolls, Hinchliffe and Elsie proceeded across the English countryside in smooth air, between layers of light cloud. After half an hour, they'd covered about 48 miles, reaching Burton-on-Trent. From there, they struck a westerly course for Cannock. This took another hour in similar weather. Next, they headed for Church Stretton in the Shropshire Hills, near the Welsh border, seventy miles off.

On his way south, Hunter called his editor at the *Daily Express*. He dictated copy in dramatic prose, describing what he'd witnessed earlier, recapping what he'd seen during the past week. He stressed Hinchliffe's terms for the exclusive. The editor knew of the previous goings on, but it hadn't yet got the paper's full attention. He instructed Hunter to head straight to the Hinchliffe's cottage to get a statement from Millie. Hunter looked forward to seeing Mrs. Hinchliffe again, though he knew he shouldn't. He wasn't one to pursue married women, but she captivated him.

Soon, Lord Inchcape's wrath was being felt at the Air Ministry at Gwydyr House on Whitehall. He called Sir Samuel Hoare again and discussed the situation. There was nothing anyone could do now, of course, and Sir Samuel told him so. Perhaps this wouldn't have happened, at least not at this moment in time, if Hinchliffe hadn't been booted off the aerodrome. That wasn't put into words. It didn't need to be. An hour later, Brancker was summoned before the Air Minister, who heaped all Lord Inchcape's angst upon him.

Brancker went back to his office on the second floor and called Cardington for the latest weather report. It looked as though things over the Atlantic were rapidly deteriorating. He sat back in his leather chair staring out into the River Thames. Depression seized him. He remembered his last words to Hinchliffe. They'd apparently fallen on deaf ears. He hoped to God, they made it. This certainly wasn't any time to go flying across the Atlantic Ocean, in winter, with storms in the offing. No sir!

16

THE ATLANTIC

Tuesday, March 13, 1928.

*E*ndeavour made reasonable time, reaching Church Stretton by 10:05 a.m., then crossing Wales to Aberystwyth by 10:45 a.m. Elsie had settled down and was smiling and making a few funny remarks. They left the Welsh coast and flew over the Irish Sea, which looked quite blue in the intermittent sunshine. Ireland lay about 130 miles off and this short crossing to Wexford, with a following wind, took just over an hour. Elsie looked confident, even joyous at times—but the air was still smooth. At 12:05 p.m., they passed Wexford.

Earlier that day, Hunter arrived at Pickwick Cottage. He pulled on the bell and Millie answered the door. She gave him a look of recognition, not one to forget a face.

"Mrs. Hinchliffe?" Hunter asked, feeling butterflies in his stomach. Indeed, she became more lovely each time he saw her.

"Yes?" Millie answered with a questioning look.

He removed his battered homburg. "The name's Hunter, George Hunter, I'm with the *Daily Express*. Did you know your husband left Cranwell this morning for America?"

Millie's mouth dropped open. "*What?*"

"I was at the Cranwell Aerodrome early this morning. I saw them leave."

"They've gone?" Millie put her hand to her mouth in distress.

Hunter looked startled, not expecting this to be a surprise to her. And then it all became clear.

"I remember you now! *You* were in the bar at the Hotel George. Oh, no. I don't believe it!" This added to her fury, as though she'd been violated.

"Yes, I was. Sorry, Mrs. Hinchliffe, I was reporting on the story. I spoke with Captain Hinchliffe this morning. He invited me to see them take off. He said I should come and see you and you'd give some photos for the paper. It's so very important, ma'am." Hunter's tone was consolatory and soothing.

Millie was devastated and now put out, learning all this from a damned, snooping reporter. Why had he gone off like that after she'd written to him? Had he got her letter? She reluctantly opened the door and let Hunter in. He glanced furtively at the ticking grandfather clock in the hall. It was 12:25 p.m. Millie pushed the studio door open and he stepped into her world. His eyes were everywhere, enormously impressed. This was all making his story so colorful.

"What time did they leave?" Millie said wearily.

"About eight thirty this morning."

"Who went with him?"

"Miss Mackay—but I won't be divulging that today. You knew they were going, right?" Hunter asked.

Millie didn't want to show any rift or difference between her and her husband. "Well, er, yes. I wasn't sure *exactly* when, that's all."

"You have photos for me—"

"Oh, yes, wait here. I'll show you what I have," Millie went to her darkroom.

Hunter scanned Millie's artwork: he focused on a painting of the Cardington sheds, ominous and dark, with towering black clouds above them. Then the unfinished portraits of Hinchliffe and Elsie. He noted the mass of color around Elsie's head—purple, red, yellow, pink, orange and gold. Beautiful! He thought it was a nice artistic effect. He then spotted the grand piano at the end of the room. Suddenly, the house was filled with a concerto of sound. He played *"Yes, Sir, That's My Baby"*. Millie came out of her darkroom. This, though his playing was marvelous, was really rather rude. Her irritation showed.

"I'm so sorry, Mrs. Hinchliffe, I just couldn't resist," Hunter said.

"I see you play."

His face lit up. It was a nice face—compassionate. Even so, he had a manly daring way about him that she thought women must find attractive. She also thought he was the type that got people to open up to him and talk. "When I see a piano, I just jump right on it! Can't stop myself. It's a compulsion of mine. I'm *so* very sorry."

After a moment, Millie smiled. He was forgiven. She was surprised at how well he spoke, considering his scruffy appearance—he needed a shave, his overcoat was tatty and had a white stain on the shoulder. He smelled of stale cigarettes. He reminded her of a gumshoe—and what do gumshoe's do? They hang around a lot, digging up facts, stamping out their cigarettes with their well-worn brogues, only to light up another moments later.

Millie cleared some of her art supplies, brushes and bits and pieces from her work table and handed him a sheaf of eight by ten black and white photographs. He shuffled through them eagerly, laying them out on the table: Elsie and Hinchliffe in front of the plane in the snow, *Endeavour* taking off, the Hotel George, views of Cranwell from the air, assembly of the plane at Brooklands, and some of their silly poses around Grantham. Hunter chuckled at these. He was thrilled.

"Terrific stuff! This'll look great in tomorrow's paper. Thank you so much, Mrs. Hinchliffe. It's very kind of you."

Kate entered the studio carrying a tray of tea and Millie introduced them. Kate still looked shocked at the news of Hinchliffe's departure, which Millie had relayed to her in the kitchen. They stood around chatting and drinking tea for a few minutes until Hunter told them he had to get back to Fleet Street.

"You haven't heard anything about the weather over the Atlantic, have you, Mr. Hunter?" Millie asked.

"No, but I'll make a point of finding out."

Hunter held up four photographs. "Can I take these?" he asked.

"Certainly," Millie replied.

"I'll return them to you—"

"There's no need."

Slightly disappointed, Hunter made for the door. "I'm sure they'll be fine, Mrs. H," he said.

Millie stared after him blankly.

The only thing Millie could think of, was to speak to Brancker. She let Kate know and got dressed in warm clothes and walked down to the phone booth in the village. It was now overcast and beginning to drizzle. She used her umbrella. She put her pennies in the slot and dialed his number. She got straight through to Brancker, still at his desk. She pressed Button 'B' on hearing his rich voice. The pennies dropped, clanking noisily. She sounded as if she were in a dungeon somewhere below ground. "Sir Sefton?"

Brancker's mood was further depressed when he heard Millie's bewildered voice. "Millie, I just heard, myself."

Millie's tone was accusing. She couldn't help it. Was he in on it? "Reporters have just been to my door. I'm devastated. I'd just sent a letter to Raymond asking him to abandon the whole thing. Now, I hear they've gone. Just like that! How could he do such a thing?"

Brancker's guilty heart sank like a stone. She sounded like a woman drowning in that echo chamber down in the country. "Millie, I'm afraid that they'd been told to get off that aerodrome. It came right from the top. Hinch must've decided to go and get it over with—he couldn't have got your letter."

"Who would have done such a thing? That was cruel, forcing them off like that."

"I can guess who was behind it. But look, Millie, when the press come around, you must keep up a united front. Don't tell anyone you tried to stop him. It'd diminish their great effort," Brancker warned.

"I'm worried sick! What's the weather doing? What can they expect?"

"I have to be honest. It doesn't look all that good. The winds are increasing—but if anyone can succeed, your husband can. In my book, Raymond is the greatest pilot in the world today. We must keep our hopes up."

"Where will they be now?"

"I just heard that they passed over Mizen Head Lighthouse about one-thirty. The weather there was pretty good." Brancker had thought about telling her to say a prayer for them, but thought better of it. When he hung up he felt dreadful. Millie trudged home. She'd not really learned much, but it was something.

Sinclair arrived home at about 2:30 p.m. in the Bentley. Kate rushed to the door on hearing his wheels. She went to him at the car. Millie stood at the door with Joan. She was glad for Kate.

Kate kissed Sinclair on the cheek. "I'm so glad you didn't go, darling," she whispered.

He looked wistful and grim at the same time. He nodded. "He's gonna have his work cut out," he said. It was clear to Millie that Kate knew her husband well enough. He'd be moody for a day or two. Millie shook her head. None of this had turned out the way she'd hoped. Sinclair handed Millie the bouquet of roses from Hinchliffe he'd bought in London, the diary with the money, and Hinchliffe's letter.

"Did he get *my* letter?" Millie asked.

"I don't know. He didn't say he'd heard from you," Sinclair replied.

Millie was forlorn. She felt powerless. She rushed upstairs to read Hinchliffe's letter.

Later that afternoon, more reporters showed up at the door. Sinclair went to the upstairs bedroom out of the way. Even though Hunter's exclusive wouldn't hit the newsstands until next morning, Fleet Street was abuzz. A wild rumor had sent reporters rushing around, getting nowhere. They couldn't raise Elsie, they couldn't find Sinclair. Cranwell couldn't or wouldn't provide a straight answer. They'd gleaned that Hinchliffe had flown off somewhere, but that was all. Stories had been circulating for months, but no one was sure if the intended destination was in the east or the west.

A plaintive man in a shabby raincoat stood on the front step. "Mrs. Hinchliffe?"

"Yes."

A flashbulb from a Speed Graphic camera popped in her face.

"I'm with the *Daily Mail.*"

"And I'm from the *Daily Telegraph*," another one said. "We understand your husband took off from Cranwell this morning for America—"

"I just heard that," Millie said.

"Was Miss Elsie Mackay his copilot?"

"Captain Gordon Sinclair is his copilot," Millie answered. She didn't like lying, but knew Elsie would rather she kept the myth alive. They asked more questions, most of which she couldn't answer. She was civil. They had their job to do, but it was all dragging her down. One had asked to use the telephone, but she told him she didn't own one. She respectfully bade them goodbye and closed the door gloomily. But there was another ring almost immediately. It was Reverend Grey. He'd heard about it on the BBC and came to offer a blessing. As he was administering this and laying his hands upon Millie's head, Barney, the blacksmith, appeared. He respectfully took off his cap and offered his best wishes with bowed head. Both men had been at Pam's christening, and both looked surprised. Millie was appreciative of everyone's concern. She didn't feel quite so alone.

That afternoon, Hinchliffe's telegram addressed to Major Scott was delivered to Cardington House. The secretary at the reception desk took it to the conference room, where a design meeting was underway. She handed it to Scott, who ripped it open. He smiled as he read it aloud.

"It's from Ray Hinchliffe. 'I promised you would be the first to know. WGRH.' That's all it says. Well bless his heart! I guess he's on his way."

Captain Irwin chimed in. "Good luck to him. He's going to need it!"

"Hear! Hear! Good luck, Hinch!" everyone said.

Johnston glared at Richmond, remembering their spat. Richmond showed no emotion.

Millie took her husband's roses into the studio and placed them on her work table beside a glass vase. She cut their stems and lovingly placed them in the vase, spacing them carefully. She took it into the living room and put it on Hinchliffe's desk under the window. They'd be there for her to look at this evening, where they'd sit after dinner, listening for news on the radio. Waiting would not be easy. Nor would sleeping—not until she knew he was safe. Her annoyance had subsided, but not her fear. She was sure he'd not received her letter— he'd not mentioned it in *his* letter.

Hinchliffe and Elsie had reached Waterford at 12:25 p.m. By 1:35 p.m. they were passing over Mizen Head Lighthouse, as Brancker had said. The lighthouse keeper had heard them, and opened his window to peer out. He'd shook his head in disgust when he saw the plane heading for the open water. The weather was still comparatively smooth. If it remained like this all the way, they'd do fine, as long as the engine remained reliable. It sounded sweet at the moment. Elsie was in still good spirits, despite looking out at a landscape of gray seas all the way to the horizon. She took out a packet of sandwiches wrapped in greaseproof paper and looked inside.

"Hmm, this one's ham and cheese. D'you fancy that?" she shouted above the din.

"Sure, and coffee please," Hinchliffe answered.

"After that, I'll need to pee," Elsie told him.

"Okay, let's eat first, shall we?" he said with a half-smile.

They ate and drank their fill, and then Elsie sat on her little bowl while Hinchliffe kept his eyes on the horizon. She noticed whitecaps on the water below as she emptied it out the window. *Endeavour* began to quiver and shake. Elsie took the controls. Hinchliffe thought it best to keep her occupied. He expected it to get worse—how much worse, he wasn't sure.

Suddenly, it dawned on him! He stared at the instrument panel in stunned disbelief. He loosened his seat belt and ran his hands around in his pockets, trying to think. He'd forgotten his lucky charm. Where the hell was it? Elsie was quick to pick up on his desperation. She knew exactly what was going on. He took his watch from his top pocket and hung it on the instrument panel by its broken strap. It was 6:35 p.m., the light was fading fast now. He turned to her as she put her fingers to the gold crucifix around her neck. He looked away and down into the sea. "We'll have to rely on *your* lucky charm, today," he said. Elsie remained silent, uncomfortable he'd forgotten his black cat. Any good luck was welcome, as far as she was concerned. She put her hand back on the wheel.

Around 8 o'clock, Hinchliffe took the controls. The winds were now severe, bringing a mixture of rain and sleet. Conditions had steadily deteriorated since leaving the Irish Coast. Elsie had become extremely uncomfortable. "How far have we come, do you think?" she asked.

"About twelve hundred miles, I reckon," Hinchliffe said, raising his voice to be heard.

"How much longer to go?"

"It depends how much stiffer these winds get."

"Do you think it'll get much worse than this?"

"It could."

Kate and Millie cooked a chicken for dinner that evening, followed by apple pie with custard. After cleaning up, they sat in the living room around the fire, listening to a play on the radio. Millie was having difficulty concentrating, but when she heard the BBC pips, the radio had her full attention.

Beep, beep, beep, beep, beeeeep.

This is the BBC nine o'clock news. It has been learned tonight that another transatlantic flight attempt is being made by the distinguished war veteran and Imperial Airways pilot, Captain Raymond Hinchliffe. The flight is shrouded in mystery, as the identity of his copilot has not been revealed. There are reports that the Honorable Elsie Mackay, the daughter of shipping magnate, Lord Inchcape, may be the one at the controls with Captain Hinchliffe. Conditions over the Atlantic have deteriorated since take off this morning, with gale force winds, accompanied by snow, sleet and freezing rain. In other news ...

Millie excused herself and went up to check on the children and then sat on the bed and reread Hinchliffe's letter. She wasn't one to pray, but tonight she prayed fervently, wringing her hands.

Oh, dear God, please, please, please ...

The winds over the Atlantic had intensified to gale force. The noise alone, was frightening. The buffeting and bouncing, terrifying. Elsie leaned against the cockpit wall and kept closing her eyes. Hinchliffe had flown in similar condition many times and wasn't unduly worried, not yet, at least.

"I'm going to fly a more northerly course and try to work our way around this storm," he shouted.

"Won't that slow us down and take longer?"

"We have no choice."

"Let me take her."

"No, not now—later," Hinchliffe said.

Elsie looked away sullenly. Suddenly, as the plane dropped, there was a loud crack and Elsie gave a bloodcurdling scream.

"What was that?" she yelled.

"Sounded like one of the struts," Hinchliffe shouted. He reached into his bag and pulled out the bottle of whiskey and thrust it in her hands. She took it and put it in her lap. She then pulled out her rosary from her pocket and twisted it around her wrist, holding its gold cross tightly with her other hand. She closed her eyes. Deafening thunderclaps rolled around them and lightning flashed, lighting up a non-stop spray of rain and sleet on the windscreen.

Millie couldn't sit by her sleeping child in her bedroom any longer. She went down to her studio and sat at the piano. In a trance, the music and her emotions flowed as she played Beethoven's Moonlight Sonata. The first movement was slow, graceful and sad. By the third, the piece had erupted into a passionate frenzy, flooding the house, her distraught face etched with pain and terror. The Sinclairs listened. They were deeply sorry for her, but knew she'd rather be alone. They maintained their vigil in the living room, while Millie's hands flayed the keyboard.

Endeavour had entered hell. The plane was being slammed around like a child's toy by the horrendous winds and turbulence hitting from all sides. In a flash of lightning, Hinchliffe saw the wing fabric beginning to tear. He began to relive that awful night he'd been shot down over France—something that terrified him until this day. He'd never spoken of it, even to Millie.

He'd been on night patrol with Sinclair alongside him. They'd run into a German Gotha bomber that had shown up in the searchlights. They got on the German's tail and chased him over the lines. Hinchliffe unleashed a few rounds, but the enemy tail gunner fired on them immediately. A hail of machine gun bullets had blasted through the cockpit, splintering the instrument panel. Then more sliced through his leg and forehead. Blood gushed down his face, filling his goggles on the left side. The Sopwith descended and he steered toward the west, to get back over enemy lines. In pain and dread, he was sure he was finished, he couldn't see the ground, let alone find a place to land. After an agonizing ten miles, with his engine sputtering, he'd seen black shapes ahead—a forest. He was now at treetop level. It wasn't going to be pleasant. He glanced up and saw Sinclair's plane abreast of him. Next he knew, his plane was ramming its way through tree limbs, finally coming to rest high above the ground. He wasn't sure if he was alive or dead, until what seemed like ages later, his good eye opened and he saw faces at the window—soldiers with ropes and tackle. "The pilot's alive," one had shouted.

Getting him down from that tree had been horribly painful. He passed out again when they put him on a stretcher and loaded him into a field ambulance. He woke up two days later, less one eye and his leg stitched and heavily bandaged. His war was over. Sinclair had visited him every day in the field hospital. He'd stayed with the German plane, blasting it out of the sky, before catching up with Hinchliffe and watching him crash into the trees. He'd alerted the medics, who saved Hinchliffe's life.

Hinchliffe felt as powerless against this storm as he had that night. His feelings of misery were reinforced, when he heard the engine begin to pop and backfire. He grabbed his flashlight and map. With great difficulty, he shone it on the islands leeward of them, to the south —the Azores. In his head, he calculated the compass bearing. He'd begun to distrust that compass—but there was nothing he could do about it.

"I'm gonna do a one-eighty and turn south. We've gotta get out of this. It's no use," he shouted across to Elsie. But Elsie didn't respond. She'd long ago given up and was preparing herself to die. She held her rosary, fingering the beads, chanting over and over in a whisper. "Hail Mary, Mother of God, pray for us sinners now and at the hour of our death ..."

Hinchliffe gripped the controls and banked *Endeavour* around onto a southerly course, dipping and dropping violently as it turned, almost flipping the plane over on her back. Once on their new course, with a forceful tailwind, the plane became slightly more stable. But the drop in turbulence hadn't registered with Elsie. She was out of it. The engine continued to backfire. Hinchliffe cursed those plugs to himself. Why had he switched them out? Dammit! Was it them? Was it fuel starvation? Icing? He didn't know.

Turbulence continued to diminish, mile after mile and the thunder grew fainter. It was a wonder the plane was still in once piece. Elsie remained in the same catatonic state, twisting her rosary over and over. Hinchliffe thought if they could make it to the Azores they'd be safe. Ruth Elder had made it. So could they. He kept scanning the horizon in the gray moonlight. He took out his wallet and slipped out the photo of Millie with Joan and kissed it and then carefully replaced it. He glanced at the wings. Fabric was hanging in long strands from the port wing. The rest seemed to be holding up. The engine continued spluttering. Hinchliffe thought they should see land soon. They might just make it. He took a swig of coffee from a flask. It was warm and didn't taste bad. As he gulped it down, he thought he saw a shape in the ocean ahead—about five miles to the east. Yes, there it was, no question. His hopes soared. He banked towards it.

"Elsie, look, look! The Azores!" he yelled. But she didn't stir.

As they approached the island, now only three miles off, the backfiring grew worse and parts of the fluttering fabric tore off and flew away. The engine note changed more dramatically, as though starved of petrol. Hinchliffe slapped the tank behind him. It sounded like an empty drum. He turned and grabbed the valve and opened it. It was useless. The engine quit. He glanced at the island, now two miles away and fought for control. *Endeavour* descended. He hurriedly checked his watch hanging in front of him. It read 3:07 a.m. He brought the plane down to the water as if it were a normal landing. They hit the sea forcefully. The remaining wheel strut broke off with the wheel attached and floated away.

On impact, Elsie's head slammed against the cockpit wall and she bit through her tongue. Blood spurted from her mouth and ran down her chin. She immediately came out of her trance and went into a full-fledged panic, grabbing at her seat-belt, trying to free herself. It was jammed.

Waves of black water crashed over the nose of the plane and seeped in around the doors. Hinchliffe was unharmed. He attempted to help Elsie free herself, but couldn't shake her belt loose. He pulled down his flying goggles, pushed open his door and slipped out into the icy sea. It took his breath away. The cockpit was filling rapidly and dragging the plane down. Hinchliffe held on to the high wing and swam around to Elsie's side, where he yanked the door open. Elsie was still struggling with her seat belt. The cockpit was submerged with the empty wing tanks keeping the plane afloat for now. Hinchliffe jerked the seat belt strap. Elsie remained tethered. He pulled her shoulders, but couldn't break her loose. He remembered his knife. He'd left it in his bag. Too late now. Out of air, he let her go and returned to the surface. He gasped and filled his lungs and ducked under the water back to Elsie. The plane continued to sink under the engine's weight, pulling him down. It was hopeless. Time stood still. Elsie pulled him to her and lovingly touched his face. She held his head in both hands and kissed his lips, then pushed him away. He hung on the surface, mesmerized by Elsie's imploring face in the windshield as the plane sank into the black depths. He remained motionless, the metallic taste of her blood in his mouth, until she and *Endeavour* were gone.

Hinchliffe struggled to the surface, his lungs bursting. As his head broke the surface, he gasped again for air. He saw the moon bright between two mountain peaks. He yanked open his coat and blew into his life vest. He began swimming for his life.

17

THE DEAFENING SILENCE

Wednesday, March 14, 1928.

Millie had spent a miserable night. She'd played the piano until about two-thirty and then gone up to lay down. All she could think of was her husband in that plane with Elsie. She tossed and turned, until she finally slipped into a light sleep.

She was awoken by the sound of Barney's hammer. It must be 6:00 a.m. She could set her watch by it. She lay listening in the darkness to a horse neighing in one of the stalls. These were sounds that had always given them comfort. But not this morning. She remembered her dream. It stabbed her heart like a knife. Minutes later, she heard the paperboy's tires on the gravel beneath the window.

She sat on the side of the bed, trying to breathe and lit her lamp. Sinclair's chickens were beginning to stir. The cock crowed. The letterbox snapped shut and the newspaper fell to the floor. She thought of George Hunter and his story. Wearily, she roused herself and silently put on her dressing gown, careful not to wake baby. She crept downstairs to the entrance hall and picked up the *Daily Express*. It was eerily quiet. She held up her lamp and was shocked to see the grandfather clock stopped at twenty minutes past three. She hurriedly wound it and reset the time to six-fifteen, before going into the kitchen. Butch and Whiskey were fussing to be let out. She opened the door and they scampered off into the darkness. She laid the newspaper on the table and sat, glaring at the headlines in the lamplight.

A DRAMATIC START FROM A SNOWY AERODROME

SECRET PREPARATIONS BY CAPT. HINCHLIFFE &

THE HON. ELSIE MACKAY

THE DAILY EXPRESS STORY THEY DENIED

As Millie was reading, Gordon and Kate entered the kitchen and read the article anxiously over her shoulder in silence. Kate put the kettle on and got the cups and saucers out. Millie turned to Sinclair,

"Quickly Gordon, put the radio on, please."

They listened to someone talking about getting your garden ready for spring planting. They were all becoming impatient. At last, Big Ben struck the hour.

This is the seven o'clock news. There has been no news of Captain Hinchliffe and his copilot who took off from RAF Cranwell yesterday morning bound for the United States. There has been some mystery as to the identity of his copilot since neither Miss Elsie Mackay nor Captain Sinclair could be reached last night, although one Fleet Street reporter has claimed to have witnessed Miss Mackay being in the plane when it took off yesterday. In other news ...

Millie spent the rest of the day dragging herself around the house in a dream. At times, she snapped out of it, convincing herself that Hinchliffe would be all right. She consoled herself with Brancker's words, *'If anyone can make it, Captain Hinchliffe can.'* He'd always come through, no matter what. He will again, she kept telling herself.

There was no news for the rest of the day and she spent another sleepless night. Everyone moped around in a listless state the next day until the Reverend Grey showed up again to give them some solace. Millie was thankful in some ways that he'd come by, but it seemed to make things worse. More dire. She started to think more about death and dying. She didn't want to think about those things. Hinchliffe had to make it. She looked for symbolism in all things—for signs. She glanced at Hinchliffe's roses and found they were dying. Two withered red petals were lying beside the vase.

One for Ray, one for Elsie?

She shuddered.

That evening Sinclair went to the village and purchased the *Evening News*. The headlines read:

NEW YORK WAITS WITH EXCITEMENT
NO NEWS OF MISS MACKAY
CAPTAIN HINCHLIFFE MYSTERY
DID THEY HAVE A SECRET DESTINATION?

By Friday, most people had given up hope. There was a rumor that they'd crashed in Newfoundland and were alive. But that couldn't be confirmed. Millie stood motionless staring out the kitchen window at the falling snow, praying.

Please God, if you exist ...

She was brought back to reality by Joan, happily munching her corn flakes, unaware of the anxiety permeating the house.

"When is daddy coming back, Mummy?" she asked.

Later, Millie was cooking bacon and eggs for Sinclair, but her mind was elsewhere. Soon the kitchen was filled with smoke and Millie was in a temper, throwing the pan into the sink with a crash. Kate took Millie up to her room, while Sinclair cleaned up and cooked his own breakfast. Later that day, reporters were at the door again. Kate tried to prevent Millie from talking to them, but she insisted. There were six. Barney was standing silently off to one side, cap in hand. Tears were streaming down his face.

"Mrs. Hinchliffe, have you given up hope?" one asked.

Millie answered forcefully. "Not at all. There's a good chance they've been picked up by a ship or landed in some remote place in Canada. We may not know for weeks."

The reporters looked at her with pity, impressed with her bravery. They asked a few more questions and she gave upbeat answers. They were kind and understanding and didn't stay around long. When they left, Barney trudged after them, back to his shop across the lane. As far as the reporters were concerned, Hinchliffe and whoever he was with, were probably in a watery grave. But they'd keep the story going for as long as they could. The public was captivated.

That Saturday, there were stories about Elsie's father. Reporters had been to Glenapp to interview Lord Inchcape.

A *Daily Sketch* headline read

I KNOW NOTHING ABOUT THESE FLIGHTS
SAY'S ELSIE MACKAY'S FATHER
I wasn't a party to any of it

Stories carried in other newspapers were similar. Some even hinted that Hinchliffe and Elsie were having an affair and that maybe they'd flown off somewhere together.

That night, Millie found herself searching in the gloom. Searching, searching, searching. The ground under her feet was black and silty, puffing up clouds around her ankles as she trudged. At last, ahead, she saw a glimmer of light in the darkness. Now, she could make out the black shape of a plane. As she moved closer, it became clear and bright. Yes, it was definitely her husband's plane—*Endeavour*, grubby and dirty with silt and brightly colored encrustations. Ah, and there was the Union Jack.

Millie moved toward it cautiously. She saw the door on Hinchliffe's side ajar. She pulled it open and peered inside. In the pilot's seat sat Elsie, her head resting against the window, sleeping, her skin like porcelain. Blood trickled from her open lips and down her chin. Her rosary dangled from her wrist. A sea snake slipped out from Elsie's flying coat and swam past Millie's head. The only sign of Millie's husband was his watch hanging from the instrument panel. It read ten minutes past three. She stared at it.

Suddenly, Elsie's eyes opened and she glared at Millie, furious at being woken from her slumber. Her voice was muffled, her teeth covered in blood. Tiny bubbles flared around her head and from her mouth, as she hissed venomously, "He's not here! Go away!"

Millie woke up with a start and sat up on her bed. She lay back down, trying to breath, her heart thumping. She remembered her predicament returning from her sub-aquatic nightmare to her real one. She spent another hour lying in the gloom, praying for God to bring news of her husband. Finally, she went back to sleep.

Later that night, someone stood motionless in the snow, staring at the unlit cottage. It looked cozy. A plume of smoke rose out of the old, clay chimney pot from dying embers in the grate. After gaining entry, the man moved past the ticking grandfather clock toward the stairs. He stopped when he saw Whiskey glaring at him from under the hall table. The cat hissed and gave a growling moo before slinking off into the living room. The man turned back to the stairs, pausing to glance at pictures on the walls, lit by moonlight.

He stealthily climbed the stairs and moved along the hallway to Millie's room. Once inside, he went to the bed where Millie lay, fully clothed, collapsed with exhaustion. The solidly built man, dressed in a full-length leather flying coat stood over her, gazing at her face, as though aching to caress her. The loudly ticking alarm clock on the side table was the only sound apart from Millie's breathing. Butch, who'd been sleeping in his own chair on the other side of the room, slowly eased himself down, half-heartedly wagging his tail, unsure of their visitor. He was confused.

The man turned his gaze back to the framed photos on Millie's side table. He studied each one carefully. Beside his diary, he saw Millie's letter, which had been sent back marked 'Return to Sender'. She'd torn it open and left it there. He read her words in stunned disbelief. His own letter to Millie was there also. He read it through, remembering that dreadful morning.

13th, March, 1928

My Dearest Millie,

We leave this morning. I hope this turns out well. Thank you for putting up with all this and for what I now realize is selfishness on my part. There's much I want to say, but there's no more time now.

Love always, Ray.

P.S. I promise I will never put you through this again.

The man turned in the moonlight. He wore a leather flying cap and a black leather eye patch over his left eye. He had a look of total sadness and bitter regret. In an act of devotion and comforting, he leaned over Millie and kissed her lips slowly and deliberately, making no sound. Millie sighed loudly, as he pulled away. She continued sleeping soundly.

Hinchliffe turned to the baby in her crib. He kissed his fingers and put them to her tiny head to wish her a good life—a life he would not be around to share. His regret was unbearable.

Hinchliffe moved to Joan's room and stood over her, looking wistfully and with great love, at her sleeping face. He kissed her cheek gently, savoring the moment. On the chest of drawers, he noticed the silver music box he'd given her before leaving for Grantham.

He went to the door and stopped. He returned to the music box and twisted the plane, so that it would be facing the girl when she awoke in the morning. It played a few notes and stopped.

Hinchliffe left Joan's room and descended the stairs. As he did so, the sound of his leathers and heavy boots on the treads could plainly be heard. He made no effort to be quiet. In her room, Millie stirred in her sleep and let out sad sigh.

Gordon Sinclair heard the footsteps and was afraid. Hinchliffe moved from the foot of the stairs and passed through the front door. The ghost of Captain Hinchliffe trudged wearily away from the house in the moonlight over the snowy ground, his gait no longer confident, his back no longer ram-rod straight, leaving footprints at first, until they and he, gradually faded away, into the night. An owl hooted far off in the distance.

At that moment, Millie sat bold upright on her bed.

"Ray!"

The baby began to cry.

18

ENTER MRS. EAST

Saturday, March 31, 1928.

A nice cuppa. Yes, that's what we need, dear. A nice strong cuppa!" Mrs. East said brightly to her ever-present companion. The eccentric old lady hummed out of tune as she poured scalding water from the kettle into her chipped, brown teapot on top of her black fireplace oven. After stirring the tea leaves, she placed the lid on the pot and turned to the picture on the wall over the table.

The wait for news about Hinchliffe dragged on endlessly, as it had done once for this sweet lady in Croydon, just seventeen miles from Pickwick Cottage. Mrs. East had lost her only son, Lawrence, in the war. Life without him was hard. He'd joined the merchant navy during the war. His freighter, *Florazam,* had been sunk on March 11th, 1915 by the infamous German U-boat, U20. *Lusitania,* was sunk two months later, off the coast of Ireland by the same skulking menace.

The wait for news of her son had been endless and soul-destroying. It was all the more distressing to find out that he was the only crew member who'd perished. Mrs. East longed for the day when she'd be reunited with her son. She wasn't melancholy about it. In her heart, she had every reason to believe it would indeed happen since she'd become immersed in spiritualism. She looked forward to being with her husband, too, one day. He'd died of cancer five years before her son had gone off to serve his country. Her spouse, a bricklayer, had been a jolly soul, and they'd been happy. So she waited. This was her life.

Mrs. East was a jolly soul too, considering her lonely existence. She lived in a little terraced house on a quiet street. Her house and furnishings were simple, as was her dress. She had little money. She got up each day at 6:00 a.m., as she'd done these past fifty years, since her marriage, and went through her routine: building the fire in the kitchen stove, washing and dressing, eating her toast and marmalade. The kitchen table, set against one wall, was always laid with a white table cloth across one half, leaving the polished wood of the other half exposed. Above the table on the wall, was a portrait of Lawrence in his merchant navy uniform. Hung beside it, his white, flat navy cap.

"Well, I think it's time for a chat, me darlin' boy," she said.

She put the teapot on the table, where a cup and saucer, milk and sugar were always set. On the sideboard, a radio was on but she wasn't listening. It was barely audible, anyway.

This is the BBC. There is still no news of Captain Hinchliffe and his companion, who it has now been confirmed as the Honorable Elsie Mackay ...

Mrs. East turned the radio off, shuddered and took her woolen shawl and draped it round her frail shoulders.

"It's a bit chilly," she muttered.

She opened the dresser drawer and took out a small board and laid it on the table along with a contraption with tiny wheels, a writing pad and a thick black pencil. She put milk in the cup and poured her tea, leaving it to one side. She placed her left hand on the planchette over the Ouija board. The indicator moved immediately, as though someone had been anxiously waiting.

"Ah, there you are!" she said, with a delighted chuckle, her eyes lighting up.

Above her head, her son smiled down at her. Mrs. East carefully watched the indicator as it rapidly moved, writing down the letters spelled out with her right hand. But it wasn't who she was expecting. She stared at her own big, scrawled letters.

PLEASE HELP ME

"What is it dear?" Mrs. East asked.

I AM A DROWNED PILOT

Mrs. East scowled. "Who are *you*?" she asked, indignantly. She was always vigilant for evil or mischievous spirits.

I DROWNED WITH ELSIE MACKAY

This piqued her interest for a moment. Her indignation turned to concern. "What happened?"

CRASHED INTO SEA

"How?"

STORM ICE ENGINE FAILURE

"Where did this happen?"

LEEWARD ISLANDS

Mrs. East wasn't happy. It probably *was* a mischievous spirit. That happened sometimes. She became impatient. *Leeward Islands indeed!* She had no idea where they were.

"Who is this for goodness sake?" she asked crossly.

Later that week, Millie received two letters. One was from the bank to say their current account was overdrawn. The second contained a personal check from Alfred Lowenstein for fifty pounds with a handwritten a note.

I am very sorry to hear about Raymond—Alfred L.

Hinchliffe had joked, 'good luck getting paid'. Well, here it was, albeit a bit late. Millie would have smiled at this, but she didn't feel like smiling. The check was for the original portrait she'd painted and sent to him. He wasn't such a bad sort really, especially since she'd quoted him thirty. Lowenstein hadn't mentioned the second one.

Perhaps I should've let him have it to burn.

She drove with Sinclair and the children straight to the bank on Croydon High Street. Looking and feeling deathly worried, she stood at the teller's window with the baby in her arms and Joan at her side. Millie handed the bank notice to the teller, asking her to check the account. There had to be some mistake.

The teller came back a few minutes later to say that the account was indeed overdrawn by nine pounds, six shillings and ninepence-ha'penny. Millie told the clerk that a deposit should've been made in the middle of March. Elsie had been paying Hinchliffe and Sinclair by direct deposit each month and it usually arrived around the fifteenth of the following month. The bank clerk informed her that no such deposit had been received. Before leaving, Millie deposited Lowenstein's check into the account. Sinclair got the same story when he went to his bank along the street. Something had gone seriously wrong.

Millie decided to pay a visit to the family solicitor a few streets down. She had to wait for half an hour before Mr. Drummond could see her. She explained matters to him. He'd heard about Hinchliffe's Atlantic bid, and was alarmed to hear about the bank situation. He promised to call Elsie's bank and look into the matter of the insurance. He'd get to work without delay.

The following Monday, the postman arrived as Millie and Sinclair were entering the front door from a trip to the village. He handed Millie two letters. She tore open the first with *Edridges & Drummond, Solicitors at Law* in the top corner. She closed her eyes. It'd been written by Mr. Drummond on Friday.

"It's from our solicitor. It says no money had been transferred by Elsie's bank because all her accounts were frozen the day they took off for America. He also says there is no insurance policy, as the premium wasn't paid for that very same reason. Oh dear, what am I going to do? I am ruined!" Millie sobbed.

She opened the second letter. Things couldn't get much worse, but they did. It was from the mortgage company asking for payment on the house. Millie was distraught.

She went back to the village and called Brancker to inform him about her predicament. He was dumbfounded, realizing Elsie's father must be behind it. He promised to do what he could. He'd call Lord Inchcape himself, and if that didn't resolve matters, he said he had friends who'd exert pressure, including Lord Beaverbrook, the owner of the *Daily Express*. He'd shake things up. He urged Millie to write to Inchcape herself—Inchcape needed to be shamed into making good on Elsie's promises. Pressure must be exerted from all sides. Brancker promised to come and see her very soon.

After speaking with Brancker, Millie called Hunter and told him about her plight. Hunter was upset to hear this. He said if there was anything he could do, she only had to ask. When Millie got home, with the help of Gordon and Kate, she immediately composed a letter to Lord Inchcape and put it in the mail.

Hinchliffe had spent most of his time around Millie, witnessing her mounting problems in horror. The stress and hardship she was enduring—not to mention her grief, filled him with crushing sadness and anxiety to a degree he'd never experienced during his lifetime. And it was all his fault. The burden of guilt was intolerable and he often wept for Millie and the children. He'd keep on trying to help them through Mrs. East and her son.

The following day, Mrs. East sat down at her kitchen table with her Ouija board hoping to communicate with her son. The planchette moved immediately. She was ready with her pencil.

MUM HINCHLIFFE IS GENUINE

HE IS HERE

Mrs. East was pleased. "Oh, thank you dear son. I didn't believe it."

Hinchliffe took up the dialogue.

HINCHLIFFE

PLEASE TELL MY WIFE I WANT TO SPEAK TO HER

"Where did you say you went down?" Mrs. East asked.

OFF LEEWARD ISLANDS

MUST SPEAK TO MY WIFE

The old lady frowned. "Where will I find her?"

TOYS HILL

IF LETTER DOES NOT REACH

APPLY DRUMMONDS HIGH ST CROYDON

Mrs. East sat and thought this through. She felt she couldn't just contact this widow out of the blue. The poor woman would be filled with grief. It might enrage her, perhaps drive her over the edge.

The next day, Hinchliffe came back to plead with Mrs. East again.

PLEASE LET MY WIFE KNOW MRS E

I IMPLORE YOU

"It's such a risk. She might not believe any of this," Mrs. East said aloud.

TAKE THE RISK

MY LIFE WAS ALL RISKS

I MUST SPEAK TO HER

Mrs. East decided to act. She went to a phone box and looked up Drummond's phone number in the telephone directory and called them. She explained that she was a friend of Mrs. Emilie Hinchliffe and that she'd lost her address. She knew, she said, that she lived at Toys Hill, but had lost the exact location. Mrs. East thought this would be the ultimate test. The girl on the switchboard came back with the address.

'Pickwick Cottage, Puddledock Lane, Toys Hill, Kent.'

·Mrs. East was both astonished and thrilled.

That same day, she went up to London. She'd been reading about Sir Arthur Conan Doyle. He'd be giving a talk that very afternoon. She decided that if she got the chance, she'd tell him about Hinchliffe's messages. She put on her best hat and off she went on the train. Mr. Doyle might be able to advise her. Hinchliffe watched these developments and accompanied her on her journey to the city.

That afternoon, she sat in a small audience at the London Spiritualist Alliance as her hero, graying, portly and mustachioed, got up to speak. Hinchliffe sat in the empty chair next to Mrs. East. The ladies applauded enthusiastically.

"Ladies and gentleman," Doyle said, (there was only one other man in the room) "as you may know, I gave up writing Sherlock Holmes mysteries some years ago to concentrate on the most important question a human being can ask. 'What happens to us when we die?'

The ladies listened in rapt attention. It was clearly the most important question on *their* minds.

"I began my professional life as a physician—trained to examine hard facts. I always had grave doubts about the existence of God and the 'After Life' and all of that. In my 'infinite wisdom', and with my 'superior intellect', I *knew* it was all just a lot of old tommyrot!

The ladies tittered happily, looking from one to another.

"Then, as I grew older, I took my reasoning a stage further, as I'd been taught to do at medical school. I examined the facts with a more open mind, trying not to prejudge as I'd done as a young man. The paranormal had always been associated with the naive, the weak and the grieving.

His audience nodded in agreement.

"I now believe it will be the scientists who will ultimately become the high priests of this world. Already, they're asking themselves about the existence of God—a marked change for science. It is *they* who have become the seekers of spiritual truth!"

When Doyle's lecture was finished and everyone had gone, Mrs. East left her seat and went to the great storyteller.

"Sir Arthur, it was a lovely talk. I enjoyed it ever so much," she said. This pleased him. But when she told him about her experiences with the Ouija board, he wasn't just fascinated—he was enthralled.

"What I don't understand is, if he was supposed to be flying to America, could he have flown to the Leeward Islands? I don't even know where they are." Mrs. East asked.

"I need to study this case," Doyle answered. "But I think you should definitely write to the pilot's wife. It might make all the difference in the world to that poor soul."

Hinchliffe was highly pleased with Mrs. East and thankful for what she'd done.

Doyle returned to his home in Crowborough, near Tunbridge Wells, and studied the world map on the wall of his study. This certainly was a conundrum. And Doyle *loved* conundrums. He talked aloud to himself.

"Now, Captain Hinchliffe, if you were heading north and got caught in a gale, and in desperation you turned south—what islands would you reach?"

What Doyle didn't know was that ghost of Captain Hinchliffe was standing right behind him staring at the map over his shoulder. And when Doyle posed his question, Hinchliffe shouted as loud as he could as Doyle traced his finger down the map and stopped.

"The Azores!"

The following day, Mrs. East, sat down and wrote a letter to Millie and posted it. Hinchliffe came through on the Ouija board in the afternoon. He'd become adept at not only exerting pressure on Mrs. East's hand, but also on her mind that controlled her left hand. Her son, Lawrence, had shown him how.

THANK YOU FOR WHAT YOU DID MRS E

MY WIFE STILL HOPES I AM ALIVE

GLAD YOU TOLD DOYLE

Millie clung to the hope Hinchliffe was alive. The Germans landed in Newfoundland on this day, Friday, April 13. Millie prayed he was alive and somewhere in that same region. She even hoped, irrationally, that those Germans would find him!

So, when Millie got Mrs. East's letter the following day, it wasn't well-received. She didn't recognize the sender's name and address on the envelope, or the handwriting. She sat with the Sinclairs in the kitchen to read it. After scanning through it, her eyes remained in a fixed stare. The Sinclairs were alarmed, waiting for her to explain.

"It's some crank!" Millie gasped.

"Whatever is the matter, Millie?" Kate asked. Tears flowed down Millie's cheeks. She handed the letter to them. They put their heads together and read it aloud.

April 12, 1928

Dear Mrs. Hinchliffe,

Will you excuse a perfect stranger writing to you? I am supposing you are the wife of the airman lost the other day. I get writing and I had a communication from him that they came down into the sea, off the leeward islands, at night. His great anxiety is to communicate with you. Of course, you may not believe in communication, but he's been so urgent. Three times he's been. I thought I must write and risk it.

Yours sincerely,

Beatrice East.

The Sinclairs grew more annoyed by the moment.

"People like this prey on the grieving," Kate snapped.

"This woman says they came down in the Leeward Islands. He could never have made it to the Caribbean! Damn these people!" Sinclair exploded.

19

HELLO MR. DOYLE

Wednesday, May 16, 1928.

Newspapers continued to report on Hinchliffe's Atlantic bid. A report out of Canada, claimed that a plane had been seen coming down over Maine, just south of the Canadian border. There were reports of wreckage on a hillside with two bodies visible from the air. This all turned out to be a cruel hoax, making Millie more ill and depressed.

Daily Sketch:

IS HILLSIDE WRECKAGE CAPT HINCHLIFFE'S PLANE?
BODIES SEEN FROM THE AIR

The *Daily Express*:

HOPE DIMS FOR ATLANTIC PIONEER TWOSOME

The *Morning Star* said, a little ominously:

WAS AMERICA REALLY THEIR DESTINATION?
OR DID THEY FLY EASTWARD?

These stories were devastating for Millie. Her hopes were up and down like a roller coaster. Finally, she went away and stayed with friends in Brighton for two weeks. But once there, all she wanted was to get back in case there was news, or he showed up. When she returned, she opened a letter which had arrived while she was away. It shook her and the Sinclairs.

May 7, 1928

Dear Mrs. Hinchliffe,

May I express my sympathy in your grief. I wonder if you received a letter from a Mrs. East. She has had what looks like a very real message from your husband, sending his love and assurance that all is well with him. I have every reason to believe Mrs. East to be trustworthy, and the fact that the message contained the correct name and address of someone known to your husband and not to Mrs. East, is surely notable.

A second medium corroborated the message. That medium remarked that you were not English and had a baby and, she thought, another child. I should be interested to know if that is correct. I am acting on what appears to be your husband's request in bringing this matter before you. According to that message, the plane was driven far south.

Please let me have a line.

Yours faithfully,

A. Conan Doyle.

The following day, Millie was searching through closets and drawers when the front door bell rang. Sinclair had asked to borrow Hinchliffe's studs, as he couldn't find his own. Millie answered the door and was surprised to find a portly gentleman on the front step. He looked vaguely familiar.

He doffed his hat. "Mrs. Hinchliffe?"

"Yes."

"My name is Arthur Conan Doyle."

She gazed at him with incredulity, suddenly recognizing him.

"Oh, hello, Mr. Doyle. Please, do come in." She called to the Sinclairs, who were in the kitchen and they all went into Millie's studio. Millie was mystified and needed the Sinclairs' support.

Doyle's eyes swept the room, taking in Millie's paintings and photographs. He was impressed.

"Oh, look at these pictures, my word! My father was a wonderful artist. I've always wished I could paint," he said.

Millie was impatient to know what the great man was doing there.

"I try," she said.

"Lovely portraits," he said and then he noticed something special about them. "I see you paint in their auras. Wonderful!" He was studying Lowenstein's and Brancker's portraits. Both had colors streaming from them, which most saw as background colors. He paused and said, "Mrs. Hinchliffe you probably don't know, but I spend my life these days writing and lecturing on the subject of 'Life After Death'.

Millie stared at him blankly. And so did the Sinclairs. It didn't sit well with them. "I read something about it. I can't say I believe in it. We're not religious people."

"Did you receive my letter?" Doyle asked.

Millie nodded as if to say, 'yes and we don't believe any of it.'

"Please forgive me for dropping in on you like this, but since I hadn't heard back from you, I decided it was too important to let slide. We've received a rather stunning message from your husband. He communicated that he came down in the leeward islands," Doyle said.

Sinclair was ready. "That's damned impossible, sir!" he exploded. He'd already heard enough.

"Just a minute, Gordon, let's hear what Mr. Doyle has to say," Millie urged him.

"Wait my dear fellow, he meant, 'leeward of the storm'. That would put them in the Azores!" Doyle beamed. "And what a coincidence. That's where Ruth Elder went down in her plane in October—*they* too were in a Stinson Detroiter. But they were lucky—they got picked up."

"That's all too fantastic. Where did these messages come from?" Kate snapped.

Doyle ignored Kate's question, keeping his kindly composure. "Mrs. Hinchliffe, it has been brought to my attention that your husband is *desperate* to speak to you."

"Oh, no. I don't think so." Millie sensed where this was all leading.

"There's someone I'd like you to meet," Doyle said.

Millie shook her head from side to side adamantly. "No! No! No!"

"*Drummond*—is he your solicitor?"

"Yes, he is. Why, has Mr. Drummond been in contact with *you*?"

"Oh no, Mrs. Hinchliffe. Your *husband* gave us his name. That's how we contacted *you*, in fact."

Sinclair interjected again. His face was getting red. "I wouldn't have anything to do with this, Millie." Even though this was the great

Sir Arthur Conan Doyle, they felt this was all a confidence trick. Maybe *he* himself was being used unwittingly as part of some big ruse.

"The point is this, Mrs. Hinchliffe. Your husband knows you're in dire straits. He has vital information affecting you and your family's future. Apparently, the plugs let him down. He said he should never have changed them at the very last moment."

Millie was wavering. This was important information that only Sinclair would've known.

"Did he change the plugs, Gordon?"

Sinclair didn't answer. He was struck dumb.

"*Gordon!* Did he change the plugs?" Millie demanded.

Sinclair looked as though he'd been kicked in the stomach.

"Yes! Yes! *I* changed them. He asked me to, at the last damned minute," he said, his head down. "God, I wish we hadn't!"

Suddenly, Doyle beamed at Millie. "Mrs. Hinchliffe, would you paint my portrait?"

Millie wasn't in the mood to paint anybody's portrait. She felt totally devoid of artistry at the moment.

"Er—"

"What's your usual fee?"

"I usually charge fifty pounds."

Doyle took out his wallet. "Will you permit me to pay half now and the rest on completion?" he said, placing five ten-pound notes on the table.

Goodness, that would pay the mortgage and put food on the table for a couple of months.

"That's too much," she objected.

"Come, come, Mrs. Hinchliffe. Your husband knows you need help. Business is business! A hundred pounds is fair. I can see you are *exceptionally* talented," Doyle said, gesturing with a sweep on his hand around the room.

"Thank you so much," Millie said.

"Please drop Mrs. East a line. She's a lovely lady. Now, like I said, there's someone I'd like you to meet *very soon*. I'll be in touch." With that, Doyle ambled out to his chauffeur-driven Humber and was gone.

"Manna from Heaven," Millie mumbled, as they watched his car disappear down the driveway. Sinclair remained uneasy. After Doyle's unexpected visit, Millie overcame her reluctance and responded to Mrs. East's letter.

Millie was surprised, yet again, the next day. True to his word, Brancker showed up at her door. He came in bearing a beautiful bouquet of flowers and kissed her on both cheeks. He wanted to know how everyone was getting along. He knew, of course, that the Hinchliffe household was devastated, and tried his best to buoy Millie up. He assured her he was working furiously on her behalf, as were many others. She felt confident she had a loyal friend in Brancker. After discussing the insurance issue and other less consequential things, Brancker sheepishly said, "Millie, I have a favor to ask."

Millie frowned. "I'll try, Sefton."

"I'm in need of another portrait."

Millie couldn't help but smile. "You've been talking to Sir Arthur Conan Doyle?"

Brancker didn't answer. He looked evasive. "No, Millie, it's something I have to have. They hung the first one in the entrance hall at the Air Ministry—and now, they want one at Cardington."

"I'd be honored, of course. When I'm feeling up to it."

He took out his wallet. "Look, here's a deposit." He placed a hundred pounds on the table over Millie's objections.

"No rush, dear girl. "

20

THE FIRST SÉANCE

Tuesday, May 22, 1928.

Over the next couple of weeks, Millie met the sweet lady who loved to chuckle. The first time was at a tea house in Croydon and the second, at Mrs. East's home, where she showed Millie a shoe box full of messages, mostly from her son. Millie remained skeptical, but at least she knew the old dear wasn't a charlatan. It was clear the lady passionately believed in all this stuff about spirits. Millie proceeded with an open mind, still harboring thoughts Hinchliffe might be alive—in the wilds of Newfoundland, in hospital somewhere, or on a ship at sea. She kept her hopes up, though after seventy-six days she knew it was unrealistic—'*but stranger things have happened*', she kept telling herself.

Mrs. East told Millie about her own life and about her son and how he'd joined the merchant marine to avoid the trenches only to get torpedoed. She told her how happy she'd been with her husband and how she communicated with her son most days with her Ouija board. It was what kept her going, she said. She told Millie how her interest in spiritualism had grown over the years and how she visited the London Spiritualist Alliance once in a while, for a 'reading'. She mentioned one of their mediums—Mrs. Eileen Garrett. She was wonderful, she said—'so *gifted* and if we could sit with her, we could learn a lot'. Millie was more than a little reluctant. In the end, after much coaxing, she agreed to go as long as Mrs. East stayed with her at all times. Mrs. East said she'd be delighted, and suggested Doyle attend the sitting, if he could be persuaded. When contacted, Doyle jumped at the opportunity.

They traveled up to London on the train. Millie took a notepad and some pencils. She was a shorthand typist, after all. She'd make verbatim notes and type up transcripts later—if any of it was credible!

At the Spiritual Alliance building in Belgravia, the two women were shown to a spacious room on the second floor furnished with comfortable armchairs, matching settees and oriental rugs. The drapes were half drawn, allowing the sunshine in. Millie didn't find anything 'spooky' about the place as she'd expected, but was still *extremely* nervous.

Doyle had already arrived and was sitting with Mrs. Garrett, a woman of about forty with short black hair. They rose from their chairs. Mrs. Garrett took Millie's hand and she felt the medium's energy. She sat apprehensively on the couch opposite Mrs. Garrett and Mrs. East sat next to her. Mrs. Garrett explained that she'd go into 'trance' and that her 'control', an Arab, would come through and speak to her. She said he was a lovely, obliging spirit, but sometimes his Baghdad accent was hard to understand, especially when he got excited. Millie was terrified.

Presently, Mrs. Garrett closed her kind, smiling eyes and breathed deeply. They sat watching her while sounds of passing traffic and horses' hooves clattering on the cobbles drifted through the open window. That connection to reality gave Millie comfort. Suddenly, Mrs. Garrett's eyes opened and she gave Millie a beaming smile. "Greetings, I am Uvani," she said. "I'm sensing doom and gloom all around you."

Millie gave a start. Mrs. East turned to her and nodded, willing her to say something.

"I suppose that's right, yes," Millie whispered. She began scribbling on her pad.

"There's a lady here in the room with you with white hair. She says her name is Sophia."

"I don't know anybody by that name."

"Are you sure? She says she's around you all the time."

"The name means nothing to me," Millie said tersely.

"She says she's been close to you, lately."

Millie was losing what little nerve she had. She wanted to get up and run out the door. "I knew this was all a mistake!" she said, looking at Mrs. East.

"Ah, now here comes a tall, gray-eyed, young man. He has light brown hair and a straight nose. He was full of life and speed—cars and aeroplanes were his thing!" the voice from Mrs. Garrett exclaimed. Millie remained skeptical. "He says he's your husband. He rubs one eye and laughs. He sends greetings and appreciation to Sir Arthur over there and waves a calabash pipe at him and grins. Now he gives me the letter E. Are you are E?"

"My name is Emilie, but I'm sure you already knew that!" Millie said, casting a suspicious look at Doyle.

"I saw you searching the drawers and closets for my studs the other day—*and* my wings," Uvani said."

"Is that so?" It was a half-sneer. Nevertheless, she kept scratching her shorthand notes.

"Millie, it's *me*," another voice said.

"Who is *me?*"

"Raymond."

Skepticism, disbelief and annoyance registered in Millie's face. Mrs. East put her hand on Millie's arm, trying to calm her.

"Okay, let's play pretend, shall we?" Millie said with a smirk.

"I'm here to help you, Millie. I want you to know, I *am* alright."

"If you're *dead*, how can you be a*lright?*"

"Millie, there was so much more I wanted to say in my letter, but there wasn't time. I wanted your forgiveness for everything I'd put you through. I saw your apprehension growing after Minchin disappeared and Elder went down. Yet I still pushed on with it. But you held it all in. I was so remorseful that morning and during the flight. Oh dear, it's all such a mess!"

"Yes, a real mess!" Millie exclaimed, forgetting her skepticism for a moment.

"I'm so very sorry, Millie."

"How could you do this to us? There's no money, your salary payments are frozen, Gordon's dead broke, there's no insurance, and soon they'll be foreclosing on the house. We'll be in the street in no time!"

"Millie! Millie! I am going to help you, I promise."

"Just *stop* all this nonsense!"

"First, you must sell our piece of land next door." Millie glared at the medium. This seemed real enough. "It'll tide you over until the insurance money comes."

Doyle leaned forward, intrigued. These were the sort of indisputable facts he yearned for.

"There *is* no insurance money. *Do you not understand!*"

"You will receive every penny of that money, I promise you, Millie."

Mrs. East beamed at Millie, but it did little to assure her.

"Oh, yes, yes, I'm sure we will."

"You must contact Elsie's father."

"If you really *were* my dead husband, you'd know I've written to him already—and you'd also know that my letter has been *completely* ignored."

"That isn't enough. You must *confront* the man."

"I'll go with you, Millie, if you like," Doyle interjected keenly.

"Yes, and I'll come too," said Mrs. East, with a chuckle.

"We'll all go to Glenapp in my car," Doyle said excitedly.

Millie was still rebelling, not convinced. How could any of this be real?

"That would be marvelous, Sir Arthur. Thank you for all you've done. You must sell that land, Millie. You'll find the surveyor's plan behind the drawer in my desk. You'll need that. Please look for it," Hinchliffe said.

Millie was in turmoil. This was all too much to accept. Although much of the information she was hearing had elements of truth in it, her logical mind couldn't accept it. Perhaps the medium was able to read her mind. She recoiled. "I don't know who's giving you details of my private affairs—"

"Dear Millie, my studs are in the cigar box in the closet in our bedroom. Tell Sinclair he can have them—I shan't be needing them. My wings are in the music box I gave Joan. As for my black cat lucky charm—that'll show up later."

Millie nodded. She looked forward to going home and finding out one way or another if any of this were true.

"Millie, please come back soon and talk to me—just the two of us?"

Millie gave a half smile. "We'll see," she said.

Millie went back to Croydon with Mrs. East. Sinclair picked her up later. Sinclair asked about Millie's experience with Mrs. Garrett. She told him she was mulling it all over. Millie remained wrapped up in her thoughts, all the way home. Sinclair said no more.

Later that evening, after the Sinclairs had gone to bed, Millie searched around in Hinchliffe's closet in her bedroom. She felt around on the top shelf until she found his cigar box. She sat on the bed and opened it reverently. There was his distinguished flying cross. A military ribbon and an old brass lighter. An envelope with a lock of Millie's hair. And, of course, *his studs!* She'd already found his wings in Joan's music box when she'd put her to bed earlier. If Millie had turned around at that moment, she'd have seen Hinchliffe's reflection in the mirror behind her on the wardrobe door. He'd been watching her every move. He smiled sadly. He was sure she was convinced now. Convinced he was dead.

Millie shook with emotion. Yes, he had to be dead. The medium couldn't have known any of this. This was incontestable. Irrefutable! She was absolutely terrified. She wheeled around to look behind her. There was no one there now. The house was silent. The grandfather clock in the hall below suddenly began striking twelve, startling her further. She took the lamp and, followed by Butch and Whiskey, went down the stairs to the living room where Hinchliffe's desk stood in the alcove under a window. She placed the lamp on the desk and opened the drawers which were full of documents, and odds and ends. She picked up a gold fountain pen Lowenstein had given Hinchliffe. She'd forgotten about that. She took out an old bible and on an impulse, opened it and read the inscription inside the cover. She stared in disbelief. It read, 'To Raymond with love. Grandmother Sophia.'

Millie pulled the side drawer out completely and looked into the dark space. There was something blue and white at the back. She reached in and pulled it out. It was a crumpled blueprint. She opened it flat on the desk. It was the surveyor's plan of the land next door. Millie sank to the floor on her haunches in shock. This was astonishing. What more proof could she ask for? There was no question. In some ways, she was almost joyful. Hinchliffe was dead. But he wasn't dead! Millie wanted to see Eileen Garrett as soon as possible. She couldn't wait to get to the village and make a phone call in the morning. She was also looking forward to presenting Sinclair with her husband's studs. The cat gave a loud meow and the dog whimpered.

Millie went back to her bedroom, dragged out her old Underwood from the closet and put it on her writing table. She began typing up the transcripts. For the next hour, the Sinclairs could faintly hear her from their bedroom. Tap, tap, tap, … tap, tap, tap, and then the occasional ding.

21

THE SECOND SÉANCE

Thursday, May 24, 1928.

I see your powers of mediumship are already strong, dear lady, and I can tell you, they will grow stronger each and every day. I expect you see auras around people," Uvani said.

"I always have. I thought everyone did. Though now, they're more vivid. Sometimes I imagine Ray is close to me."

"It's not imagination. You'll soon sense spirit around you, as all mediums do. Your husband is here," Uvani paused and Hinchliffe continued speaking through Eileen Garrett.

"My darling Millie, I'm so glad you came. I wanted to tell you how much I love you and how much you mean to me. This sounds silly, but I did it all for you and the children. Stupidly, I thought I could do what others had failed to do. Pride kills!"

"My dear, dear husband. It's done now—but life is so miserable without you."

"Thank you for keeping it from Joan. I had the picture of you both with me. I kissed it just before we went into the water."

"Oh, Ray—"

"I want to help you, Millie. Inchcape and the insurance business is so maddening! I see you doing your best to cope. It's been unbearable for me to watch."

"Things can't get much worse, can they?" Millie replied.

"The sale of the land should tide you over for six months. I see you found the plan."

"Yes, I took it to the estate agent yesterday. I think the owner wants to buy it himself," Millie said.

"Good, let him have it."

"Then, I may have to sell the car."

"No. No need yet. But on the insurance, you must go on the offensive. It'll take a while, but you *will* get it eventually—I can assure you of that."

"What should I do?"

"You'll need to speak publicly and tell your story. The papers will pick it up and shame him. You'll be getting a lot of help from influential people *very, very* soon."

"We're going up to Glenapp on Saturday," Millie replied, and then, "How is Elsie?"

"Recovery from her crossing over has been hard. She had a terrible time. That poor girl sat down there on the ocean floor in the darkness for many days, before they came for her."

"Oh, dear God," Millie whispered in dismay, remembering her nightmare.

"She's riddled with guilt over the muddle she's put you in with the insurance, and for deceiving her family, of course. She'll be fine. She's really a nice soul. She was a bit ditsy and was trying to impress her old man. She's learned a lot from this experience. I've become quite fond of her."

"I think she was head over heels in love with you, Raymond," Millie said.

"You may be right. But how could she not?" Millie laughed. That was her husband, all right. "She spends a lot of time around her brother, Jonathan," Hinchliffe said.

"And what about *you*? I want to know what happened that night— I want to know *everything*."

Hinchliffe described their flight in detail—how Elsie had been in a bad way for many hours due to sheer terror. He told Millie how he'd eventually decided to turn sharply south. They couldn't fight the horrendous gale any longer. They'd try and reach the Azores. Hinchliffe paused and sighed heavily, thinking. The medium's face showed the strain of their terrible ordeal.

"We came down within sight of land after the engine quit. I tried to restart it by switching tanks. I thought maybe there was an airlock. After we hit the water, I tried to save Elsie. She was trapped in that seat belt. I can't believe we didn't fix it. Still, it wouldn't have done her any good—she couldn't swim anyway. I watched her go down and then tried to swim for the island—Corvo it was called. I saw it at first, and then became disoriented. I soon got totally waterlogged, cold and exhausted. In the end, I floundered, not knowing in what direction to go. After about five or ten minutes, I passed out in the numbing cold.

Later, much later, I came round. I was in some horrible place; it was half-light. I thought I must've washed up on the island I'd seen. The beach was like black mud. I knew the beaches in the Azores were black and thought I must have washed up there. I laid in the surf for a time, unable to move. Then after a while, I dragged myself out of the water and crawled up the beach. I could hear rooks or ravens cawing and carrying on around me. I looked toward the trees—they were ugly black shapes—gnarly and broken. I saw vultures along their branches. I thought they were waiting for me. I crawled on across the filthy beach to the woods, where I heard things. Nasty things. Squeals, gnashing of teeth, howls and cackling. My nostrils were filled with the stench of death and decay, my mouth the taste of stale blood. I crawled on through mildewed bracken, which I sensed was infested with snakes and rats."

"Oh, Ray. That's horrifying."

"At one point, I slumped down in the slime to rest my throbbing head, listening to the wind hissing in the trees. I was totally distraught —scared out of my wits! I kept thinking—where am I? What is this place? Later, I heard noises and looked up. Two entities were leaning over me. Their faces evil—eyes, terrifying black pools. It seemed like they'd come for me—to claim me. They didn't speak. They grunted and squeaked, pawing at me. They wanted me to go with them. I was *very* afraid.

They were driven off by another being who appeared out of the forest. I perceived him to be good. He'd not only come to claim me, but to protect me—rescue me! He warded them off, and they slunk away into the gloom. He was an old sage, his face craggy, his hair long and white to the shoulders. He was wearing a monk's robe, once white, now grubby and worn. In *that* place, it could hardly have remained flowing white! He raised me to my feet and stared into my face, willing me to follow him. His face was angelic, his eyes huge, and blue—totally mesmerizing.

I trudged behind him for what seemed hours, days, even weeks. It's impossible to say. I gradually came to realize I was dead. I must be dead! Where was he taking me, I wondered? To hell? Is this hell? It seemed like the fringes of hell. We passed by all kinds of entities, mostly horrible. I wanted to get away from there. *God help me!* I cried.

In the distance, I saw flames and molten lava. I became more afraid. Later, we came to a body of black water, wide and smooth and then to a dock of rotten black wood. He led me along it. I stepped carefully in case the boards collapsed. He waved for me to get into a wooden boat moored alongside. We clambered in and he nodded to the boatman, who pushed us off. Beneath the surface, I saw dark shapes— I dreaded to think what they were. Without a word, the old man rowed us out into the estuary and across to the other side. We got out onto another dock, and the boatman rowed away.

This side of the river felt better, calmer. I followed my guide again, for how long, I don't know. We passed nicer people and animals, more pleasant. Things became better with every step. My spirits began to lift. The sky brightened and colors went from black, to dark earth-tones, and then to pleasing pastels. Later, as we came to green pastures the colors became more vivid. In fact, I saw, or sensed I saw, colors I'd never seen on earth. I began to hear sounds—such soothing sounds— birdsong, beautiful music, choirs, children's laughter and welcoming whispers. My spirits soared. Perhaps all was not lost. Presently, I saw a church, a Gothic church, like St. Saviour's in our village, set in fragrant gardens. He took me inside, now smiling at me for the first time. Inside, he handed me over to a portly monk who gave me the biggest welcome you could ever imagine.

'Raymond,' he said, putting his arms around me and patting my back. 'Walter George Raymond Hinchliffe.'

'Yes,' I said. 'I am he.'

'What a life it's been!' he said. He seemed to know all about me. All I could do was agree weakly with him.

'You know where you are?' he asked me. I nodded. I suppose I did, sort of. 'You will remain here with us in this place until you recuperate —spiritually, of course. Bodily there is no problem.'

'I must get back to see my wife and children,' I said.

'We'll see about all that,' he said. "All in good time."

So, my dear Millie. I rested there in that place. Later, I was told I would be allowed to come and visit you, and I did, as you know. It's all been traumatic, but I'm coming out of it. I've been given tasks to accomplish. It's been healing."

"I'm so glad, Ray."

"Death gives you a whole new perspective on life, Millie!"

"It must."

Hinchliffe paused for some time, as though considering what he was about to say. Millie waited.

"I've talked to a lot of people here about something that's been bothering me a lot."

"What's that?"

"I've spent time at Cardington and I'm gonna be there a lot. That airship's a deathtrap. Our friends there will die on her maiden voyage unless—"

"What can we do about that?"

"Somehow we must get it stopped. But first, we must concentrate on getting you the insurance we were promised."

Before returning home, Millie decided to act on Hinchliffe's advice and took a bus to the *Daily Express* offices on Fleet Street. The people on the front desk were more than interested when Millie introduced herself. She told them she wanted to tell her story to Mr. George Hunter, who knew her quite well.

Millie was immediately taken to the second floor by a young intern through a bank of telegraph machines, and then a huge office, packed with people at desks, surrounded by clattering typewriters or on the phone.

Hunter was in a small, glazed office on one side. He was on the phone facing the wall with his back to Millie, his feet on the desk. The young man left Millie at the door, where she waited patiently. Hunter was talking about her, mumbling through his cigarette. "So, what are the odds of Mrs. Hinchliffe getting the money she was entitled to?"

Millie was excited that Hunter was already working on her behalf. She wished she could hear the other end of the conversation.

"I see ..." Hunter said pessimistically.

He removed his feet from the desk and spun round in his chair. He was surprised to come face to face with Millie. His eyes lit up.

"Er, well look, see what you can do. I'll call you back, okay?" Hunter said, putting the phone down. "Mrs. Hinchliffe, I had no idea you were coming in to see us."

"Please forgive this intrusion. I thought I'd take a chance and drop by."

Hunter had been very taken with Millie and was upset for her sake when Hinchliffe disappeared. He didn't dare think of making an approach to her, certainly not for a long time to come, but doubted he was in her league, anyway. He killed the cigarette in the ashtray.

"I'm very glad you're here—it's wonderful seeing you again."

"I came to ask for your help."

"Anything, Mrs. Hinchliffe. You may have just heard the tail end of that conversation. I'm working on another story about you right now."

"Good. If you want my story, I'll tell you everything."

He smacked his hand on the desk. "Fabulous! How are you faring?"

"We're barely surviving. I'm selling things. I'm doing portraits and I'm thinking about giving piano lessons and art lessons. I've been asked to play the organ at the village church—although it doesn't pay much!"

"Would it be right say you're penniless?"

"Soon will be. We have no means of support. Despite everything Miss Mackay promised us."

"Thanks to Lord Inchcape?"

"You might say that!"

He took out another cigarette, lit it with his gold lighter and snapped it shut. "I've been hearing that you've been in touch with your husband through a psychic medium—is that true?"

"Er, yes." Millie wasn't sure about this avenue.

"I heard Sir Arthur Conan Doyle is assisting you?" he said, raising an eyebrow.

"Yes, he's been exceptionally kind. He's a wonderful gentleman."

"This is great! What did your husband have to say?" Hunter said, smiling. Millie couldn't tell if he was being sarcastic.

"He said we'd get the money."

"Did he indeed?" Hunter sounded intrigued.

"He said *without question,*" Millie emphasized.

"Well, that's going to be *very* interesting, isn't it—and quite a story. Our readers will be fascinated. They can't get enough of that stuff—or of *you,* come to that. They're out there rooting for you, you know, Mrs. Hinchliffe. We get letters all the time."

"My husband also mentioned something else you may find interesting."

Hunter leaned forward in his chair. "Go on."

"He says the *Cardington Airship R101* is a deathtrap and won't survive her maiden voyage."

"Wow! I'll put that nugget in the file for later," Hunter said. "First things first."

Millie told Hunter about her life, being raised in Holland and meeting Hinchliffe. She gave him the full story about his war years, before they were married and then his days with the airlines. Hunter took notes while they chatted for an hour or so. They arranged to meet again in the future as a follow up. Before Millie left, Hunter offered his help on a personal level, as a friend. Millie was pleased and flattered. He really was a nice person to be around and seemed to genuinely care.

A few days later the *Daily Express* ran a story about Millie's heartbreak and hardship.

WIFE OF ATLANTIC PILOT NEARLY PENNILESS
PROMISED INSURANCE POLICY STOPPED BY FAMILY

22

GLENAPP CASTLE

Saturday, May 26, 1928.

It was a sunny morning. Millie and Mrs. East set off with Doyle, very early, for Scotland in his Humber. As they traveled north along country roads, Millie told them the results of her search for the items Hinchliffe had mentioned during the first séance with Eileen Garrett. Doyle was delighted. After the second séance, Millie thought it appropriate to wear black and had purchased a few items in Croydon.

Along the way, Doyle told them about his experiences with the spirit world, even touching on his up and down relationship with Houdini, great American showman and master of escape. Houdini had been devastated by the death of his mother. Hearing of Doyle's interest in the 'afterlife', Houdini had contacted him and they'd become fast friends, until intensive research and attempts to contact his mother ended in failure. Houdini became bitter and their friendship came to an end. Doyle, remained open minded.

They arrived in Glenapp at 4:00 p.m. after 10 hours on the road with two stops for petrol and a bite to eat. The old stone castle appeared foreboding. Millie felt intimidated, even before they'd pulled the old bell cord. After a few minutes, the creaking oak door was opened by a hostile-looking butler who glared at them. Doyle introduced himself. The butler appeared unimpressed they'd driven up from London, but asked them, in a rather snooty Scottish accent, to step inside. He'd see if Lord Inchcape was available today, or at any time in the foreseeable future.

Their luck was in. Eventually they were shown into what reminded Millie of a dungeon or a torture chamber. Lord Inchcape sat scowling in the gloom behind a colossal hand-carved desk. Doyle stepped forward, his hand outstretched. Inchcape took it reluctantly.

"Lord Inchcape, I'm—" Doyle began.

"I know exactly who you are, sir—and this is the airman's wife, I presume?" Inchcape said, glaring at Millie in her widow's black. He rudely ignored Mrs. East, who stood frozen in shock.

"Yes, I'm Emilie Hinchliffe—" Millie said nervously.

"I've been reading hard-luck stories about you in the *Scottish Daily Express*. What can I do for you, madam?" Inchcape said harshly.

Millie and Doyle had prepared what they'd say on the way up. Nonetheless, Millie already felt browbeaten, her voice weak and wavering. "First, let me say how sorry I am for your loss. Your daughter was a fine, brave woman with high ideals."

"I will stop you right there! My daughter was not fine, or brave, and she had no ideals at all. She was a stupid, immature, publicity seeker, who deserved exactly what she got!"

Millie was shocked, not expecting such a vitriolic response, but regardless, she soldiered on bravely. "Your daughter made an agreement with my husband—"

"You are all liars and deceivers. Because of your greed and your husband's recklessness he, too, is dead. That's what comes of skulking around in the night, deceiving people. And if I may say so, all this flying around is an affront to God Almighty. If that was His intention, He'd have given us wings!"

"It was your daughter who approached Mrs. Hinchliffe's husband —" Doyle began.

"Enough! She'll not get a penny out o' me!"

Millie was by now enraged.

"You keep Elsie's damned money for yourself! But you remember this 'til your dying day—it was *you,* who forced them off that aerodrome, and it was *you* who forced them out into that storm. All that girl ever tried to do was to impress and please *you*—you *wicked* old man!" she screamed, her eyes like daggers.

Lord Inchcape showed no sign of relenting. In fact, quite the reverse. There was no more to be said. Doyle put his arm around Millie and led her out. Once outside, she burst into tears and was comforted by Mrs. East.

"Grief shows itself in different ways, dear. Don't you worry," she told Millie.

After staying the night in a hotel in Carlisle, they drove back to Croydon the next day.

On Monday, Millie got up after sleeping late. She looked ill. It was while she was preparing a meal in the kitchen and Joan was busy with her crayons, that she heard of Lord Inchcape's latest move on the radio.

This is the BBC news. Lord Inchcape, the father of the Honorable Elsie Mackay, announced from Glenapp Castle today that his daughter's entire fortune is to be placed in a fund for the next fifty years, after which time, it will be donated to the government.

Within a week, the mood in Britain regarding this whole affair was one of concern for the 'airman's wife', as the press called her. The atmosphere in the House of Commons was likewise, rapidly becoming hostile toward Inchcape. One MP gave an impassioned speech on Millie's behalf:

"Without detracting from the generosity of Lord and Lady Inchcape, is the Chancellor of the Exchequer aware that Mrs. Hinchliffe is in dire straits as a result of her husband's accident, who in normal circumstances would have claims against Miss Mackay's estate for promises not honored?"

At this, there were cries from the left.

"Hear, hear!"

"Shame!"

"Shame!"

Winston Churchill, the Chancellor of the Exchequer, got to his feet. "Sir, as regrettable as the circumstances are, this has absolutely nothing to do with the Chancellor of the Exchequer!"

The MP would not let it go. "It is unconscionable for this house to treat the widow in this way. Her husband was a decorated war hero and a great aviation pioneer."

"The Chancellor of the Exchequer has no control over what Lord Inchcape does, or does not do, with his daughter's money," Churchill responded.

There were now cries from the right.

"Hear, hear!"

Whilst all this wrangling was going on, the Atlantic Ocean was as smooth as silk. The sun's rays upon it were like a kaleidoscope of broken glass, reflecting the vivid colors of sunset from the May afternoon sky. In all this wondrous beauty that no one saw, something bobbed in the clear blue water—a rubber tire attached to a splintered, wooden aeroplane strut.

23

BRANCKER BRINGS NEWS

Thursday, June 7, 1928.

illie's anxiety over money grew worse, even though they had enough for the short term. The estate agent in Croydon had purchased the land from her and that would tide them over. But she knew this, and the generosity of friends, couldn't last forever. Millie was determined to survive and was working on ways to make some money. Sinclair had planted out more of the rear gardens beyond the walls and hedges and had vegetables growing in abundance. They'd sell most of them. Also, the chickens were doing well and producing plenty of eggs, which they also sold. Sinclair had added a huge chicken coop to house another fifty birds. His beekeeping honey-producing venture would also contribute. None of this was a fortune, but it helped sustain them.

Millie decided to capitalize on her own talents and began giving art classes and piano lessons as she'd told Hunter she would. She was also painting portraits of local people. The newspapers had been helpful—many readers asked for their portraits doing. Some even sent money or checks. The whole nation was becoming obsessed with Millie's story, but Elsie's father was unyielding.

Millie took down the portrait of a young choirboy in his surplice and cassock from her easel and laid it on her work table. A woman waited, her son at her side. Three other paintings were propped on a wall shelf, waiting to be picked up. The boy stared in fascination at Millie's paintings of *Endeavour,* one in the hangar, and one in the air, while Joan proudly explained that they were pictures of 'her daddy's aeroplane and that he was away flying it'. Joan told him that sometimes he came back—while she was asleep. Millie pretended she hadn't heard as she wrapped the portrait in newspaper. She tied it with string and handed it to the woman. The doorbell rang. Millie excused herself and opened the door to Brancker, who stood with a sympathetic smile. He thrust another bouquet of flowers at her, put his arms around her and kissed her cheeks.

"I have some news," Brancker told her grimly. Millie led him into her studio, where her clients patiently waited. Millie handed her the painting, and the woman gave her a check. Brancker watched all this with interest and smiled as they were shown out. She returned to find him inspecting her latest artwork. He was studying his own finished duplicate copy and Sir Arthur Conan Doyle's portrait, now in progress.

"These are magnificent, Millie. Wonderful likenesses," Brancker exclaimed.

"Thank you."

"This is a wonderful idea. I'm sure you're going to do well. How are you making out?"

"It's a struggle, but everyone's been very kind." Millie said.

"Yes, yes, it must be hard. I'll do what I can. I spoke to Beaverbrook yesterday. They're all coming out to bat for you Millie," Brancker said.

"Everyone except Lord Inchcape, Sir Sefton," Millie said. She was itching for Brancker to get to the point of his visit.

"Millie," he said, and then hesitated, his eyes down.

She waited.

"I told you as soon as I heard something ... you might ask the Sinclairs to come in, if they're around," Brancker said. Millie hurried off to fetch them.

When they came in, Brancker looked at Joan pointedly, and Millie asked Kate to take Joan into the kitchen out of the way.

"The wheel of a plane has washed up on a beach in County Donegal," he told them.

Millie gave a small startled cry. "Oh!"

"I contacted the Stinson factory in Detroit yesterday. They've confirmed that the tire was the type used on Raymond's plane. The wheel had the special brakes they used, too. They are the only manufacturer using that system. I also gave them a description of the wooden strut attached to the wheel. It all matches, sad to say."

Sinclair put his hands to his head. "Sweet Jesus!" he whispered.

Millie stood woodenly still. "I suppose that's it then," she said finally. Although she already knew Hinchliffe was dead, this was still painful—like reading his death certificate.

"I'm afraid it looks that way, my dear. But please know that everyone has their shoulder to the wheel," Brancker assured her. But Millie looked doubtful.

Later, in the evening, Millie took Joan to bed and kissed her goodnight. The baby was already in her crib, fast asleep. Joan glanced at the plane on her music box. She asked about her daddy, as she did every night and Millie told her the same thing—she wasn't sure when he'd be back, but not to worry, he was somewhere nice, and he was thinking of them all. Joan lay her head on the pillow looking at the little silver plane facing away from her. "I do love Daddy's present Mummy. And I do love Daddy."

The following morning Joan slowly opened her eyes focusing them on the plane on the music box. It was now facing her. She slowly got out of bed, not taking her eyes from it, and crept downstairs to her mother who was standing at the kitchen sink.

"Daddy was here again last night, Mummy," she said.

Millie wasn't the least surprised. "How do you know, darling?"

"He keeps moving the plane. I know he's doing it. He comes when I'm asleep," Joan said.

Millie wasn't fazed. She knew Hinchliffe probably *had* been in Joan's room. She stood at the window, remembering the day he'd returned from his Fokker-retrieving expedition. She saw a vision of the scene reenacted in the garden. Hinchliffe playing the fool with the sheet over his head, pretending to be a ghost, the dog barking, and then the three of them coming together in a big family hug. The scene faded away. She turned back to the cooking stove in the hearth.

The following week, Millie was in her studio, working on Brancker's second portrait. She heard the sound of a vehicle on the driveway and went to investigate. It was the biggest, shiniest, black Rolls Royce Millie had ever seen. She didn't recognize the man emerging from the backseat while the chauffeur held the door. He looked impressive in a black pinstriped suit; his hair was slicked back, with a razor-sharp parting. He strode to the door.

Millie waited until the bell rang before she opened it. The visitor smiled broadly, his teeth even and sparkling white. "I am presuming that you are Mrs. Hinchliffe. Please forgive me showing up like this. I'm Max Aiken," he said, holding out his hand. Millie stared up into his piercing, intelligent eyes, none the wiser. "You may know me as Lord Beaverbrook."

Millie gulped.

"I was wondering, could we talk? I heard you're one of the best portrait painters in the country," he continued.

"Why don't you c-come in," Millie stammered. She'd heard of Lord Beaverbrook, of course. He was a Canadian business tycoon who'd settled in England and was a member of the government. He also owned the *Daily Express,* amongst many other newspapers, making him the biggest newspaper proprietor in the world. She led him into her studio, where he marched up to Brancker's portrait.

"Ah, I recognize this gay old dog—it's Brancks. He's a jolly good man!" he said. "He was the one who told me where to come to get my portrait painted." He cast his eye warily over Lowenstein in the corner and frowned.

"That was very kind of Sir Sefton," Millie said.

Beaverbrook looked around and out the window at the garden.

"Lovely place you've got here," he said. "Mrs. Hinchliffe, I want to help you. I know all about you and your husband. Believe me, I am sorry. He was a great pioneer. Planes and pilots fascinate me—they're incredible people—certainly gave those Huns a run for their money! His Atlantic attempt was not a waste. He's contributed immensely to this country's aviation—more than you could possibly know."

Millie was very touched. Tears welled up in her eyes.

"I must have a portrait. Can you fit me into your schedule? I know you're busy. There are at least six MP's I know of who want you to paint them." He gestured over to Doyle's picture. "I see Sir Arthur is on your list of clients, too."

Millie was astonished. Word must have got around fast in higher circles.

"Yes, of course, er—"

"Max. Call me Max."

"Yes, Max."

"Now, about your situation, a syndicate has been formed and a fund is being set up for donations to assist you until Inchcape comes to his senses," Beaverbrook said.

"I don't know what to say—"

"Now, where shall I sit?" He pulled the wooden armchair Millie used for sitters toward the French windows. "How about here—will this do?"

Millie was in awe of this man. He was a powerhouse. He sat down and she took some photos. She set up an easel and started roughing out his likeness. After about forty-five minutes he jumped up.

"You have enough to be getting on with?"

"Yes, I think so," Millie said.

"One more visit do?" he asked.

"Yes, I'm sure you're a busy man."

He took out his wallet. "Two hundred, all right?"

Millie screwed up her face. "That's *way* too much," Millie protested.

"Absolutely not!" He placed two hundred pounds on the table and left.

She knew he might show up any day in the future and she'd have to drop everything. This was a man who got things done, and who expected immediate results. He reminded her of Brancker. Their auras were similar, well-balanced, with generous amounts of red, yellow, pink, green and orange.

A couple of weeks later, on July 4th, a strange event occurred. Millie was shocked to hear about it on the radio and read about it in the newspapers later. Alfred Lowenstein had left Croydon Airport aboard his Fokker Trimotor bound for Brussels. On board were the pilot and the mechanic in their own sealed cockpit. Lowenstein was in the main cabin with his valet, his male secretary and two female secretaries. The weather was perfect.

About half way across the English Channel, Lowenstein put down the documents he was working on and went to the back of the plane to use the toilet. After twenty minutes or so, his valet became concerned and went to check on him. He found the toilet empty and the exit door of the plane open. Lowenstein was nowhere to be found.

The pilot was informed and decided to land on a deserted French beach near Dunkirk. The beach turned out not to be deserted, but in use by the French military. After the facts were eventually revealed by the pilot the local police were called. No one was charged, although it was all very mysterious. Had old Lowenstein committed suicide? And if so, why? Or was it foul play?

24

THE THIRD SÉANCE

Monday, August 6, 1928.

Millie arranged for a third sitting with Eileen Garrett. She needed to tell Hinchliffe how pleased she was and to thank him for all he was doing. She knew he'd worked behind the scenes coaxing people, even though they weren't aware of it. She also knew he needed cheering up. But on the way from the train station, she had a shocking experience.

She saw an airship in the sky. It dipped its nose violently, as if it were going to crash. It leveled out for a few moments with smoke billowing from its nose. Then she saw flames. It dived again more precipitously, disappearing into a black cloud bank below. Millie knew this must be a vision—although it was so vivid—because behind the ship, she saw the Eiffel Tower. Millie stumbled on, feeling sick, toward the Spiritualist Alliance building.

She was still shaking when she was shown into the sitting room on the second floor, where Eileen awaited her. After a few minutes relating her experience to Eileen, the medium went into trance.

"I see by your aura your psychic powers have developed enormously," Uvani said.

"I just saw a terrible thing in the sky. It seemed so real—" Millie said.

"It was a vision, my dear. A warning. Be not afraid. But first things first. Your husband's here."

Millie calmed down quickly, astonished to hear what Uvani had said.

"Dear Raymond, thank you for all you do. I'm getting so much support from friends and influential people. I know it's your doing. Lord Beaverbrook is now helping us," she said.

"You must keep your hopes up about the insurance, Millie. It's definitely coming. The month I've been given is July—the last day of July," Hinchliffe told her.

"We'll see. I hope you're right, dear," Millie replied.

"I've been around Lord Inchcape recently, with Elsie. I should tell you she's pleased with the help you're getting. She's furiously working on the old man. I wouldn't be surprised to see him taking an interest in spiritualism when this is all over. Elsie's passing has changed him a lot. He's become very thoughtful—he misses her a lot—more than he thought possible. I'm seeing movement there," Hinchliffe said.

"Ray, the one thing I can't get out of my mind is—where did your body wash up—if it did?"

"It wound up on the rocks in Jamaica, nothing but skin and bone was left by August—scattered between the rocks. The other wheel came ashore down there too, a few miles away."

Millie could hardly speak for a few moments. The thought of it was sickening. She held her head. "What happened to Lowenstein? You heard he was missing from his plane over the English Channel?" she asked.

"Yes, I heard about that. I'm not sure he's really dead. I've tried to find him, but no one here knows anything." Hinchliffe changed the subject of dead people in the water. "And now Millie, we have work to do."

"You mean regarding the *Cardington R101*?"

"I'm worried about our friends. The vision you just had in the street *was* a warning."

"What shall we do?"

"Tell the world. Your words and paintings will speak volumes."

As soon as Millie got home, she went to the studio and sketched a picture of her vision of *Cardington R101* near Paris in flames. The Sinclairs stared in horror when they saw it. From the sketch, Millie did a large canvas painting in vivid color. Sinclair had become a true believer, scared to death of it all, but a true believer. He looked at Millie's painting and shook his head, sadly as if to say, 'what can we do?'.

Over the course of the coming year, they seemed to live in a state of limbo. In reality, they were not. They felt as if they were eking out a living, but were lucky in many ways. Millie taught photography and art classes. She reproduced many of her paintings and sold them in an art shop in Croydon. Grantham Hunt was a favorite. With Doyle's permission, she'd sold several copies of his portrait too. She'd managed to bring out much of the beauty of his character, his kindness, his naivety, his heart—both that of a child and of a lion. All this was clearly displayed in his aura.

Someone wanted to buy the Lowenstein portrait, but she wouldn't part with it—she didn't really know why. Maybe it was a link to her husband, because he'd flown him around so much in the past. Perhaps she had a slight connection to the man. She continued to wonder what had happened to him.

It turned out that his body became entangled in the nets of English fishermen in August. Millie asked Hinchliffe about it again during one of her sessions with Eileen. He told her Lowenstein had finally turned up. He'd come to Hinchliffe in a very bad state, telling him that he'd been allowed to seek him out. Lowenstein begged and pleaded for help. He needed someone to vouch for him he said. Someone who'd say a kind word for him. He'd had difficulty on that score. Hinchliffe was the only person he could think of. Hinchliffe was pleased to do it, especially since he'd been the first to send Millie money—even though it was money he owed and was late.

It appeared Lowenstein had done wrong in the manner of his death, but explained that he couldn't stop himself. His compulsion to die had exceeded his urge to live. It wasn't until he was out in the freezing air, hurtling toward the icy sea that he realized he'd made a horrible mistake. A mistake he couldn't undo. During his descent, his life had played out before his eyes—it seemed for an agonizing eternity. On hitting the water, he immediately found himself in a worse place than Hinchliffe had done.

It had filled Lowenstein with terror and he called out to God, to Jesus, to the Mother of God and the Holy Spirit to have mercy on him. His cries were heard and he managed to escape and gradually he came to brighter places and then to Hinchliffe. Hinchliffe said that he was a changed man, very humble. He'd never seen Lowenstein like that.

It was all very strange. It seemed that Lowenstein's wife would inherit the money—but no one would say how much—or if indeed there was a great fortune. Millie read that his wife hadn't attended the funeral and Lowenstein's name hadn't even been put on his gravestone. Millie remembered Lowenstein's fuss over the magpie. It made her sad.

Sinclair was enterprising with his end of things; he also worked at the Coach & Horses as a relief barman four nights a week and during the day, sometimes. He also worked in the local garage part-time, putting his mechanical skills to work. He even helped out across the road with Barney at his forge some days. He became adept at shoeing horses. He'd put a sign out on the road advertising vegetables, eggs and honey. His efforts contributed to the household income.

Millie played the organ in the village church. She earned a pittance for that, but she did it more for the love of the community and the comfort she got out of it than anything. Millie started receiving a monthly check from the Airman's Wife Fund organized through the Beaverbrook organization. This usually ran to about twenty-five pounds per month. Millie and the Sinclairs felt truly blessed. They had diverse talents and they had each other. But still the feeling of being in limbo remained. The fund couldn't continue forever.

Millie saw Eileen Garrett once a month, usually traveling up to London with Mrs. East. Mrs. East became one of the family and loved to babysit sometimes. Her life had become enriched and more meaningful. Over the coming months, Millie began seriously developing her powers of mediumship, sitting 'in circle' with others under the supervision of powerful mediums of the Spiritual Alliance in Belgravia.

She often visited the homes of well-known mediums around London where she had illuminating experiences, often seeing Hinchliffe and other loved ones of attendees in 'transfiguration séances', where their spiritual image overlaid that of the medium, and in other cases where spirits actually materialized 'in the flesh'. Millie entered into these meetings with skepticism as fraud in these activities was notorious. Once or twice, she actually got up and walked out, realizing it was a scam.

During this time, there was a great deal of growth in Millie's character and psychic development, not to mention her soul. She began visiting women's groups, who enthusiastically sought her out to come and speak to them about life after death. Once it was revealed that she was a wonderful classical pianist, they would coax her into playing for them whenever a piano was available. Gradually, she overcame her dislike of performing in public. She also spoke about her art, often bringing some of her best pieces to display. Hinchliffe was immensely proud of her.

Doyle frequently accompanied Millie to these meetings and, naturally, he was a huge hit. At other times, Hunter went along; he, too, the ladies found interesting, as a successful journalist. Mrs. East never missed these meetings, becoming a popular figure herself. During this year, Hunter had proved himself to be a good friend, although he would have liked to be more. He trod carefully. He knew her heart remained with her husband and probably always would. He came to Pickwick Cottage once in a while and played the latest hit tunes to cheer Millie up as he did at the women's group meetings when he was there. Millie had become quite fond of him.

Hinchliffe had been keeping tabs on his friends at Cardington ever since his own demise. He'd looked over Captain Irwin's and Navigator Johnston's shoulders constantly, following their day-to-day activities. Captain Irwin continued monitoring construction and updating engineering drawings. Johnston worked on all matters concerning planning and navigating new routes to far-off places.

During the course of the year, Hinchliffe passed on a lot of information to Millie—things he'd seen and heard concerning the airship's faults—things that seriously worried him.

Hinchliffe had heard their comments about him after he'd been missing for over a week. He'd followed Irwin down the corridor to Johnston's office. Irwin looked extra glum as he'd poked his head inside Johnston's door.

"Looks like poor old Hinch is a gonner, then, Johnny," Irwin had said mournfully.

"Don't count him out yet, old son," Johnny had replied.

Hinchliffe was saddened by that exchange. Why hadn't he heeded their advice? And why don't they heed *his*! He was becoming increasingly worried about his friends. He didn't have the least faith in their project.

Hinchliffe also moved around the sheds. He liked to listen to the workmen. No one took any notice of him; obviously, they couldn't see him. Then, one afternoon, he realized that a certain young man *could* see him quite plainly. Hinchliffe recognized him from their Cardington visit the previous September. He kept staring at Hinchliffe as if to say, 'I know you. I saw you here with your pretty wife not long ago.'

"What are doing here?" he'd mumbled. "You're supposed to be dead, ain'tcha!"

"What's your name, son?" Hinchliffe had asked him.

"Me name's Joe, Joe Binks."

Hinchliffe put a finger to his lips. This was to be their little secret. Binks's jaw dropped open. Binks's coworker heard him.

"Talkin' to yerself now, Joe, are yuh? What's up, mate? Are you goin' barmy?" he said.

Hinchliffe had smiled at Binks mischievously and then sauntered off to find out more about what was going on at the Royal Airship Works. When Hinchliffe was making his recovery from his Atlantic ordeal and his passing, he found that he could move at the speed of thought. He could visit Pickwick Cottage or Glenapp Castle in the blink of an eye. It was the same with the Vickers company in Yorkshire where the sister ship *Howden R100* was under construction. He liked to pop up there to look around and compare what was going on. It wasn't long before he felt the animosity between the two teams of airshipmen. That made him even more worried, believing it would make them prone to take unnecessary risks. Heaven knows he knew all about that!

25

ANOTHER VISIT TO CARDINGTON

Wednesday, June 19, 1929.

Millie had been keeping up with the political goings on during this past year. The morale in Britain during the early months of 1929 had fallen drastically, with the popularity of the Conservative Government dropping to new lows. A general election was called and the Conservatives won 260 seats. Labour won 287. This was not enough for Labour to form a majority until Lloyd George threw in his 59 Liberal Party votes. Thus, the Labour party took up the reins of power once again and Lord Thomson was back in his old job as Minister of State for Air. Thomson was anxious to get up to Cardington to view his brainchild, HMA *Cardington R101*. Much was made of this in the newspapers and Hunter let Millie know that he, along with the rest of the press, had been summoned to Cardington House where Thomson would give an address concerning progress of the Airship Program. Millie knew it was important to be there. Doyle agreed to go with her.

The train driver leaned over the rail in a sooty vest, a cigarette in his mouth, his eyes on Millie as she and Doyle walked along the platform. She took no notice. They'd reached St. Pancras in good time, climbed aboard the train and sat beside the window, opposite each other. Millie felt nervous. These were important people whose feathers she'd be ruffling. But she was resolved. Hinchliffe was adamant that they should do whatever they could to prevent another airship disaster. Millie cringed when she recognized Brancker coming along the platform accompanied by the statuesque Lord Thomson, together with another man she didn't know. She saw a railwayman acknowledge them. "Mornin', sir," he said brightly.

"Good morning to *you*, my dear sir!" Thomson gushed.

"That's the man we've got to stop, right there!" Doyle said, suddenly noticing Thomson.

Millie's heart missed a beat. She smiled weakly and nodded. She kept her eyes down, as the three men moved past their window to their own carriage. When she looked up, she saw two men following Thomson and his companions. They wore bowler hats and black raincoats, white shirts and ties. One was tall with a beaky nose, and beady eyes. He reminded her of a raven. The other was short, and he had a limp—he seemed to scamper to keep up. They had to be Thomson's security detail.

Millie was glad Doyle was with her. He gave her strength. She tried to keep calm. Doyle appeared relaxed, untroubled by the disruption they were bent on causing. He opened *The Times* and began reading. A loud whistle blew, and innumerable doors slammed down along the train. Suddenly, Hunter dashed through the platform barrier and ran along the train peering in the windows. He spotted Millie, grabbed the door handle and jumped in as the train juddered forward.

"Ah, Mrs. Hinchliffe, I thought you'd be on this train."

"Mr. Hunter!"

"Mind if I join you?"

"Not at all, my boy! Come and sit down with us," Doyle said happily. They made a good trio, having seen a lot of each other over this past year.

Meanwhile, their fellow travelers—that is Lord Thomson and company—had settled down contentedly in their first class compartment. This was a big day for Thomson. He couldn't wait to reach Cardington.

"Well, here we are again, Sefton, back where it counts!"

"It's good to have you back, CB," Brancker said.

"We'll need to visit Egypt—make sure everything's on schedule with their mooring mast and shed. Damned pity we lost our man, Hinchliffe. He'd have been ideal to fly us out there," Thomson said.

Brancker shook his head sadly. "It was a terrible loss."

"Did the widow ever get the insurance money?"

"No."

"They should have taken care of that woman," Thomson snapped.

"Perhaps you'll come back with another magic carpet," Knoxwood said brightly, getting back to the subject. Knoxwood was Thomson's private secretary at the Ministry. He knew that one of Thomson's most prized possessions was a Persian rug presented to him in Iraq.

"Our magic carpet, Knoxwood, will be His Majesty's Airship *Cardington R101*, which will transport us first to Egypt and then India."

"Well put, CB," Brancker chortled.

Millie watched the squalid backyards of Camden Town pass slowly by. Doyle lowered his newspaper and gave her a reassuring smile. The train entered a tunnel. In the gloom, Millie noticed Hunter's aura for the first time. There was a lot of blue and pink, emphasizing his writing skills. Orange showed he was good-natured, and yellow that he was a good communicator, which he seemed to be. Green showed he was practical at doing stuff around the home, such as decorating and gardening, like Millie herself.

She looked at her own worried reflection in the window. Gradually, Hinchliffe's image appeared behind her, startling her at first. This alerted Hunter, who wondered what she'd seen. After taking a deep breath, Millie smiled. Hinchliffe smiled back lovingly. Doyle lowered his newspaper again and caught sight of the exchange. Although he couldn't see what she saw, he guessed. He grinned at Millie. Hinchliffe had galvanized her. Millie spent the rest of the journey making notes for a speech she'd be making on Friday in Brixton at Lambeth Town Hall.

The wheels clacked along rhythmically over the tracks. In first class, the airship discussion was still going on, while the train glided unhurriedly through grimy rows of terraced houses. Thomson loved that sound. Train rides always put him in a good mood.

"Now gentlemen, let's see what's what, shall we?" he said, delving into his red ministerial box. After reading his memoranda for a few moments, he looked up suddenly, shooting a glance at Brancker, who was busy studying the form of a young woman pegging out her washing in her back yard.

"What happened to those trial flights to Egypt? We were going to use *R33* and *R36* for that purpose. What happened to them?"

Brancker turned back to Thomson. "Er, er, the trials got scrapped—budget cuts. Well er, …not budget cuts exactly …those ships needed a lot of money spending on them—especially after *R33* got wrecked."

"*Got wrecked!* What do you mean *'got wrecked'*?"

"Collided with her shed—"

"Collided with her shed! Who was in command?"

"Scott, of course."

Thomson looked away in exasperation. "Whatever is the matter with that man?"

Brancker raised his eyebrows and made no comment.

"Well, they should have rebuilt those ships," Thomson muttered.

"The funding just wasn't there CB," Brancker replied.

"Budget cuts? Damn the Tories! Wish I'd been around. What else did they cut?"

"Nothing I can think of, but the emphasis is on heavier-than-air aircraft nowadays. Many in government just don't like airships," Brancker replied.

"We'll see about that! I hope we don't live to regret cutting those test flights with those older ships. We could've learned a thing or two from a few trial runs. My main concern is the schedule. The Germans are getting way out in front of us. Our ships should've been in the air by now."

"Quite so, Minister, quite so," Knoxwood agreed.

The train rushed into another tunnel and they sat in the gloom. Thomson continued. "So, let's recap. Both ships are running three years late. We've taken twice as long to reach this stage. But on the brighter side, we've only spent half as much again. So, I suppose we can say, we've given employment to *more* people, for a *longer* period of time. Fair assessment, Sefton?"

"I suppose you could put it like that, CB, yes."

Even in the semi-darkness, Thomson sensed Brancker was amused by his nutty logic. The train rushed out of the tunnel into sunshine, revealing lush green fields and blue skies. A happy omen.

"India by Christmas then!" Thomson exclaimed. Brancker and Knoxwood exchanged knowing glances.

The train slowed as it came into Bedford Station. Millie, Doyle and Hunter watched Thomson scoot past and out of the station, followed by the two bowler-hatted gents. When they got to the station entrance, they were just in time to see them climbing into the Cardington Works Humber. The security men went behind in a black Morris. Millie's party jumped into a cab and followed. When they got to the Cardington gate, Thomson's car stopped momentarily and was then hastily waved through. At the gate, Millie spoke to the gatekeeper, telling him that Squadron Leader Johnston was expecting them, which was true; she'd called him and told him they were coming. They then followed Thomson up the hill to Cardington House, where they saw him leap out of his limousine and rush up the stone steps to where Colmore, Scott, and Richmond were waiting, along with a whole gaggle of reporters and photographers.

Hunter got out. "I'd better join that lot. I'll see you both again later. And good luck!" he said with a wink to Millie.

After waiting a few minutes for the fuss to die down, Millie and Doyle mounted the steps and entered the main door. The reception hall was now empty of dignitaries. They went to the desk.

"We're here to see Squadron Leader Johnston and Captain Irwin," Millie said.

"Your names please?"

"Mrs. Emilie Hinchliffe and Sir Arthur Conan Doyle—they're expecting us."

The girl gave a start at the mention of Doyle's name. A few minutes later, Johnston appeared and took them to his office on the second floor. Johnston hadn't seen Millie since Pam's baptism on Boxing Day of 1927. He'd taken Hinchliffe's disappearance very hard, as had all his friends at Cardington. Presently, a doleful Captain Irwin came in and they all sat down to tea and biscuits.

Millie wanted to get down to the subject of the Airship Program and to deliver her husband's message, but first she asked where Hinchliffe's body and other wreckage might have ended up. They discussed Brancker's revelation about the wheel, which had washed up on an Irish beach last June. Johnston pointed to the map of the Atlantic on his wall (he had many such maps of the world), and indicated the motion of the North Atlantic Drift. He pointed to the mid-Atlantic.

"If they came down here somewhere, the Drift would push the wreckage to anywhere here along the Irish coast—the same as the wheel."

"Millie pressed a dainty finger against the Azores. "What if they'd come down here?"

"That's most unlikely, Millie," Irwin said softly, "They'd be miles off course."

Johnston nodded in agreement.

Millie gave them a blow by blow account of what she'd learned from Hinchliffe during the séances. Johnston and Irwin looked at one another as if Millie had lost her mind. They gently played along with her—humoring her was the least they could do. It was well known that Millie was into all this spiritualism stuff and that she was very much against the airship program. They liked and respected Doyle. He was a kindly gentleman, but regarded him as a bit 'potty'. They'd read his column in the Sunday papers and about his belief in fairies and suchlike, as well as his run-in with Houdini, which the newspapers had thoroughly enjoyed.

Millie explained that Hinchliffe had told her he'd flown on a north-westerly course, and then later a more northerly course after getting into a violent gale. She told them that they'd lost a wheel early on in the battle, but kept going until they couldn't tolerate the storm any longer. At 12 o'clock, they'd turned south and flown at great speed with the wind behind them for three more hours, until they crashed in the water in sight of the island of Corvo, in the Azores—also known as 'the island of the crow'.

"Based on that, where would his body have ended up?" Millie asked.

Johnston pointed to the map, and indicated that the body, and the other wheel if it had broken off, could've been pushed by the currents down as far as the Caribbean.

"As far as Jamaica?" Millie asked.

Johnston stared at that location and nodded, noncommittally. "Yes, I suppose so." He pointed to the Drift currents. "The Drift splits here. This is the North Atlantic Drift, and this is the Canary Current, sweeping south. So, wreckage could go either way—across this way to Ireland or south to the Caribbean."

"So, if they came down near the Azores, the currents could've pushed wreckage down and then toward the Caribbean," Doyle confirmed.

"Yes, if indeed they came down that far south," Johnston answered.

Millie seemed to have the answers she wanted. They'd confirmed what Hinchliffe had said. She wondered what was left of her poor husband. She remembered his words.

Nothing but skin and bone scattered between the rocks.

She shivered.

They sat down around Johnston's table and finished their tea.

"How are you coping, Millie?" Johnston asked, trying to brighten things up.

"Quite well. Friends like Sir Arthur have been a great comfort," Millie said, looking fondly at the aging writer.

Irwin glanced at Doyle. "Hinch was here in September, before they left," he said.

"You chaps were close?" Doyle asked.

Johnston let out deep sigh. "He and I were great friends, we flew together to India in early '27. Hell, I *do* miss him!"

"We warned him not to go. But he was more concerned about *our* safety than his own," Irwin said.

They sat in silence for a moment, "He's *still* worried about you, Johnnie," Millie said softly. The silence dragged on again until Johnston spoke.

"Millie, I do understand. But, I'm sorry, I don't believe in communication with the dead."

Irwin's face was expressionless—as if he was more on the fence about such things.

"Captain Hinchliffe has asked—nay, I should say, *implored*—Millie to deliver a warning to you," Doyle declared. It all sounded too melodramatic. The two airshipmen looked at each other uncomfortably, shuffling in their chairs.

"Ray has described things to me in your airship which he says are unsafe," Millie said.

They were immediately curious. "Such as?" Irwin asked.

"It's going to come out too heavy," Millie said.

"That's been in the papers. We can always add another bay and give her more lift. That shouldn't be a problem," Johnston answered dismissively.

"Ray knows that's a possibility. But he says that'd take away her resilience," Millie countered.

Irwin coughed and Johnston rubbed his chin, frowning. This was inside information. "Millie, where are you getting all this stuff?"

"Bird, Johnny, please listen. Ray wants you to give up on this Airship Program. Your lives are in *great peril!*" Millie implored them.

There was a knock on the door and a young RAF man stuck his head in. "Gentlemen, the briefing of the Air Minister is about to begin."

Reprieved, Irwin and Johnston stood up. Doyle got to his feet and explained that he and Millie would attend Lord Thomson's speech in the afternoon, after they'd had lunch at the local pub. Johnny told them he'd arranged to have front row seats reserved for them.

A full agenda had been laid out for the Air Minister's visit. After morning tea, he and forty members of the Royal Airship Works would be briefed by Colonel Richmond in the conference room; then they'd adjourn for a lunch of rack of lamb; on to the great shed for an inspection of the ship; a visit to the singing ladies in the gasbag factory; then afternoon tea, with the promotion of a young American Lieutenant; all followed by the Ministerial Address in the garden to be attended by all, including members of the press and public. It was there, that Millie planned to make a speech of her own—unbeknownst to poor Irwin and Johnston.

26

LORD THOMSON'S GARDEN ADDRESS

Wednesday, June19, 1929.

Millie and Doyle had a pleasant walk to Cardington village, where they visited St. Mary's Church. Although not deeply religious, they enjoyed the peace found within its walls. Millie knelt down in one of the pews and said a prayer for strength for what she had to do. They came out from the church and seeing the graveyard, they crossed the lane and entered its gate. They ambled from one tombstone to another reading names. When they reached the area at the back, looking across the field toward the airship shed, Millie saw a new grave with mounded earth, wreaths and fresh flowers. But it wasn't real. It was a vision. She read the name chiseled in the headstone.

Freddie Marsh

Born 16th October 1913

Died 16th October 1929

in the shadow of the great shed

Millie became upset. "I'm seeing a young boy's death foretold," she stammered.

Doyle put his hand on her arm. He was secretly thrilled her psychic development was progressing so rapidly. "It's all right, my dear. You're going to see such things long before they happen. You have the gift. Truly, you do. You'd better get used to it."

"The poor boy will die on his birthday," Millie sobbed.

"That's his fate, my dear."

As they turned away from Freddie Marsh's future grave, Millie looked toward the cemetery wall and the church across the street. She was mesmerized when she saw a great multitude gathered around a vast open grave and heard their whispered conversation. She heard the tolling of bells from many churches surrounding the area. In the grave were forty-eight coffins draped with Union Flags. She didn't need to count them. She knew. Standing in the grave amongst the coffins was one man she recognized—the Prime Minister, in black, his shock of hair and mustache like a lion. In one hand he held his hat, in the other, two roses. He looked forlorn, not knowing on which coffin to place them, although Millie knew full well, which one contained his best friend. When he came up the ramp out of the grave, she heard a drone of aeroplanes overhead. At the same time, a covey of crows swarmed over the graveyard like a school of fish in the ocean. They made no sound except for the beat of their wings.

Millie faltered and Doyle caught her arm and led her to the gate, where she stopped and turned around. The mass open grave had disappeared. So had the mourners. In their place, stood a pristine tomb of white stone with names of the dead airshipmen etched on all sides. Wreaths of flowers were heaped around its base. Moving unsteadily down the lane towards the village green, they passed a blue Rolls Royce at the curb. But a few moments later, when Millie looked back toward the cemetery gate, the Rolls was nowhere in sight. It too, had been part of her vision.

At the Kings Arms Pub, Doyle found a table and brought them both a brandy. After a few sips, she emotionally recounted what she'd seen in the churchyard. When she was recovered, they had lunch of steak and kidney pudding, mashed potatoes and gravy, washed down with a bottle of Claret. Her face flushed, Millie was now, more than ever, determined to press forward with her mission.

While Doyle and Millie spent time in the village. Hinchliffe had been following Thomson's movements. After his visit to the gasbag factory, they'd returned for afternoon tea at Cardington House where Thomson made an announcement. He gently tapped a silver spoon against his cup and the room fell silent.

"Last year, I had the honor, as chairman of the Royal Aero Club, to represent Great Britain at the International Conference on Aviation in Washington, D.C. Whilst there, I had the pleasure of meeting the Secretary of the United States Navy." Thomson's eyes fell on Remington, at whom he smiled benignly. "We spoke of many things concerning aviation and the Secretary takes quite an interest in their man over here—Lieutenant Louis Remington—who has diligently assisted in our endeavors over these past five years."

All eyes turned toward Remington. Thomson continued. "The Secretary asked me to personally convey his thanks to the lieutenant, along with his warmest personal regards. Captain Irwin, I would be grateful if you will do the honors."

On cue, Irwin walked to the head table at the top of the room and stood with Thomson who glanced at Remington. "Lieutenant, if you would kindly step forward," Thomson said. Surprised, Remington joined Thomson and Irwin. Thomson held something in his hand which he handed to Irwin who spoke next.

"Lieutenant Remington, it is my pleasure to inform you that your rank has been raised by the United States Navy to that of Lieutenant Commander."

Remington stood to attention while Irwin pinned the insignia to his collar. Irwin then stepped back and saluted. Remington returned the salute and everyone applauded. Remington glanced around the room at Colmore, Scott, Irwin and Atherstone—all in dress uniform.

While he twisted the gold ring on his wedding finger, he looked at them as if to say, 'Heck, all these guys knew in advance!'

"Thank you, sir," Lou said to Irwin, and then to Thomson as they shook hands, "I'm very grateful, sir."

Thomson smiled, obviously pleased. The chief steward appeared to be swooning and nodding enthusiastically at Lou as he pointed to an iced cake he'd put on the front table.

"Now, if you will kindly move to the garden, I'd like to say a few words to you and the good people of Cardington and Bedford," Thomson said.

After their stroll around the village, Millie and Doyle made their way to the Cardington House garden, where hundreds were gathering to hear Lord Thomson. They were met by an RAF man who showed them to their seats at the front. People noticed them. Most had no idea who the portly, gentleman in a posh mohair sports jacket was, until they were told he was the most popular author in the world. Others had read about the plight of the younger woman with him—Mrs. Hinchliffe, swathed in black.

The murmur of the assembling crowd drowned out the gentle splash of an ornate fountain positioned beside the steps up to the rear of the main house. It was a romantic creation, tinged with green and peopled by stone cherubs clutching bows and arrows.

The garden, an area some two hundred feet square, was flanked by boxwood hedges and flowering trees. This had once been the previous philanthropic owner's outdoor theater, complete with a stage built of stone, where Shakespearean tragedies had been performed. Rough-cut flagstone paving covered much of the area. Two hundred folding chairs were occupied by a group of people similar to those present when Thomson unveiled his New Airship Program in 1924: Royal Airship Works personnel, local bankers, businessmen, and solicitors. In addition, there were contractors, and general workers from the factories and sheds connected with the airship program with their families.

Crewmen and construction workers stood along the sides and at the rear, leaving seats for VIPs and the elderly. Journalists were seated in the front row with photographers positioned in the aisles down each side. The crowd chattered excitedly. Thomson was pleased with the size of the gathering. They were all here out of self-interest. Times were tough. Work was scarce. It was satisfying for him to know he'd created jobs in two counties. Once Millie and Doyle had sat down, Irwin and Johnston arrived to sit next to them. As they did, Thomson appeared, having marched down from the main house. He'd heard that Doyle was there and wanted to make a point of greeting him.

They stood while Irwin made introductions. "Lord Thomson, permit me to introduce Mrs. Hinchliffe."

"My dear lady, your husband and I flew together to Egypt and Iraq. And of course, he's flown the Prime Minister and I to Lossiemouth on many occasions. Such a *terrible, terrible* loss!"

"You're most kind, Lord Thomson."

"And this is Sir Arthur Conan Doyle, who, of course, needs no introduction—" Irwin said.

"Yes, yes, of course, Sir Arthur, it is an *honor*, sir." Thomson paused and then gave him a crooked smile. "Although, I must say, we were all a little cross with you for killing off poor old Sherlock Holmes!"

Doyle came right back at him. "But *I* don't propose to kill any real people, sir!"

Thomson turned abruptly on his heel. "I must get started. Please excuse me," he said, hurrying off to the steps up to the stage. He walked stiffly across to join Colmore, Brancker, Knoxwood, Scott and

Richmond. As he approached, they got to their feet, applauding and smiling. Thomson sat down. Colmore went to the lectern and waited for the applause to die down. All seats were occupied and the aisles down each side were filled with people standing between the chairs and hedges.

Colmore cleared his throat and adjusted the microphone, causing a screeching whine from the speakers each side of the podium.

"Good afternoon, ladies and gentlemen. It is my distinct pleasure to introduce the Minister of State for Air, Lord Thomson of Cardington, whom we all know and admire. He'd like to say a few words concerning our progress and the future of the British Airship Program. Before I turn over the microphone, I must remind you that we owe him a debt of gratitude, not only for revitalizing the program, but for making the Royal Airship Works central to his great vision."

There was more enthusiastic applause. Thomson got up and stepped up to the lectern. He adjusted the microphone up six inches, causing another ear-splitting screech.

"Wing Commander Colmore is *much, much* too kind," Thomson said. "I'm just one man doing my small part. It is *you* who will make this program a success, not *I*. My job is to jolly things along. This great endeavor that you've worked upon with such selfless dedication —and I must say, I've seen it with my own two eyes today—is one that will open the skies for the benefit of *all* mankind.

"We've reached a critical stage in the development of the program. In some ways, we're out in front—from the *technology* standpoint. But in other ways, on the *practical* front, we're falling behind. The Germans made their maiden flight last year, crossing the Atlantic in their *Graf Zeppelin*. They're preparing to make a round-the-world trip in August, and if we're not careful, we'll be in a position where we cannot keep pace."

He scanned the dejected faces.

"With this in mind, I say to you: We must push hard to produce results as quickly as possible. We must show the world what we can do. It's been more than five years since I announced the start of the program and our ships are *still* in their sheds! I'll leave it there. I know you appreciate what I'm saying, and why."

Thomson was careful not to single anyone out with his icy stare, but could see the audience understood only too well. Richmond and Colmore had taken his words to heart. It was time to build them back up.

"Having said that, I'm certain we'll come out on top. When this ship emerges from her shed this year, she'll be the finest airship ever built—about that, I have *no* doubt at all.

Thomson looked reassuringly at Richmond, but Richmond didn't exude confidence. Thomson went on.

"Now, we've embarked upon a great journey, you and I, and I look forward to the day when we fly together in this magnificent airship down the route of Marco Polo to India. And thereafter, we shall press forward with airship services linking our great empire around the globe and build bigger, more advanced airships that will be technological marvels of the world."

Thomson stepped back and the crowd was on its feet, applauding. He'd rallied the troops. Hunter stood up as the noise died down.

"Lord Thomson, George Hunter, *Daily Express*, I have a question," he called.

"Well, all right, just one or two," Thomson said brightly.

"Just how safe do you think this airship really is? Our experiences to date have been quite abysmal!"

Thomson remembered having trouble with this one before. He grimaced. "That's a perfectly fair question, and I'm so glad you've asked it. This will be the safest airship ever built. It'll have diesel engines, making her much safer from fire."

But Millie's soft voice from the front row came like an explosion.

"But the starter engines are petrol-driven are they not, Lord Thomson?"

Thomson was floored by this question out of the blue—and from a woman! He looked helplessly at Richmond who nodded—'Yes, she's right'. Reporters were scribbling furiously, sensing a story here.

"So, with five million cubic feet of hydrogen, it would only take one small spark, would it not?" Millie pressed.

Thomson was furious. How did this woman get in here?

Millie was surprised at her own boldness. Her voice grew stronger.

"Even static electricity could be *highly* dangerous, could it not? My husband says that these railway engines are too heavy. He says they're underpowered and their massive surging thrust will cause them not to be properly stabilized. He says the cover will also be a big problem. It'll flake off. You're planning to dope it with a highly dangerous flammable mixture of iron oxide and powdered aluminum ..."

Thomson was completely flummoxed. He switched off the microphone. The audience at the back couldn't hear Millie, and he was glad of that.

"I don't know where you're getting all this information from, madam—much of this is top secret," he snapped.

Millie shouted; most couldn't hear her, but the reporters at the front did. "I got it from my husband, Captain Raymond Hinchliffe. He has sent me here to deliver a warning: This Airship Program *must be stopped at all costs!*"

This was all very embarrassing for Thomson. There was a collective moan from some workers. Reporters were looking at one another, eyebrows raised, smirking and puzzled, as if to say, 'Now this is a right turn up for the book!'.

Thomson controlled his seething anger well, and tried a soft tack. He switched the microphone back on. "My dear lady, I know you have been through a lot. We all do. Your husband was a brave and gallant man. He was the type of man who helped build this great empire. All heads had turned in Millie's direction, muttering and nodding.

Thomson continued, "As far as your claims are concerned, however nebulous they may be, I want to assure you that the team here at Cardington have gone to *extreme* lengths to ensure the safety of all those who fly in this great airship. Safety first is our motto and *safety second as well!* Thank you all for coming."

Without further ado, Thomson descended and marched up the aisle to the steps of the great house, followed by those on the stage. They reached the throng of people at the top of the aisle which parted like the Red Sea. Thomson climbed the steps, followed by the multitude. When he reached the top, he gave the crowd a jubilant wave. He swept into the reception room and stopped.

"What the hell are those people doing here?" he growled.

"If you don't mind, CB, I'll go and talk to her," Brancker said.

"Be quick!" Thomson answered, pacing around.

Brancker retraced his steps and shouldered his way through the crowd to Millie, who was still seated. "Millie, God Bless my soul!" I had no idea you were here!" he said breathlessly, grabbing Doyle's hand and shaking it. "Sir Arthur! Millie, I wish you'd spoken to me before you did this."

"I didn't expect it to happen quite the way it did. We need to talk, Sir Sefton, it's important" Millie answered.

"I'll be away for a day or so. I'll contact you on my return, I promise," Brancker replied. He apologized and returned to Thomson at the main house where they continued their exit down the front steps to the Humber. The driver held the doors open and the threesome climbed in. They drove off slowly, the driver tooting his horn, Thomson waving his royal wave. The men in bowlers followed behind.

"Well, I think the day went off all right, except for that damned Hinchliffe woman at the end. We'll need to keep an eye on her—she's a threat to national security," Thomson said. "What did you say to her?"

"I told her I'd contact her. I'll try and smooth the waters when I see her."

"Fwankly, Minister, I thought you were marvelous. I shouldn't worry about her," Knoxwood said.

"I'd better talk to Doyle. Get him to come and see me—soon as possible!" Thomson thundered.

"Right you are, Minister. Will do," Knoxwood answered.

27

WHEN THE SPEECH WAS OVER

Wednesday, June 19, 1929.

The press was abuzz after the unexpected turns in the garden and clamored for more. Reporters milled around Doyle and Millie as they left the garden. On her way, Millie received a sympathetic smile from a young airshipman in American Naval uniform. She remembered him from when she'd met him in the Kings Arms, when she and Hinchliffe had visited two years earlier.

Such a good-looking man!

George Hunter was among the reporters, but he was playing his role at arm's length. Photographers took pictures as they climbed into a taxi.

"Mrs. Hinchliffe, are you planning to do any more about your husband's warning?"

"Definitely. Everyone should take it *very* seriously!"

The reporters were feverishly writing. A flurry of questions came through the open window. "What do you think about the situation regarding Miss Mackay's estate?"

"I'm deeply shocked at the way we've been treated by her family," Millie replied.

"Do you think you'll ever get the insurance money?"

"My husband tells me I will."

"Do you have any plan of action regarding the Airship Program?"

"I most certainly do. Starting this week, I'll be giving a series of speeches around the country. It must be brought to an end."

The reporters got everything down. They stared after their disappearing taxi—they had a great story here!

After Millie had gone, Hinchliffe jumped on the back of Lou Remington's motorcycle and rode with him over to the great shed where they waited beside the control car. It was eerily quiet. Soon they heard the captain's footsteps approaching.

"Ah, Lou. Let's go aboard," Irwin said.

The three of them climbed on board and Irwin led the way up to the lounge where they sat in the wicker easy chairs at one of the card tables which Remington had set up for Thomson's visit earlier in the day. Hinchliffe could see that Remington was puzzled, not knowing why the captain wanted to speak to him.

"You and the crew did a great job, Lou. The Old Man was thrilled," Irwin told him.

"He ought to be pleased, sir. It's a beautiful ship," Lou responded.

"Looks can be deceiving," Irwin said. "We'll see what she's made of when we take her up." Irwin glanced down at the table for a moment, then back at Lou. "Congratulations on your promotion today."

"Thank you, sir. That came as a big surprise."

"Everyone was pleased about it. You've done a great job at Howden. You're a natural diplomat. You've helped keep the peace."

"Thanks."

"How's Charlotte? Is she taking kindly to all this?"

"I think she'll be pleased with my promotion, and proud. She's settled down fairly well here now. She really didn't want to come down south."

"Yes, I got that impression."

"She's been worried about safety, naturally, but everyone's assured her these new ships will be safe."

"Let's hope so," Irwin said.

"Charlotte's pleased I'm happy and doing what I like. I think once we've got a few trips under our belt, she'll be okay."

"She's a wonderful girl."

"What Charlotte needs is a child. In fact, she wants lots of children! But no luck so far. That's what makes her most unhappy," Lou said.

"We want a family one day—we've even chosen a name for our first-born," Irwin said.

"What is it, sir?"

Irwin looked away, concentrating on an image in his mind. "D'you know, when I close my eyes sometimes, I can see that child. His name will be Christian. I see his black hair and blue eyes."

"Just like his dad."

"It's all up to the good Lord," Irwin said.

"I guess so."

Irwin turned his eyes back on Remington, his expression now business-like.

"Lou, I'm going to propose you for another promotion—to third officer—if you want it. You'll be under my command aboard this ship and Captain Booth on *Howden R100*."

"Thank you. I don't know what to say, sir."

"You've got a good head on your shoulders and the crewmen look up to you."

"I suppose they do."

"You survived *R38* and that experience will make you careful."

"That was just luck."

"Nothing wrong with that. I need men with good luck on my ship."

"Kind of you to say, sir."

"If all the things the Old Man says come true, the sky's the limit. He'll be in need of captains for the fleet."

They got up and shook hands then went down to the shed floor and stood alongside the ship. Hinchliffe followed them.

"Oh, one more thing, Lou. I like to see my officers and crew in church on Sundays." Irwin looked up at the ship, a hint of skepticism in his eyes. "We'll need all the help we can get," he said, before abruptly marching off toward the exit.

Hinchliffe had listened with interest. Irwin obviously had reservations about his ship. He'd get Millie to work on him somehow. Out of curiosity, Hinchliffe decided to stick with Remington and see what his wife had to say. She had doubts by the sound of it. He rode home with Remington and the chief steward's iced cake.

They arrived at a red brick three-story terraced house on a quiet street ten minutes later. Before Remington could even put the key in the lock, the door was flung open. A very beautiful girl, obviously Remington's wife, threw her arms around him, kissing him feverishly.

Hinchliffe smiled. He wondered if Remington was greeted like this *every* time he came home. *That couldn't be bad!*

"Oh, Remy, my darling. I love you so much. I'm sorry I was so mean to you this morning. You will forgive me, won't you?" the girl said breathlessly. Remington looked surprised, but relieved. Hinchliffe supposed they must've had an argument earlier—maybe about his job.

"Of course, Charlie. You must've been tired. I'm sorry I had to be out all day."

"Who was that riding on the bike with you?"

Remington looked puzzled. "What do you mean? No one. I was alone."

She looked equally puzzled. "I could swear a man was sitting behind you when you arrived. I was watching for you from the window."

"You must be seeing things, honey."

"Well anyway, I want to talk to you tonight about things."

Ah here we go. Hinchliffe thought.

"What about, Charlotte?"

"Well, about *us—and 'things'.*"

This girl's definitely got some issues. Might be interesting, Hinchliffe thought.

He followed them downstairs to the breakfast table that looked out into the garden. It was still sunny. Flowers were in bloom. Remington unwrapped and placed the chief steward's cake on the table.

"What's that?" she asked, reading the icing.

" 'Congratulations!' On what?"

"I'll tell you in a minute. It's a present from the chief steward," Lou said, remaining expressionless. Hinchliffe could see Remington was trying not to laugh.

"Oh, I see. What's his name?"

"Er, I don't know."

Charlotte batted her eyes and pursed her lips. "Oooh, should I be jealous?"

Remington chuckled. And so did Hinchliffe. Charlotte opened a bottle of white wine and poured two glasses. She held one out to her husband. The kitchen was warm. He breathed in the dinner cooking in the oven. "Smells good," he said.

"Roast beef and Yorkshire pudding—your favorite."

Mine too, Hinchliffe said to himself.

"Mmm, lovely."

"Well, how did it go today?"

Remington's face lit up. "So much to tell!"

She was intrigued. "Why? What happened? Tell me!"

"I took the lads fishing for a while and after that we went to the ship and finished setting up the furniture and I must say, it looked pretty damned good! Then the Old Man arrived. I was stuck on board while Irwin showed him over the ship. I stayed out of sight—I couldn't very well announce my presence. I heard everything they said. It was pretty damned embarrassing, actually."

"What did they say?"

"Well, Lord Thomson got a bit flowery about the ship and the future and how he was depending on the captain—and a lot of stuff I should *never* have heard."

"What sort of stuff?"

"He talked about a woman he hopes to marry one day."

"Goodness. Did the captain know you were there?"

"Nobody knew and I'm not gonna say anything. Anyway, they all went off to the gasbag factory. I put on my uniform and joined them. The Old Man had them old gals over there eatin' out of his hand. Funny as hell."

"What did he say?"

"Oh, he told them they were special and doing important work and all that old jaboni. He gave them all a boost. They were tickled to death."

"That's good. He must be a very nice man," Charlotte said.

"Yeah, he's all right, I guess. Anyway, we all went to the big house for afternoon tea and sandwiches. And then, you can't imagine what happened next!"

Charlotte couldn't contain herself, "Well, tell me then!"

"The Old Man got up and gave a short speech."

"What about?"

"*Me!*" Remington said, cracking up.

"*What!*"

"He said he'd been speaking to the Secretary of the Navy in Washington and he'd asked about me and how I was doing over here."

She was all agog. "Oh, go on! ... *Really?*"

"Yes, and then everyone stood up and Captain Irwin did the honors and I got promoted! I'm now Lieutenant Commander Louis Remington! Ta da!" Remington stood to attention, saluted and then bowed with a flourish, as though to the Queen.

"Oh, Lou, I don't believe it! So, what is a lieutenant commander?"

"It's the same rank as a major in the army."

"That's *amazing!*"

"But that's not all. The captain talked to me afterwards."

"What did *he* say?"

"He said I'd done a great job not only with the furniture and how the Old Man was pleased, which of course I already knew because I'd heard him with my own ears—but he said I'd done a good job at Howden and with the liaison work between them and Cardington."

"Well, it's true. You've done a *bloody marvelous* job!"

"Anyway, he's nominating me for promotion to third officer."

"Two promotions in one day! Lou, I'm so, so proud of you."

Remington finished his wine and put the glass down on the table.

"You said you wanted to talk about us and '*things*'," Lou said.

"Oh, it doesn't matter. It was nothing important."

Remington gave her a puzzled stare. She wrapped her arms around him and put her luscious, wet lips over his mouth, kissing him gently, at first. Then things rapidly got out of hand.

"I think we'd better turn the oven down low—we'll eat later," Remington said, and then taking her hand, he led her up to the bedroom. As they climbed stairs, Charlotte looked back over her shoulder, sensing Hinchliffe's presence. Hinchliffe felt very drawn to her—something about her—she was *very* special. It appeared that this lady wouldn't be expressing her reservations about the Airship Program tonight. Reservations or not, he could see these were two people very much in love, though their relationship might be complicated.

He thought it was about time to leave.

28

LAMBETH TOWN HALL

Friday, June 21, 1929.

The next day, newspapers full of the great kerfuffle at Cardington caught everyone's attention, including Lord Inchcape's at Glenapp Castle.

Daily Express

MRS HINCHLIFFE DELIVERS WARNING
FROM THE GRAVE

Daily Mirror

MRS HINCHLIFFE BROKE
MISS MACKAY'S FAMILY UNYIELDING

Daily Sketch

PILOT'S WIDOW DELIVERS WARNING
TO LORD THOMSON FROM DEAD HUSBAND

Daily Chronicle

R101 NOT SAFE MRS HINCHLIFFE
TELLS AIR MINISTER
LORD THOMSON SAYS WIDOW IS UNHINGED

"I think it's time for a little more practice, Millie," Doyle said.

Millie looked up from her easel at Doyle. He'd been watching patiently from a chair by the fireplace as she painted her vision of the tomb in St. Mary's churchyard. She dabbed at the painting gently until she was satisfied. She wiped her brushes and began cleaning up.

"Looks pretty good. Sad though," Doyle said.

"It looks well enough, I think," Millie said, leaving it to dry.

Doyle had come to help her get ready for the speech she'd be giving tonight at Lambeth Town Hall. He'd made her practice a number of times. He took a chair and stood it at the end of the room. "Here's your lectern."

Millie took off her smock. "Okay. But it's so nerve-racking."

"You'll get used to it." Sinclair looked in the door. "Come in Gordon, we need an audience. Bring Kate," Doyle said. Sinclair brought his wife in and they sat down to watch Millie standing behind the chair.

"Ladies and gentlemen, thank you for coming, I want to tell you about things that have been happening to me this past year or so—"

"Introduce yourself first, Millie. And keep your head up," Doyle told her.

"You'll be all right, Millie love. Don't worry," said Kate.

"I feel sick. I've never done anything like this before in my life," Millie said.

"You've been speaking to women's groups all year. Just be yourself, Millie, you'll be fine," said Sinclair.

Millie began again. "Ladies and gentlemen, my name is Emilie Hinchliffe. Oh, I don't know if I can do this!" Under stress, Millie was suddenly jarred by another vision.

She saw a boy running across a field in semi-darkness. Overhead, was a groaning, massive black cloud. No, it was a big black airship. It was trying to dock at its tower. The boy was reaching for one of the ropes dropped to the ground from the ship. All around him was commotion, yelling and screaming for him to stop. But he didn't heed their warnings. He grabbed the cable. Blue sparks flew from his body. His back arched and he fell—electrocuted. Water cascaded down upon him from the ship, around him an atmosphere of chaos, mayhem and death. Millie instinctively knew this boy was Freddie Marsh. She'd seen his grave. She was overwrought and had to sit down to catch her breath.

Doyle realized this wasn't just stage fright. Her psychic powers were highly developed. He comforted her.

"What did you see this time, Millie?"

"It was awful."

"The airship?"

"I saw how that boy died."

The front door bell jangled. It was Hunter. "I'm covering the story tonight. I thought I'd come over in case Millie needed moral support," Hunter said.

When she heard his voice, a sense of relief washed over her and her unsettling vision subsided. Hunter seemed to have that calming effect. Sinclair showed him into Millie's studio. They spent another hour with Millie, going over her speech with everyone giving helpful advice.

Later, in her bedroom, Millie couldn't get the vision out of her head. Her visions were becoming more powerful and frightening. She wasn't sure she wanted it. She listened to Hunter playing the piano downstairs while she applied make up in the mirror. He was playing "Toot Toot Tootsie Goodbye". She smiled. He'd become such a good friend. A comfort to have around.

As she stared at her reflection, Hinchliffe's image appeared behind her. He was showing his support with a smile. But there was a hint of sadness in his face. While Hunter continued playing, she combed her hair, not paying him much attention—she had a lot on her mind. They were interrupted by Kate entering the bedroom. Millie didn't own too many dresses. Katie had ironed one of her own to loan Millie for the evening. She slipped it over her head and pulled it down over her shapely waist and hips.

"Oh, yes! Lovely. You look so elegant in black," Kate said.

Later that evening, Millie stepped onto the stage before a small audience to cheers and light applause. Doyle and Hunter weren't the only ones she noticed. At the back, she saw Hinchliffe sitting in an end seat on the aisle. He lifted his hand and smiled. She smiled back. Her gaze then refocused on Doyle and Hunter. She smiled at them too.

Then, she noticed two men sitting off to one side in black bowler hats. They seemed out of place, their faces grim. She had them pegged as Thomson's people, but she was determined that they weren't going to intimidate her—not now, not ever—she'd draw strength from her husband, her friends and the audience. When she spoke, she was confident. It was as if her voice was coming from someone or somewhere else—an experience she'd never had before, but one she'd have many times in the future.

"Good evening ladies and gentlemen. My name is Emilie Hinchliffe." There was a burst of applause. "Thank you so much for your love and support. I can really feel it. You're very kind. I have come here tonight to give you the answer to questions I believe you really want to know about life after death. What happens to us when we die? I also want to tell you about warnings my husband has sent."

One of the bowler-hatted men cleared his throat noisily. It was the Raven. Millie glared at him, undeterred.

29

DOYLE SUMMONED

Monday, June 24, 1929.

W hen Millie got back from her speaking engagement at Lambeth Town Hall, she went straight into the studio and donned her smock. She began sketching the vision she'd had of *Cardington R101* docking at the tower on the fateful night Freddie Marsh would be killed.

She worked on it for hours into the night, long after the Sinclairs had retired. She finished it the next morning. It was dramatic and jarring to the eye. It depicted young Freddie grabbing the cable and getting shocked with his fellow workers screaming their warnings. The scene was lit by searchlights on the tower and from the multi-colored fairground nearby. The Sinclairs were speechless when they saw it—seeing into the future. Not only were Millie's psychic gifts developing, but the speed at which she painted her visions was astonishing, and her visual artistry amazing.

"You must show this when you speak next time, Millie," Kate said.

"Do you think anyone will listen?" Millie asked them.

The following Monday morning, Doyle presented himself to the receptionist at Gwydyr House, the home of the Air Ministry on Whitehall. He'd been invited for 'a chat' with Thomson at his 'very earliest convenience'. As far as Doyle was concerned, it couldn't be soon enough. He was anxious to assist Millie in any way he could to put the wind up these people. He'd traveled up to town with her and left her at Eileen Garrett's tea house at Charing Cross, drinking tea and eating a cream scone. He told her he'd meet her back there when Thomson was 'done with him'.

Thomson's spacious office was located on the ground floor, overlooking the Thames. He sat behind his walnut desk, facing the wall behind him. He was staring at a huge painting of the Taj Mahal which his valet, Buck, had hung earlier in the day. He was contemplating the question of Mrs. Hinchliffe. He grimaced. This whole business was distasteful and annoying, not to mention embarrassing. When Knoxwood knocked and showed Doyle in, his demeanor changed to one of sweetness and charm. He spun round in his chair.

"Ah, there you are, Doyle, my dear fellow."

Thomson saw Doyle glance at the painting. "Nice, isn't it?"

Doyle frowned. "What's its significance, may I ask?"

"It's there to remind me every day of our goal. *Cardington R101* will fly to India in the *very* near future."

Doyle showed no enthusiasm for that notion and didn't bite. "You asked to see me, Lord Thomson."

"Yes, indeed I did. Come, let us sit over here." Thomson said, leading Doyle to the comfortable armchairs set around a grand marble fireplace. "I wanted to speak to you about the pilot's widow." Now his expression was one of pain and sorrow. "We can ill afford to lose men like him—"

"Quite."

"I'm sure his lady is overwrought and at her wit's end, poor thing."

"All this has been extremely tough on her, to be sure, sir."

"She has little ones—one only a babe in arms, I hear?"

"Yes, that's right."

"Everyone's in an uproar about her not getting the insurance money. I'd like to help her somehow, if I can."

"Wonderful!"

"Now, about her performance at Cardington last week. All that's got to stop. I want no more naysayings and rambling on about airships and messages from the dead and all that tripe! She needs to keep her mouth shut from now on. You understand?"

"Er, I don't know. I'll have to—"

"I'm trying to help the woman—if she's got sense enough to realize it!"

"But, Lord Thomson, we have reason to believe disaster awaits you."

"Based on what?"

"Messages we've received from Captain Hinchliffe."

"Good God man! That's poppycock! I have no time for all your dabbling with the dead, sir!"

The interview had not gone well. It ground to a halt with everything said within the first few minutes. They shook hands without the least sincerity. Doyle dejectedly trooped back to Charing Cross, trailed by one of Thomson's security people. Doyle reached the teashop and went inside followed by the Raven, who made no attempt to stay out of sight. He sat in the corner glaring at them.

When Doyle reached Millie, his face was flushed and he was out of breath. "That man is not going to be stopped. He's hell-bent!" he wheezed.

"Goodness!" Millie exclaimed, but she was more concerned with the condition Doyle was in. She was picking up his condition and could feel his pain in her own chest.

"He's offering to help put pressure on Inchcape, if you'll keep just quiet."

"What!"

Doyle sat opposite her huffing and puffing, holding his chest. He didn't look good at all. Millie was getting panicky.

"We must get to Brancker," Doyle whispered.

"Right now, we need to get you to a doctor!" Millie said.

"I *am* a doctor!" Doyle snapped. He took out a jar of pills from his coat pocket and slipped two in his mouth. "I'll be fine in a few minutes. It's nothing," he assured her.

After a rest and a drink of water, Doyle was back to his old self and they made for the station. They went back to Pickwick Cottage, where she showed Doyle her latest creation, *The Death of Freddie Marsh*.

He was dumbfounded.

30

OFFER REJECTED

Wednesday, June 26, 1929.

illie's next vision came two days later. She was in her secret garden, relaxing after baking bread. As she sat with her eyes closed, she found herself in the darkness of a storm, close to a little Frenchman who was bundled up in his overcoat and cloth cap. A great shape was coming towards them, very low to the ground. It was *Cardington R101*. She just knew it. The Frenchman sneered and swore at the dirigible in disgust. As it came, it faltered once and then returned to straight and level. Then it dived again, and crashed within a hundred feet of them. There were two great explosions. The Frenchman, who'd just retrieved a rabbit from one his traps, sank to the ground in shock, clutching the animal. Both their eyes bulged in terror at the horrific sight of the burning airship. Millie could see men inside, screaming in agony. She could smell them burning.

As the horrific vision faded, Millie sat still without opening her eyes for ten minutes. She was brought back by Kate bringing tea on a tray. Kate could see she was once again in distress.

"What's the matter, Millie dear? What have you seen now?" she asked.

Millie didn't answer her question directly.

"I have to go to London to see Thomson myself," Millie said.

"Is that wise?"

"What do I have to lose? They've decided not to give me the money. I must do what Ray wants me to do. I have to keep trying, Kate. I couldn't live with myself if I didn't *try*, at least."

The next day, Millie went to Charing Cross and tramped down Whitehall in the rain under her matching black umbrella. She didn't call to make an appointment. She wanted to surprise him. If he wasn't there, she'd try again another day. She got to Gwydyr House and marched in. She'd learned from Doyle exactly where his office was—at the end, on the ground floor. No one bothered her at first, as she sauntered through the entrance hall and along the corridor. She made for the first door on the right, a heavy, white paneled door, where a man sat outside, a bowler hat resting on his lap. Millie ignored him and barged right in. The man jumped up and tried to stop her. He was too late. Thomson was seated at his desk examining some papers through his pince-nez glasses low on his nose. As she stormed in, he peered over them, frowning.

"Miss, you can't go in there. Come out immediately," the security man shouted.

But Thomson had recognized Millie. And waved him away. "It's okay, Smethers," he said. "Let her be."

The door closed behind Millie, leaving her alone with Thomson. "Lord Thomson, I must speak to you," she snapped, stepping forward, water dripping from her black raincoat onto the carpet. She was stopped in her tracks momentarily when her eyes fell on the Taj Mahal. It sent shivers down her spine.

"Mrs. Hinchliffe ..." Thomson began, a smile curling at the corner of his mouth. He was pleased at her reaction to his treasured painting. His recovery from her invasion was commendable. "I see you've noticed my painting. Funny that you should call by. I heard you're quite the artist—this must be Fate indeed. I'm looking for someone to paint *Cardington R101* over the Taj for me. I was going to ask Mr. Churchill, but maybe you'd like to do it for me instead?"

Millie looked at him with incredulity. She studied his aura. It hadn't been easy to see at Cardington in the garden sunlight. It was of many shades sparkling reds, blues, greens and yes, blacks and browns. But the predominant color was purple. Unlucky in love.

"Certainly not, sir! It'd be sacrilege to spoil that picture. I won't encourage you with your impossible dreams—dreams that will end in *disaster!*" she said finally.

"That's a jolly pity, madam. Then I'll ask Winston."

"I want you to know that your financial offer is rejected!"

"Please yourself," he replied disinterestedly. He'd recovered well again.

"All that matters to my husband and I is the safety of those men at Cardington."

"With all due respect, Mrs. Hinchliffe, your husband is dead!"

"I beg your pardon, sir, his spirit is *very* much alive. He's warned us that your airship will not survive."

"My dear Mrs. Hinchliffe, the Germans have flown airships for millions of miles without mishap."

"Oh, they *will* have their 'mishap', *believe* me, sir,—*they will have their mishap!*"

"You're causing a great deal of embarrassment to the Air Ministry and to me personally, Mrs. Hinchliffe—"

"Your embarrassment really is the least of my concerns, Lord Thomson."

"What you are doing is tantamount to sedition… And if you do not cease and desist, I will have—"

"Your bowler-hatted dogs harass me some more! Is that it?"

"I don't know what you're talking about, madam." He sat back in his chair peering at her. "You know, I was going to ask you to paint my portrait. I was going to sit for you. And I would've paid you well for it —"

"I would *not* paint your portrait sir, not for a thousand pounds. And if I needed to, I could paint it from memory. A sitting wouldn't be necessary. Your image has been indelibly burned into my brain!"

Millie started for the door and as she reached it, she turned back to him. "I've got one or two more paintings for you to stick on your wall. They're *much* more colorful than that one!"

Thomson didn't respond. Millie left the room without saying more. Thomson sat pondering her interruption. He turned to meditate on his painting, as he liked to do when mulling over a problem. And Mrs. Hinchliffe had definitely become a problem. Still, he wasn't one to bear a grudge. She was one hell of a plucky woman, and he *loved* plucky women.

31

THE NIGHTCLUB

Saturday, June 29, 1929.

Millie hadn't heard from Brancker. She called his office at the Air Ministry a couple of times without success and decided to track him down in town somehow. She called Hunter, who was, of course, more than glad to hear from her. He suggested that he pick Millie up and take her to a few nightclubs in the West End. He knew some that Brancker liked to frequent. Millie was pleased to accept his offer. She'd been leading a pretty dull existence for a very long time. He was a nice chap and when he cleaned himself up he was quite attractive. Hunter was tickled to death.

Millie decided it was time to dispense with the widow's weeds. There didn't seem to be any point in going about in black any longer, especially since she knew her husband had not ceased to exist. Katie loaned her a turquoise cocktail dress, a jazzy little number, which turned out to be perfect for the evening. It was the third nightclub on Hunter's list that bore fruit. As soon as they entered, Millie spied Brancker in the middle of the dance floor amongst a feverish group of writhing bodies, fashionably clad. The orchestra was going wild with American jazz. Brancker, monocle glued in its socket, gyrated, all the while smiling at his beautiful partner.

Millie and Hunter were shown to a table close to the dance floor. As Brancker and his partner were coming off at the end of a number, he noticed Millie, not for who she was, but as a beautiful woman. He did a double take, and then came to their table. He suddenly remembered his unkept promise.

"Millie! How lovely to see you," he said eyeing her dress. "You look *absolutely* splendid. I'm so sorry I've not called on you. I've been terribly busy. It's been crazy," he said breathlessly.

"Please, sit with us," Millie said, looking from Brancker to his partner.

"Oh, this is a very dear friend of mine, Bubbles Carlisle," Brancker said, pulling out a chair. The girl fluttered her eyelashes with studied perfection, enough to impress any movie director.

They shook hands and sat down. A waiter came.

"I vote we have champers," said Brancker. They agreed. "Bring us a bottle of Dom Pérignon, please waiter," Brancker said. After a few pleasantries, and they each had a bubbling flute in front of them, Brancker raised his glass. "To us!" he shouted, and then, "To your success, Millie." Millie realized he was talking about the insurance. "We're all working on it for you. I know you don't realize it, but there's a lot going on behind the scenes." Millie nodded her thanks as they chinked glasses. "The papers are full of stories about you Millie. It's relentlessly being kept alive."

"Yes, I know. George here has been very kind in that regard," Millie said, glancing at Hunter.

Brancker looked at him with interest. "The *Express*, right?"

"Yes, sir."

"I've been in touch with your boss, Lord Beaverbrook, on a regular basis, regarding Millie's situation," Brancker told them.

"Yup, we've all felt the pressure," Hunter replied.

"I'm not sure they can withstand the heat much longer. Something's got to give up there in Glenapp Castle," Brancker said.

Millie was astonished and pleased. She'd begun to give up hope, despite Hinchliffe's assurances. "Do you really think so, Sefton?"

"Yes, indeed I do. I've heard rumblings. Keep your spirits up, my gal!"

Hunter leaned forward over the table. "I've been following Mrs. Hinchliffe's story very closely. The public can't get enough. Especially about the latest developments—you know about the predictions?"

Brancker became decidedly uncomfortable, fidgeting with his champagne glass. "I heard something about it, yes."

"Millie has a message from her husband for you. That's why we're here tonight," Hunter said. "We've been in three clubs tonight, trying to track you down."

Brancker sighed. Bubbles put a cigarette into a long pearl holder. Brancker lit it for her. She took a look drag and blew smoke over the table.

"It all sounds simply *intriguing*, darling," she purred.

"How s-strange," Brancker stammered.

Millie looked directly at Brancker. "He's asked me to appeal to you, to give it all up. Airships are a *lost* cause."

It was as if he hadn't heard. "*Cardington R101* will be launched any time, Millie. She'll show herself over London soon. Lord Thomson is talking about making a flight to India over the Christmas holiday."

Now it was as if, by saying it out loud, it was inevitable.

"Millie has been having vivid visions, Sir Sefton," Hunter said.

Brancker jerked his head toward Millie. "What have you seen?"

"I've seen terrible things. First a boy will be killed at the tower, very soon. Then, I've seen an airship crash and explode in flames," Millie told him.

"*Cardington R101* is not the only airship under construction, you know, Millie. A second one is being built by Vickers at Howden—her sister ship. *She's* scheduled to fly to Canada. You may have the wrong ship," Brancker offered hopefully.

"Yes, we know all about that," Millie said.

"In your visions, have you seen any markings?" Brancker asked.

"Yes, *R101,* as clear as daylight. It's you who have the wrong ship, Sefton," Millie said.

Brancker was crestfallen—his evening totally ruined.

Bubbles was now quite concerned. "*Your* ship is *Cardington R101*, isn't it Sefton?"

Brancker took out his handkerchief and wiped his brow. "Just my luck. Can't say I believe in all that stuff ... Although, I do remember having my fortune told once in Paris, during the war."

"You've never told me that, Sefton. What did they say?" Bubbles asked.

"It was jolly accurate for the most part. Astonishingly so! Trouble was, she said she couldn't see anything in my future after 1930 ... isn't that a *riot!*" He threw his head back and roared with nervous laughter.

Bubbles was now extremely upset. Clearly, she believed in those things. "Oh, Sefton!" she exclaimed, her eyes filling with tears.

Brancker gulped down the rest of his champagne.

"Nothing you can do about yer fate, my darling. Must go and change me collar. Can't dance with a soggy collar can we!" he said.

Brancker always traveled with two or three spare collars in his pocket. As was his custom, he went to the gentlemen's luxurious, Victorian bathroom to change this one. Dancing was a sweaty business and being the dapper gentleman that he was, he was always prepared. While the muffled strains of "My Melancholy Baby" drifted through the walls from the dance-floor, Brancker washed his face in cold water. He brought his dripping, haggard face up from the basin and stared into the mirror. An attendant handed him a clean, white towel. He pressed it to his face with trembling hands.

The man in the white jacket asked. "Are you all right, sir?"

"Oh, yes, yes, perfectly fine, my good man. Yes, thank you," Brancker replied.

He removed a collar from his pocket and fumbled with his studs, trying to position it around his neck. Fear showed in his eyes all the while.

Damned bad show!

After receiving help from the toilet attendant with his collar stud, Brancker returned to the dance floor fit and ready to dance the night away. And to make the most of the time he had left on this earth with gorgeous girls like Bubbles Carlisle.

With the object of Millie's mission complete, she danced with Hunter well into the night. This, for Hunter, was bliss. Millie found herself looking at Hunter once in a while. He really was a handsome chap, about her own age, and such a good dancer. How had she not really noticed him before?

32

WINSTON CHURCHILL

Tuesday, July 30, 1929.

M illie's next visitor came unannounced, as they frequently did. A black Wolseley sedan rolled into the driveway bearing Mr. Winston Churchill. He arrived at the door carrying a bottle of champagne and two glasses.

When Millie appeared, he said. "You, Mrs. H. have become something of a celebrity. I presume you *are* Mrs. Hinchliffe?"

Millie laughed and her eyes sparkled with delight and astonishment. "Yes! Mr. Churchill?"

Churchill carried on his school-boyish face a look of mischievous pleasure and a twinkle in his eye. "Indeed, it is, my dear lady, and *I* am the bearer of good news," he said, holding up the champagne and glasses. A dumbfounded Millie led the balding, cherub-like man into her studio, where at the sight of her artwork, his eyes lit up. He put down the champagne and glasses and removed the unlit cigar from his mouth. He was in his element and went charging around from one painting to another. The first he saw was the one she'd just finished: *Cardington R101* crashing beside the French rabbit poacher. Then he gazed at the airship exploding with the Eiffel Tower in the background.

"This all looks *terribly* alarming," he said.

"It is, I'm afraid."

"You've been busy. Nice work. Nice colors," he commented. "What's it all mean, young lady? Well, don't answer that now. I've got news for you."

Millie had been holding her breath. "What is it, Mr. Churchill?" she gasped.

"This morning I met with Lord Inchcape—"

"Yes—" Millie's eyes had become like saucers. She pressed her palms together.

"And today he's instructing his bank. He's had enough. The sum of ten thousand pounds is being placed in the hands of the Chancellor of the Exchequer, to be done with as he sees fit. That means the insurance money will be yours by tomorrow."

Millie almost fainted. That would be the last day of July!

Oh, Raymond! My dear, dear Raymond! God Bless you. God Bless you!

She was brought back from her thoughts and to her senses by the sound of a champagne cork blasting from the bottle. Churchill poured out two glasses and held one out to her. "My heartiest congratulations to you!" he said.

Millie took a gulp, still in a daze, as Churchill continued. "You know, this reminds me of a day back in 1919, when I personally presented a check for ten thousand pounds to Alcock and Brown after they'd made the *very first* Atlantic crossing. The circumstances today are tinged with terrible sadness, but nonetheless, I'm still *delighted* to be the bearer of this news."

After they'd drunk their champagne, Churchill continued his inspection of Millie's work. Portraits of Doyle, Brancker, Elsie, Lord Beaverbrook, Mrs. East, and sketches of personalities at Cardington. He then looked at *The Death of Freddie Marsh*. "Now, tell me, what are all these pictures about, hmm?" he asked.

Millie couldn't help looking sheepish. "They're paintings of visions I've had."

"Well, it doesn't look at all that promising for these damned airships, does it?"

"Absolutely not, Mr. Churchill."

"I'd keep all this quiet for the time being, till that money's safely tucked up in your bank account. You've already put a burr under Thomson's saddle. I saw him last week in his office and he told me all about it. Said he'd asked you to paint an airship on that lousy painting on his wall—done by some fifth-rate dauber."

Millie gave an embarrassed laugh. "Yes, that's right, he did and I refused."

"I wish you'd done it for him. Now *I've* got stuck with it!"

"I'm so sorry."

"I'll have to go to Cardington to see that hydrogen bomb for myself!"

"Just don't go for ride in it, sir."

"I'll probably take your advice." He glanced at Lord Beaverbook and Sir Arthur Conan Doyle and cocked an eyebrow. "Now, I see you're an excellent painter of portraits, Mrs. Hinchliffe—I also see that you observe people's auras. I wonder what you see in mine!"

Inevitably, Churchill asked Millie to paint his portrait and, of course, she willingly agreed. He posed while she took his photo. He stood with a hand on a coat lapel, the other holding a fine Cuban cigar. He said he'd come back and pose again, since he only lived 'just up the road' at Chartwell. As a fellow artist, he seemed completely comfortable with Millie and being in her studio. They'd become instant chums.

"I like to paint, myself," he said.

"I read that you were a prolific painter," Millie said.

"It helps keep the old black dog away, that and the brandy, of course."

Millie laughed.

I have a nice studio in my back garden. It's my sanctuary. Keeps me sane," Churchill said. "You must come sometime. We'll have some great conversations, you and I. I'm out of office now, so I'll have plenty of time."

Millie studied him and his aura. She saw plenty of black—she thought *that* must be the 'old black dog'. It was mixed with many other strong colors. She saw wisdom and fortitude. She also saw death and destruction. "You'll be back. Your greatest time is yet to come, Mr. Churchill," Millie said.

"Is that so? What do you see?"

"There is much you will do for this country. True greatness is in your future and we shall all be thankful."

"Yes, you are absolutely right. I know it myself," he said. "The Devil is out there waiting in the shadows again."

The following morning, the House of Commons was relatively quiet, but rumors had been swirling all morning. Members of

Parliament jabbered excitedly when they saw the Chancellor of the Exchequer rising from his seat. He coughed gently before beginning.

"Members of this House, it falls to me as the Chancellor of the Exchequer to make this announcement on behalf of Lord Inchcape, regarding the matter of his daughter, the Honorable Elsie Mackay, and her estate. Lord Inchcape, being desirous that the Elsie Mackay Fund should not be the occasion of any complaint, has placed at the disposal of the government, the sum of ten thousand pounds for the purpose of meeting any complaint in such a manner as the Chancellor of the Exchequer may think fit."

Raucous cheers broke out on both sides of the chamber.

Millie and Kate were in the kitchen when the BBC News came on.

Beep Beep Beep Beep Beep Beeeep.

'This is the BBC Home Service. Here is the six o'clock news. It was announced today in the House of Commons by the Chancellor of the Exchequer that the father of the Honorable Elsie Mackay has set aside the sum of ten thousand pounds for the purpose of meeting any complaint against the Elsie Mackay Fund. Miss Mackay disappeared earlier this year while attempting to make a record Atlantic flight from east to west with Captain Walter George Raymond Hinchliffe, the famous war ace. This means in effect, that the widow of Captain Hinchliffe will receive the equivalent sum of the insurance money promised by Miss Elsie Mackay ...

Later that day, a telegram arrived. Millie sank into an armchair in the living room to read it. It said:

JULY 31, 1929.   TO MRS E HINCHLIFFE.

MY GREATEST PLEASURE TO INFORM YOU INTENDED INSURANCE AMOUNT HAS NOW BEEN SET ASIDE FOR YOU AND AT MY DISPOSAL FOR DISBURSEMENT   STOP CHANCELLOR OF THE EXCHEQUER STOP HM GOVERNMENT WESTMINSTER

This was the final confirmation they'd been waiting for. Millie and Kate hugged and Sinclair rushed out to the local off-licence and bought a bottle of cheap red wine. They had their dinner of ham and eggs around the kitchen table and toasted Millie. Their long-term financial problems were over. Next morning, Millie went to see Mr. Drummond to handle the matter on her behalf.

Millie arranged a meeting with Eileen Garrett immediately.

"Hello, young lady. He's here and wild with joy," Uvani said.

"Raymond, it happened just as you said. I'm sorry I ever doubted you," Millie said.

"Oh, Millie, Millie, Millie. I am absolutely thrilled!" Hinchliffe exclaimed. With that, he jumped from the chair Eileen was occupying and grabbed Millie and pulled her to her feet. He put his arm around her and danced her around the room. "Just Millie and me, and Joanie, makes three, I'm happy in my green heaven ..."

Millie was blown away, feeling his happiness. It would have been a strange sight for Mrs. East or Doyle to see if they'd been there. She was glad she'd come alone.

33

THE DEATH OF FREDDIE MARSH

Wednesday, October 16, 1929.

On October 14th, His Majesty's Airship *Cardington R101* was launched and Hinchliffe was on the spot to witness the momentous occasion. He watched as five hundred able-bodied men and one not so able-bodied boy pulled out the gleaming silver ship from her shed. No one, except Freddie Marsh and his family, knew of his health problems.

Everything went without a hitch. Thousands watched the great airship walked to the center of the airfield and then allowed to ascend to six hundred feet for all the world to admire. The next day, she was taken on a short flight around Bedford. On the third day, Lord Thomson, the Air Minister, and Sir Sefton Brancker, the Director of Civil Aviation, were to take an extended flight. There was much ballyhoo in the press.

Thomson and Brancker arrived early that morning, shaking hands and making a fuss of everyone. This included ground crewmen in a line at the tower, among them Freddie Marsh, whose birthday it was. On being informed of this, Thomson patted the boy on the shoulder and wished him a happy birthday. Then the ship departed on its highly touted flight around England, taking in London en route, then Cambridge, Sandringham, Leicester, Birmingham and Northampton.

Hinchliffe was on board, taking a close interest in matters concerning airworthiness. He was in the control car when Brancker and Colmore came down for a look round during the flight. Hinchliffe listened to their conversation. His fears were confirmed. Brancker was effusive at first. Colmore, now Director of Airship Development, didn't say much at all. He looked worried. Hinchliffe figured Colmore knew a lot more than he was letting on.

"This is magnificent!" Brancker ran his hands over the hardwood and his eyes over the instrumentation. "The workmanship and finish are extraordinary." After a few minutes, Brancker, himself an experienced pilot, couldn't resist. "May I?" he asked.

"Of course you can, sir," Irwin responded. The coxswains left the control car and Lou Remington attended the elevators. Brancker took the rudder and turned the wheel gently around from port to starboard. The massive bulk moved like a great sea galleon of old under canvas.

"I say, she seems awfully responsive. What do you say, Irwin?"

"She's responsive to the helm all right, but she's underpowered and grossly overweight," Irwin answered.

"You mean seriously overweight?" Brancker asked.

"Fully loaded, this ship wouldn't get off the ground, sir."

"Hell, you don't say!" Brancker exploded. "He's all set to go charging off to India at Christmas!"

"That would be suicide. This ship's quite unserviceable at the moment, sir," Irwin replied.

Hinchliffe saw Colmore gritting his teeth.

Later, Hinchliffe was given more reason to be worried. They were nearing Cardington. In the control car, with Atherstone, the first officer and Remington at his side, Irwin was becoming concerned.

"She's getting heavy and losing gas. It's happening so rapidly," Irwin said.

"Do you want to dump ballast yet, sir?" Remington asked.

"Yes. Dump five tons from Frame two and five tons from Frame eight."

"Right you are, sir," Atherstone said, grabbing the ballast release valves.

"I'm going to drive her hard and keep her nose up. Increase all engines to eight hundred."

"All engines to eight hundred, sir," Remington repeated, as he sent the message to all cars. They heard engine notes increase.

"How are we off for fuel?" Irwin asked.

"We got plenty. Enough for eighteen hours," Atherstone replied.

"Now dump water ballast on Frames 3 and 6," Irwin ordered.

"Dumping ballast on 3 and 6, Captain. We're down to five tons of water ballast," Atherstone said.

"Save that. We'll need it at the tower. Damn! She's sinking like a rock. Dump five tons of fuel from Frame 5."

"Did you say *fuel*, sir?" Lou asked.

"Affirmative. Start dumping *fuel*."

Atherstone carried out the order. From the control car, they watched diesel fuel cascade over the fields.

"That'll be good for the animals and crops," Atherstone said with a grimace.

"Can't be helped," Irwin muttered

Finally, they showed up near Cardington Tower, and the fair that came to the village every year at this time. After four attempts, the majestic gleaming ship passed over the fairground at about 200 feet, stunning the wildly screaming girls and boys on the Ferris wheel.

Another witness to this dangerous, terrifying event was George Hunter. He'd got permission to stand at the tower to see the docking operation up close. He'd certainly have a story to tell after this. Within a few hundred feet of the tower, cables were dropped for pick up. These cables were pulled in by an electric winch, which would then draw the airship up to the tower to be locked to the nose cone.

Freddie Marsh was one of the new boys in the ground crew. The dream of all these young men was that someday they'd get a job on the ship as a rigger or an engineer. As the ship come over the field, Freddie looked up and saw the open hatch at the front. His friend Sam Church was holding the cable, ready to throw it down. Freddie waved and grinned up at him. Church dropped the cable and Freddie shouted to another friend in the ground crew. "I'm gonna be first on that line!" At that, he took off at a sprint to gather up the line. Above him, Church was yelling at him to leave the line alone.

"Freddie, no!" Church yelled. "It's live!"

It would be alive with static electricity and would pack a severe punch if someone touched it without using rubber mats. It wasn't Freddie's job to work with the lines and he hadn't been instructed on that procedure. As he ran, a dozen other experienced ground crewmen ran after him, to stop him.

"Don't touch that line, son!" they hollered.

"Freddie, don't!"

The droning engines overhead, together with the carousel music of the fair, drowned out their warnings. As Freddie ran, he looked behind him and saw them running like madmen behind him. Thinking it was all a lark, he ran even harder. It was great fun! The boy couldn't have wished for a better birthday.

As soon as he grabbed the line, Freddie was hit by a huge burst of static electricity. He curled, clutching his chest and fell backwards, bashing the back of his head on the ground. That amount of electricity wasn't enough to kill most people, but Freddie had a weak heart. He certainly wouldn't have been allowed on that field if those in authority had known. Times were hard and Freddie's family needed every penny they could earn to survive. No one saw this coming, particularly his cousin, Joe Binks, who witnessed the whole thing from his engine car. The boy wasn't supposed to be rushing about like that or touching those lines.

Hinchliffe was present in the control car, where things were also chaotic. The ship was becoming dangerously heavy and Captain Irwin had to get rid of more excess weight, fast. Irwin shouted across to Remington. "She's sinking fast! Dump the last five tons of ballast at Frame No 7 and five tons of fuel from Frame 8!"

Hinchliffe saw the American hesitate, questioning the order. He was obviously thinking about poor, Freddie lying on the ground under the ship.

"Do it, right now!" Irwin yelled.

Remington grabbed the ballast and fuel discharge levers and let everything go. Hinchliffe moved from the control car down to Freddie's side. The boy lay there, his eyes open, while water and stinking diesel fuel gushed over his young face. Hinchliffe saw he was dead. His spirit was stirring. He looked up at Hinchliffe. "Who are you, sir? What happened?" he said, bewildered.

"Come on, son. Come with me," Hinchliffe said. He reached out to Freddie and pulled him to his feet and led him away toward the setting sun. Hinchliffe wanted to make sure the boy didn't go through the misery he'd endured during his own crossing over.

Chaos remained on the airfield until the ship was finally docked. The yelling stopped and the engines were cut. All that remained was the sound of the carousel and the screams of girls on the slowly turning Ferris wheel, its colored lights vivid in the descending darkness.

When the VIPs got down from the tower, they were met by a gaggle of reporters, including Hunter. They asked Thomson how his flight had been and he extolled the virtues of airship flight. He was, of course, more than ever convinced after this. The weather had been kind and the flight exceptionally smooth. He'd even sat up there in the heavens, working on ministerial business in perfect calm and serenity on the promenade deck.

They'd flown over Sandringham where the King and Queen had come out and waved to them from the terrace. Thomson was elated and answered questions gladly. He told them he'd had a feeling of safety and well-being throughout the flight.

"Do you look forward to going on a voyage soon, sir?" one reporter asked.

He told them he was hoping to make a voyage to India during the Christmas recess and that he was much looking forward to it. The reporters reminded him that Christmas was less than three months away. Did he mean *this* Christmas? Thomson bristled. He stressed that he would not put pressure on his Cardington team. His motto would remain, he said, 'Safety First, and Safety Second, as well!'

The mood changed when Hunter put up his hand and called a question from the back of the group.

"Lord Thomson, George Hunter, *Daily Express*, do you have any comment about Mrs. Hinchliffe's warnings?"

In a split second, Thomson's demeanor changed from joy to irritation.

Damn, not him again!

He grimaced.

"No, I do not, except to say that obviously, this woman has not been of sound mind since her husband's death. It's all *very* unfortunate."

Things went further downhill when Hunter followed up with another question. "Sir, are you aware that a young ground crewman died this evening?"

This came as a bitter blow out of the blue.

Thomson searched around into the faces of his Royal Airship Works team. They stared back at him blankly. Half of them didn't know either.

"Are you sure? What happened?" Thomson asked.

"We believe he was electrocuted, sir," Hunter said. "I saw it happen with my own eyes."

Thomson was genuinely saddened by this news. He made his way to the car with Brancker, who was also deeply dejected now. He remembered Millie's warnings at the nightclub. Irwin's pronouncements in the control car were also still ringing in his ears. But Thomson was ignorant of all that.

34

AN APPEAL TO CAPTAIN IRWIN

Saturday, October 19, 1929.

DEATH AT CARDINGTON TOWER
MRS. HINCHLIFFE'S VISION

Underneath the *Daily Express* headline the next morning was a picture of Millie's painting with the caption: *The Death of Freddie Marsh.* The photo was in black and white, but it graphically showed young Freddie sprinting after the mooring line dropped from *Cardington R101.* Behind him were other ground-crewmen, chasing him, waving their arms and shouting. The tower was behind them with the lights of Cardington Fair and the Ferris wheel in the background. Hunter had raced over to Pickwick Cottage and Millie had given him a photo for use with his piece.

Hunter's article gave a vivid description of the tragedy at the tower. It also pointed out that it had been Freddie Marsh's birthday. The report went on to mention Lord Thomson's description of the flight and his hope to fly to India at Christmas. The newspaper mentioned cryptically that he may have meant Christmas 1930.

Millie decided to keep the pressure up and her mission in full swing. She went to the village and called Captain Irwin at Cardington House. He was happy to hear from her, although wary after the hullabaloo at Thomson's Garden Address. But he did agree to meet her. He was obviously concerned for Millie, as the wife of one of his best friends. He asked if she wouldn't mind meeting him at the fair on the green at lunchtime instead of coming to Cardington House. Word had gone out, Mrs. Hinchliffe was *persona non grata*. The boys in the bowler hats from the Air Ministry had made that clear. He said he'd be at the Ferris wheel at 1:00 p.m.

Millie enlisted Hunter's help and he drove her to Cardington. They got there before the appointed hour and waited. They had a clear view of the Ferris wheel from there. *Cardington R101* was close by, tethered to the tower. That thing gave Millie the creeps. Its foreboding presence contrasted with the colorful rides and happy sounds of fairground music and laughter. While they waited, they munched on cheese and tomato sandwiches Millie had brought. Hinchliffe watched from the backseat, invisible.

They spotted Irwin in uniform coming toward the chestnut fencing entrance. Millie got out of the car and went to the Ferris wheel as he arrived. Hinchliffe went beside her. Hunter watched from the car. Their body language told the full story. Irwin looked sheepish at first, but nonetheless pleased to see her. They embraced and he kissed her cheek.

"Millie, we were all so relieved to hear the insurance came through," Irwin said.

"My dear Bird, I'm thankful you came," Millie said anxiously.

"You sounded so urgent, I'm very concerned about you Millie. Is there anything I can do for you?"

"Bird, I'm okay. It's you we're desperately worried about."

Irwin put his hand on her shoulder. "Millie, don't be. We're doing everything conceivable to make this airship *absolutely* safe."

Hinchliffe smirked and shook his head. He knew just how worried Irwin really was.

Millie searched Irwin's eyes as he spoke. Underneath his apparent confidence, she sensed concern. His words didn't ring true. It wasn't that he was trying to deceive her—more like he was trying to convince himself. She sensed a nagging doubt in those eyes.

"I've heard all that from Thomson. I'm sure what you say is true. You're all doing your level best, including Thomson." Millie looked at him in desperation. "But that's not the point, Bird. It doesn't change the fact that the damned thing's going to crash and burn." She pointed at the airship floating innocently at the tower a thousand yards away. Her eyes filled with tears. She took out her handkerchief from her handbag and wiped her eyes.

Irwin shook his head. "Oh, Millie, don't. You can't possibly know that, can you?"

"Oh, but that's where you're wrong. I *do* know."

"Millie, how could you possibly?"

Millie took his hand and looked into his eyes. "Raymond has told me." Her eyes appeared wild.

Irwin looked dismissively at her and pulled away.

"Please Bird, don't just turn away. Please listen to me. Raymond is desperately worried. He's following everything closely. He *knows* exactly what's going on—he *knows* the ship is overweight. He *knows* the engines are too heavy and underpowered. He says corrective measures they have in mind aren't going to work. He talks about stuff —stuff I know *nothing* about. He *knows* all its faults—don't you see?"

Irwin looked worried by this. There was truth in what she was saying. Hinchliffe knew they'd been discussing modifications to increase the ship's lift just this week. Irwin was doing his best to keep his composure. He simply smiled and put both arms around her and kissed her cheeks. He shook his head again sadly. "Sorry Millie, old girl. You may be right about all this. Chances are, you're more right than you know. But I'm an officer and I have my duty. There's no way out for me, or anyone here. It's as simple as that, my dear. We're all in a box. We're committed."

"Bird, the boy that was killed here last week ..."

Irwin winced. "Yes, what about him?"

"When's his funeral?"

"Not sure, they're doing an autopsy. He had a weak heart, apparently."

"That was an omen, Bird."

This only irritated the captain. Millie knew she was beaten. They stood for a few moments looking into each other eyes, as caring friends. There was nothing more to be said. Millie turned away and trudged toward Hunter's car, drawing her coat around her. Gusty winds blew the leaves around her feet. Irwin walked off toward the chestnut fencing and his airship, the mighty *Cardington R101*.

35

BLACK TUESDAY

Tuesday, October 29, 1929.

M illie made up her mind to attend Freddie Marsh's funeral at St. Mary's. Hunter had asked if she wanted to attend. He was covering the story. Freddie was buried on October 29, a day of misery that became known throughout the world as 'Black Tuesday'. Panic ran rampant when the American stock market crashed as soon as Wall Street opened for business. In New York, people were throwing themselves out of skyscraper windows.

Freddie's burial had been delayed due to the requirement of an autopsy. Mourners weren't concerned with what was happening in the world of finance, but it added to the somber mood. The focus was on the boy's family.

Freddie's grave had been dug at the back of the churchyard in the ground where Millie had seen her vision. It was close to the great shed from which *Cardington R101* had been launched. The higher echelon of the Royal Airship Works, including Irwin and Johnston, didn't attend lest the airship program garnered more adverse publicity.

Under a darkening October sky, Millie and Hunter stood with the crowd in drizzle and blustery winds, the air heavy with smoke from burning leaves. Across the grave, Millie saw Commander Remington, his arm around a woman, presumably his wife—an exquisite dark-haired beauty. She appeared to be on the verge of collapse, her skin deathly white against severe black garb.

Millie sensed Remington had seen her, although he showed no sign. The clergyman muttered prayers. Everyone stood rigidly still and grim-faced as the coffin was lowered into the ground. From the sad faces of dozens of young men, it appeared that young Freddie had been very popular. Millie also noticed Binks, the engineer. He, too, ignored her.

Also standing with the crowd, although invisible, were Hinchliffe and Freddie. Hinchliffe kept his hand on Freddie's shoulder throughout the ceremony. The boy was deeply distressed to see his mother and father weeping for him. Hinchliffe noticed Remington's wife studying him. She'd seen him on the back of her husband's motorbike and later in their house. He'd learned since that she was a nurse. He knew the poor girl had suffered much these past few years. He also knew Freddie's death had caused her unbearable sadness.

Millie had been torn—in two minds about going to the funeral. Was it pointless? Was it out of curiosity? She wished she'd made a real effort to prevent the boy's death somehow, but she knew everyone would say again that she was out of her mind. She'd known when it would happen—on October 16. She'd known where it would happen— at Cardington Tower. So why hadn't she done more? She had no answer for that. But come hell or high water, she'd do more, even if everyone thought she was completely mad.

Standing at the grave, with *Cardington R101* swaying in the breeze nearby, Millie vowed she'd increase her efforts to warn the world about the dangers of these dirigibles. She'd go on an all-out offensive this coming year—she now had the resources to do so.

Hunter didn't attempt to interview anyone. The funeral was reported in three lines the following day.

36

MILLIE'S COUNTRYWIDE TOUR

1929–1930.

During August, the sum of ten thousand pounds, set aside by Lord Inchcape, had been safely deposited in Millie's account at Barclays Bank. Millie wrote a nice letter expressing her profound gratitude to him and his family. Mr. Drummond had wisely given Millie the names of reputable investment advisers in town and she'd met with two of them. Within a month, her mortgage was paid off. She waited to make investments until she understood the workings of the financial world as best she could. Hinchliffe told her to wait to invest any money in the stock market until November, which she did. She made a series of safe investments in blue chip stocks and municipal bonds. So soon after the stock market crash, her advisers had been cautious and conservative. The good thing was that stock prices were a steal at that time. Millie also bought back their piece of land, together with another adjoining parcel, from the estate agent whom she'd sold it to. He made a very nice profit, but Millie didn't mind. She had ideas about letting the Sinclairs do something with it; build a house, start a small farm or whatever they wished. She'd help them in any way she could. Sinclair had expressed the desire to own a gardening shop one day.

Millie's countrywide speaking tour began in December of 1929, and ending in September of 1930. She visited many municipalities in London and traveled to Birmingham, Liverpool, Manchester, York, Leeds, Sheffield, Newcastle, Cardiff, Bristol, Wakefield, Doncaster, Edinburgh, Glasgow, Brighton, Bournemouth and many more. Sometimes she visited two cities a week, usually Friday and Saturday. Millie was always accompanied by Hunter or Sinclair and sometimes Mrs. East. She usually began by playing a classical piece. It set the mood. The reception Millie got was always overwhelmingly positive, though the government and the press were not so enthusiastic, painting her as the grieving widow who'd gone round the bend.

The Birmingham audience sat enraptured by the gentle sounds of Chopin's Nocturne E Flat major Op 9 No. 2. This was the opening of Millie's second speech. It was billed as *Mrs. Hinchliffe Speaks – A lecture about life after death.* On the stage around Millie were her paintings: a portrait of Elsie Mackay, *Endeavour,* a black and white enlarged photograph of Hinchliffe standing beside his Sopwith, a painting in poster colors of *The Death of Freddie Marsh,* and her two latest creations: *Death of R101 Near Paris* and *R101 and The Rabbit Poacher.*

After coming to the end of Chopin's masterpiece, Millie stood at the microphone, where she had to wait two minutes for the end of a standing ovation. They'd followed Millie's story since Hinchliffe's disappearance. Millie glanced at the end seat on the back row of the auditorium. Hinchliffe was there, as usual. He'd made it a practice of occupying a similar seat during her lectures. She was comforted and strengthened by his presence.

"Ladies and gentlemen, there is a hunger across this land for enlightenment," Millie began.

It was the same where ever she went during her tour. Millie, now beautifully dressed in the most up-to-date fashion, oozed charisma and stage presence. And people were fascinated by her art display. Pictures with predictions! The newspapers were also fascinated, but refused to print her pictures. They found them too provocative and too weird for comfort, as prestigious organs of record. They weren't organs of *prediction*, Hunter told her. They'd leave that to psychic fringe magazines, which no one took seriously. The Air Ministry continued to keep an eye on her, with the boys in bowlers regularly attending her lectures.

In Liverpool, she played Rachmaninoff's Prelude in G minor Op 23 as a rousing start to her talk and captivated her audience. She told them: "My husband has been telling me of his progress in his new state. He's been working to influence those in aviation—you may have heard something about it!" There was laughter at this—Millie had earned quite a reputation as an activist. "He's been warning of the dangers surrounding these airships. He says they are deadly and that the Airship Program must be stopped, before it's too late."

Millie went from city to city. The newspapers followed her—especially the *Daily Express,* which of course, usually had Hunter at her lectures. Hunter, was by now, an established close and loyal friend. He willingly helped organize and transport Millie's artwork.

In Edinburgh, Millie played the haunting, Chopin Etude No 3 in E major 'Tristesse' op 10, which was received with rousing applause. That evening she inspired them with her uplifting message. "My husband wants you to know that life is a precious gift, which is your opportunity for spiritual growth. Ask God and you will be given the answers. He says there is no death—only *everlasting life!*"

The audience there was just as mesmerized. That evening, there was one person present of particular interest—Elsie Mackay's brother, Jonathan. Once the auditorium had emptied, which took ages as many people wanted to meet Millie (her developing psychic power enabled her to console the grieving and bring messages from deceased loved ones), Jonathan came to her on the stage. He'd waited patiently. He was obviously filled with admiration. Millie didn't recognize him at first.

"I liked your talk, Mrs. Hinchliffe," he said.

"Thank you," Millie said, now quite weary.

Jonathan stood sadly in front of Millie's painting of Elsie, his shoulders slumped. "She was so beautiful. I loved her so *very* much."

"Oh, it's Jonathan, of course!" Millie said, her eyes registering surprise.

"Such a lovely painting," Jonathan said, not taking his eyes from it. "I came hoping you could give me some peace of mind."

"I liked Elsie very much, Jonathan. I can tell you this: my husband has told me your sister is around you *constantly.*"

"Really, he said that?" Jonathan said, turning to Millie, his face shining with hope.

Millie took the painting down from its easel and thrust it into his hands. "I want you to have it," she said. Millie was happy to do that.

"Oh, I couldn't," he said, touched by her generosity and overcome with emotion. "At least, let me pay for it."

Hunter, who'd been watching from a seat in the auditorium, came on stage and slid the painting into a box then gave it to Jonathan. After they'd sent Jonathan on his way, they packed up the rest of the art and went to the hotel.

When Jonathan returned to Glenapp the next day, he went to the library and opened the package containing Elsie's portrait. He propped it up on the conference table and stared at it. A moment later Lord Inchcape entered. "Oh, my God!" he exclaimed, breaking down.

Jonathan held his grieving father.

Millie continued her tour, spreading not only the word about the dangers of airships, but more importantly, about life after death.

In the auditorium in York, Millie played Für Elise for an adoring crowd. They actually swooned when she played the first few bars. Doyle's portrait was displayed prominently at center of the stage, surrounded by her other paintings. It was particularly sad for Millie. It expressed her somber mood. She'd learned while she was away, that Doyle had died of a heart attack at his home in Crowborough. She felt his loss deeply. They'd become very close. Mrs. East was also cut up. They both attended his memorial service at Windlesham Manor, two days later.

Between her trips around the country, Millie had been busy in her studio all year. She kept up her art classes and piano lessons for enthusiastic clients. She was still producing portraits for a never-ending demand from people of all walks of life, although some politicians were now avoiding her due to her activism. She produced more paintings based on her visions.

One vision she'd had she found puzzling. It was of eight men carrying a carpet on their shoulders, much the same way as they'd carry a coffin. It was in close-up of the men, their faces in the chilly wind, an angry, pale-faced officer behind them in the lights. Whatever it depicted, it was dramatic, and that's why she painted it. She called it *The Last Straw,* though not sure why.

Millie also completed the other visions she'd seen earlier. *The Tomb* and *The Mass Grave* which she'd seen when she was in St. Mary's graveyard with Doyle and a later one she called *Westminster Hall,* depicting coffins lying in state. These paintings went with her on stage. And they always caused a stir.

Another one she painted was of Commander Lou Remington. She wasn't sure why she painted it. She just felt compelled to one day and so she did. His image seemed set in her mind and came to her easily. In uniform, he looked so fine, his aura in beautifully balanced colors.

She studied the finished portrait. She knew he was married. Maybe it was a crush.

In July of 1930, the Vickers airship *Howden R100* set off on its transcontinental voyage to Canada. It'd become a dual between the two behemoths. Despite backdoor requests for postponement from Cardington, the Vickers team set off for Montreal. On the way there, two incidents occurred which could have easily spelled disaster. They were lucky and survived to make a faultless return journey. Many of the Royal Airship Works team were on board for the trip, including Lou Remington, who traveled as the official representative of the United States.

After surviving serious mishaps on the outbound leg of the voyage, some of the R.A.W. staff believed they could survive anything, including the trip to India aboard their own *Cardington R101*. They felt they had no choice but to make the voyage. Vickers had thrown down the gauntlet. Rivalry between the teams had reached boiling point.

37

A FAREWELL CELEBRATION

Friday, October 3, 1930.

A ll was noise and hullabaloo in the Kings Arms when Millie and Hunter arrived around 8 o'clock, that Friday evening. The atmosphere was one of great excitement. All being well, the village's very own airship would embark on her maiden voyage tomorrow. The pub was full of locals, as well as crewmen and construction workers who'd worked on the ship. Millie chatted with crewmen. Most were delighted about the voyage. They were getting paid and jobs were scarce—yes, they were getting paid to see Egypt and India. You couldn't beat that! Adding to the crowd were spectators who'd arrived from all corners of the country to see *Cardington R101* take off. Already, thousands were gathered at the fence around the aerodrome.

Millie listened to droll comments and banter between young men, their graveyard humor depressing. She stood next to the out-of-tune honky-tonk where Hunter bashed out one tune after another. Right now, it was "I'm Sittin' On Top of the World" and everyone was singing along happily.

Through the smokey haze of cigarette-smoke, Millie recognized some of the people in a small group over by the bar. There was Binks. He looked over and raised his beer mug to her. He wasn't ignoring her this time. She smiled. They seemed to be enjoying a small celebration of their own. By the way they kept looking at one young man and the blond he was with, it looked like an engagement party. That was confirmed when she saw the handsome American commander arrive. She'd last seen him at Freddie's funeral a year ago. She wondered what he'd think if he knew she'd painted his portrait. She felt a bit silly about it. He joined the others and inspected the girl's diamond ring as she held her hand up to him. It glinted in the light. Millie saw him order champagne and they drank a toast. As they did so, Millie caught a glimpse of Hinchliffe's image in the mirror over the bar behind them.

Millie kept an eye on the American. It might be useful to talk, though at this stage, perhaps it was all a lost cause. But she wasn't going to give up until she saw that airship leave the tower tomorrow evening. As she looked over and smiled, the commander spotted her. He grinned and waved, though half-heartedly. He didn't look in the mood to talk—to her, or anyone else. There certainly were a few good-looking girls in the bar who had their eye on him. It amused her. He could have his pick.

After a while, she saw the commander nodding to his crewmen. He'd had enough. He moved toward the door. Millie leaned down to Hunter and whispered, "I'm gonna go and talk to that chap, I know him. I won't be long."

Hunter appeared disappointed as he watched her go. He'd noticed the way she'd looked over at Remington. She left the pub behind the commander, who crossed the road and started across the green. Hinchliffe came out too, but waited there. Hunter's haunting rendition of "Blue Skies" drifted behind Millie, until it was drowned by carousel music from the bright, colored lights of the fairground.

Beyond the fair, *Cardington R101* was bathed in searchlights, putting the ship on display. It looked magnificent, that could not be denied. Millie felt like a stalker. She was close to the commander now. He turned around on hearing her rustling footsteps, and then her soft voice.

"Do you think she's beautiful, Commander?"

He grinned ruefully. "No, I wouldn't call *that thing* beautiful." He was looking at her. He obviously thought *she* was.

"*My* husband flew away, too."

"Yeah, I remember."

She paused and stared sadly at the night sky, remembering the last time she'd seen Hinchliffe on the platform at Grantham.

"Every day since then I've wished I'd stopped him." She closed her eyes, reliving that awful moment. "Oh, how I've wished it!" she sighed.

"Do you think you could've?"

"Good question." She stopped to consider. "I think so. In fact, I tried, but I was too late." She paused again. She blamed herself for not putting a stop to it earlier on. "He'd been so confident, and to me he was invincible—but I had misgivings at the last moment."

"Now you warn others?"

"I try to—especially when I have those same feelings."

She noticed him fidgeting with his ring finger.

"Wears your ring? I thought you were married?"

He raised his hand looking at his finger. He seemed surprised to see it missing.

"Technically, I am, I suppose."

"Then give this up for her sake."

"I would, but it's too late, she's gone off."

Millie pointed an accusing finger toward the tower.

"Was that damned thing anything to do with it?"

"I guess it may've had something to do with it."

"I'm sorry," Millie said, picking up on his sadness.

"I met you and your husband not long before he left," the commander said.

"Yes, I remember. We were all right here in this pub."

"It must be tough for you to set foot in that place," Remington said.

"He wants the airship program stopped," she said.

"Your husband, you mean?"

"You think I'm crazy?"

"I'm not sure what to think."

"Take it from me. I'm not crazy," Millie said.

"Mrs. Hinchliffe, I must go. I have a busy day ahead."

"I suppose I'm wasting my time?"

"I don't think you've a snowball's chance in hell of stopping that thing taking off tomorrow."

Millie took his hand to shake it, and then clasped it with her other.

"I'll be here to see you all leave tomorrow," she said, looking up into his eyes.

"Goodbye, Mrs. Hinchliffe."

Millie sensed, like her, he was a lost and lonely soul. They came together, he put his arms around her and they hugged. She put her lips up to his and they kissed, softly at first, and then with passion. It felt good. It'd been more than two years. She'd forgotten what it felt like to be held in a man's arms.

"Are you going back to the pub?" she asked.

"No, I'm gonna call it a day."

She kissed him again. "Come with me," she pleaded, her voice an urgent whisper.

"You wanna to save me from all this, huh?"

"Yes, I do. I *really* do!"

"Perhaps we'll meet again, Mrs. Hinchliffe," he said.

"Yes, I hope so. Good luck, and may God be with you … And next time we meet, please call me Millie."

"You sound confident I'll make it back," he said with an amused grin.

"I don't know, but I pray you do, Commander."

He nodded. "Okay, Millie. And it's Lou by the way."

She smiled. "Lou. All right Lou. I guess we're on first name terms now."

He turned away and walked across the field, heading for the fairground. She ambled wearily back toward the pub, an ache in her body and in her heart.

Ships that pass in the night.

The carousel grew faint and Hunter's honky-tonk and the laughter in the pub more distinct. He was now playing the mournful song "What'll I do?"

Hinchliffe was still outside the pub, patiently waiting. He followed Millie back inside.

38

DEPARTURE

Saturday, October 4, 1930.

Millie had found a room at The Swan in Bedford, near the old bridge. Hunter had recommended it. He stayed at the White Bear nearby, with the other journalists. Just before she drifted off, Millie had a vision. In closeup, she saw a man's hands polishing a woman's shoe. The shoe was dated, but stylish in its day—black and dark green with a Louis heel, steel beaded and embroidered. When it gleamed, the shoe was held up to the man's lips and kissed tenderly, as though it were 'she'. The hands wrapped the sacred memento in a square of azure silk and tucked it inside an old, brown leather briefcase. The lips belonged to Lord Thomson. Who 'she' was, was not revealed.

The next day was Saturday. Millie and Hunter met in town, where they saw many young crewmen in new dark blue uniforms making their way to Cardington. After lunch, they went to Cardington Field. Millie tried valiantly to get into Cardington House to see Colmore and Major Scott, or anyone of rank, but was refused admission. An RAF man had been posted on the door to keep people out, including reporters. Millie decided that after another meal, they should come back and hang around the entrance gate, near the tower. They could possibly get to someone as they entered. For Hunter, it'd be easy, he'd be allowed access to interview the VIPs and officers for the big feature in tomorrow's Sunday papers.

The weather was cold and gusty all afternoon, and as dusk fell, the sky grew more ominous by the hour. Millie wondered if departure might be postponed. As the daylight faded, the lights of the fair grew brighter. Millie looked up at the girls on the Ferris wheel. It didn't look like a comfortable place to be sitting on a night like this, but the view from there must have been spectacular.

She surveyed the crowds gathered at the fence around the circumference of the field. People had come from all over, eager to witness this historic event. They sat in their cars, many asleep, covered in blankets, after their long drive. She watched clowns on stilts weaving their way through the multitude, encouraging people to visit the fair. Sounds were mixed, shouting from the crowds, hollering from vendors eager to sell souvenirs and hot dogs, screaming and laughter from the fair and the never-ending carousel music. Capping all this, was the thumping brass band near the tower, with its oom-pah-pah, oom-pah-pah, its clarity ebbing and flowing with wind gusts.

At around 6 o'clock, Millie spied Thomson's black Daimler rolling onto the field toward the gate. It was followed by a gray Air Ministry van. She pushed her way to the gate as it opened and the limousine slowed down. The lights were on inside, so that spectators could catch a glimpse of Thomson. He waved gaily while the crowd cheered. He looked extremely happy—royal even, as he doffed his hat. Millie got alongside the car and shouted through the open window.

"Lord Thomson, I must speak to you, sir. Please, it's vitally important!"

Millie could see he'd spotted her, and was irked. She heard him bark to the chauffeur, "Don't stop, driver!"

The limousine sped forward, leaving the gray van behind. Millie kept close to the fence, as the van slowly rumbled through, stepping alongside it and walking in, unseen. She ambled slowly down toward the tower in the dusk, blending in with invited guests. The Daimler reached the tower where a BBC crew waited with a dozen reporters from the national dailies, including Hunter. Thomson jumped out smiling and waving. The van moved off to one side, where a crew was ready to unload it. When Millie reached the crowd of reporters, she stood in the shadows listening.

"How do you feel about the flight, sir?"

Thomson gazed up at the airship. "All my life, I've prepared myself for this moment."

"Any second thoughts?"

"Absolutely none. There's certainly nothing to fear," Thomson answered.

"The weather is kicking up, sir. Sure she can take it?"

Thomson held on to his hat. "This airship is as strong as the mighty Forth Bridge!"

"Do you think your departure will be delayed?"

"The experts will be looking at the weather. *They'll* make that determination."

"Will you be making the whole voyage, bearing in mind you have a tight schedule?" Hunter asked.

"The Prime Minister has given me strict instructions to return by the twentieth of October. Yes, I'll make the entire journey in this great airship."

Behind her, Millie heard a moan go up from the unloading crew as the van doors were flung open.

"Gordon Bennett!"

"Someone's gotta be jokin', right?"

"Cor blimey!"

"Bloody 'ell!"

"Holy smoke!"

Millie realized it was all about Thomson's luggage. Suddenly, she felt a tap on her shoulder. She looked round and up into the face of one of Thomson's bowler hatted stooges—the Raven.

His accent was London. "Mrs. Hinchliffe, Lord Thomson would like a word."

"Er, all right," Millie stammered. She hoped she wasn't going to be arrested.

"Follow me, madam."

As she followed him, Millie witnessed the scene she'd painted weeks ago. It snapped in her brain like a color photograph. Eight men were carrying a heavy, rolled-up Persian carpet on their shoulders—as though it were a coffin. They walked in her direction. Behind them, coming from the tower, Captain Irwin was striding toward them, his pale face like thunder. She felt it was significant in some way. Old beaky-nose led her to a wooden building beside the tower and then to a small, dimly-lit room with a desk and a chair and not much else.

"Wait here, please, madam." He left, closing the door behind him. Millie worried she might hear it being locked from the outside, but she didn't. She was left alone for ten minutes or so, until the door swung open and Thomson entered. Up close, in that small room, at six-foot-five, he was intimidating. Nevertheless, he removed his hat respectfully and calmly.

"I see you've snuck in, Mrs. Hinchliffe, despite this being a restricted area," he said.

"Lord Thomson, I've come one last time—"

"Mrs. Hinchliffe, I know why you've come. But you're wasting your time. I realize you're in a delicate state of mind. I'm prepared to give you a few minutes on the understanding that you will *not* make any more fuss. Will you agree to that?" He smiled sympathetically.

Millie considered for a moment. She supposed he was being reasonable. There would be little she could do. Having a tantrum wouldn't solve anything. "I'll agree—if you'll hear me out."

"Very well, I will listen—but we've been all through this before, haven't we?" he said patiently.

"This flight must not take place. I know you think I'm crazy because I talk to my dead husband."

"Well, yes—"

"The point is, sir, he's told me things about this airship which are indisputable. It's too heavy—built too strongly. The cover's gone brittle. It's going to tear off. It's doped with highly inflammable chemicals that'll burn like mad. They've loosened the gas bags to get more gas in them—now they're unstable. The engines are underpowered—"

"Yes, yes, Mrs. Hinchliffe! You've been saying this over and over. Most of these things have been mentioned in the press."

"This ship is going to crash and burn along with everyone on board —including *you*. My husband wants to prevent this tragedy."

"Mrs. Hinchliffe!" he said, shaking his head vehemently. "This maiden voyage *will* take place as scheduled."

"And you're *all* going to die!"

"No one's going to die. This ship is virtually *unbreakable*."

"They said the *Titanic* was *unsinkable!* Lord Thomson, if you think all this, why did you make out your will last night. Is it because you don't have as much confidence in this airship as you pretend?"

Thomson was stopped in his tracks. He looked troubled. He was the only person who knew he'd done that. Even his personal secretary didn't know. He'd stashed it in his desk drawer 'just in case'.

"A normal precaution—" he replied after a moment.

"You carry a woman's shoe in your briefcase. You keep it polished and wrapped in a piece of vivid blue silk. It's a memento. Something you treasure—it belonged to someone you love *very* much."

Thomson was stunned. His jaw dropped. "How—"

"You think it'll bring you luck. *It won't!*"

Thomson choked into his hand. "We are honor and duty bound, madam," he spluttered.

"I knew someone just like you. A person who was trying to impress someone *they* loved," Millie said. "And that's *exactly* what you're doing."

"Who was he?"

"*Her* name was Elsie Mackay," Millie answered.

Thomson understood, but didn't comment. He made for the door. "Don't forget our agreement. No fuss."

"God be with you, Lord Thomson."

Thomson turned back to her, now with resignation and humility, his aura a blaze of purple, set in black with streaks of crimson. "And with *you*, Mrs. Hinchliffe."

After he'd gone, Millie pondered his character. He was a man on a foolish mission, but she'd misjudged him in some ways. He was obviously very much in love with someone and she sensed that love wasn't returned in full measure. She knew that unrequited love would cost a lot of men their lives tonight.

Millie followed Thomson out after a few moments; the bowler-hatted one was waiting. He escorted her to the gate, where he left her with the crowd in the wind and drizzle. She felt beaten, but understood her chances of success had been slim to none. Maybe the weather would cause a postponement. Conditions were certainly getting worse. She remained in the crowd, watching the tower. Presently, she saw a young man, who'd been in the limousine with Thomson, coming through the gate. He was in a hurry. She ran alongside him.

"You were with Lord Thomson in the car, weren't you?" she asked.

"That's right, ma'am. I'm his valet," he said proudly, his head in the air.

"I must talk to you," Millie said, trying to keep up. He stopped at one of the souvenir stalls along the fence, doing his best to ignore her. He called to the vendor and pointed to the key rings.

"I'll take a couple of them, please. One red and one blue."

"Right you are, sir," said the vendor.

The valet looked at postcards with the union flag and *'R101'* emblazoned on the front in bold letters. "Oh, and I'll take a few o' them." He paid and started off again.

"Please stop and talk to me," Millie implored.

"No, miss. I mustn't. Got orders not to."

"Listen to me, you must not—" Millie began. But he was gone in a flash on his way back to the tower.

As Millie watched him disappear, she noticed Remington striding toward the gate with an RAF man. She was about to approach him when she saw a gray-haired man in his sixties, huddled in a dark raincoat, waiting for him. She stood to one side. The commander hadn't seen her. The older man looked upset. The two men embraced warmly. She listened.

"John, you shouldn't have driven all the way down here," the commander said.

"I had to come. I've been brooding all week. Mary said 'Go on, John, you go and see him off.' So here I am."

"That was thoughtful of you—you know I'm real pleased to see you."

"Charlotte isn't here anywhere, I suppose, is she?" the old man asked, peering around.

"No, she's washed her hands of me."

"I can't believe that. I hope you'll try and see her when you get back."

"I've tried. I went to her parents' house, but they wouldn't open the door to me."

"Oh, no—" the old man said, screwing up his face.

"I'll definitely come visit you, when I return, John. Then, I guess, I'll head back to the States."

The older man was heartbroken. "God, I'm so sorry. Look, if anything changes—the cottage will always be yours, you know that."

"Thanks, John."

Millie watched them shake hands and embrace again. The old man's eyes were filled with tears. "Good luck, son. Make sure you come back safe," he said and then, turning away abruptly, he disappeared. No sooner was he gone, than Brancker appeared beside the commander. After they'd greeted one another, Millie stepped beside them.

"Good evening, gentlemen," she said.

"Millie. What on earth are you doing here?" Brancker snapped. "I'd give you a hug, but my hands are rather full."

"Then I'll kiss *you*," she said, planting a kiss on his cheek. She smiled at the commander and kissed him too. "I've come to tell you what Ray— " she began.

Brancker exploded. "Millie, Millie, don't! Just go home! The ship will leave tonight. Thomson has decreed it." He turned away. "Come, Lou, we must go. *Goodbye*, Millie!"

The American gave Millie an apologetic smile. He grabbed Brancker's case and they marched off through the gate to the tower with many others, ambling trance-like to be consumed by the tethered beast. Millie thought they were all under its evil spell. To Millie's surprise, she saw Commander Remington turn back toward her. He plonked down Brancker's case.

"I apologize for Sir Sefton. He's on edge," he said. He then took Millie in his arms and kissed her lips. Millie was somewhat astonished but kissed him back passionately.

"I needed someone to kiss me goodbye, Millie," Remington said finally, still holding her tight.

"I am glad to be that someone, Lou."

"Me too."

"Please come back safely home," Millie urged.

He let her go. "I'm gonna try like hell."

With that, he was gone. A clown appeared with a handful of flyers and stuffed one in Millie's hand. It said:

LET THE GREAT CLAIRVOYANT
MADAM HARANDAH
THE ROMANIAN GYPSY
TELL YOUR FORTUNE
PSYCHIC READING
PALM READING
TAROT CARDS
3d each

She wondered what this gypsy would have to say about all this. Millie looked up from her reading and there was Joe Binks, the young engineer. He grinned at her as he entered the gate.

"What you doin' 'ere, Missus?" he said.

"It's Joe, I remember. You're on this voyage, are you?" Millie asked.

"Yes, indeedee, sure am!"

"Joe, this is important. Keep a look out for my husband. I know you've seen him. He's told me about you."

Binks looked confused and puzzled. He looked about them with embarrassment, in case they were overheard. "What for?"

"Listen to him, Joe! Listen to him! Do *whatever* he says. Do you understand?"

Binks nodded uncertainly. He kept walking, looking over his shoulder at Millie until he was out of sight. A few minutes later, when Binks entered the tower, he caught a glimpse of Hinchliffe standing amongst the officers surrounding Thomson. Hinchliffe gave him a casual salute and a wink.

Hunter exited the gate and found Millie. "Millie, I saw that big roll of carpet the men were carrying in your last painting," he said.

"Yes, I saw it, too."

"It's Thomson's Persian rug. He's having it laid down in the ship for a banquet they're having for the King of Egypt."

"Ah, yes of course. That's it!" Millie said.

"Damned thing weighs a ton! What a to-do that was. Captain Irwin was fit to be tied," Hunter said.

"So, what's happening?" Millie asked.

"They took it on board. The visitors have come ashore and the press has been told to clear off."

"When are they leaving?"

"There's some doubt. I heard they're having a big pow-wow about the weather," Hunter said.

Millie and Hunter hung around at the fence with the crowd, their backs to the wind. Rumors were circulating about postponement, but nobody really knew anything. About forty minutes later, one of the engines started and a cloud of foul-smelling, black smoke drifted over the field. The crowd cheered. Soon, three of the other engines were cranked up. The airship sat for another ten minutes. They appeared to be having trouble with the last engine. Eventually, they got it started and its propeller whirled in the searchlights. After a few minutes, all five engines sounded smooth. The crowd cheered wildly and the headlights of hundreds of cars flashed and horns sounded.

Millie looked at the crewmen's families' faces in the crowd. Some looked fearful as they signaled to the ship with hand-held flashlights. Sickened, she heard them expressing reservations. While the ship was still moored to the tower, water ballast was dropped at the bow. A fine mist appeared sparkling in the lights, close to the tower. Then one of the engines got louder as its revs increased and the ship backed away. The bow fell away to starboard and it drifted over the crowd, dropping more ballast. Screams and moans went up along the fence from the unfortunate ones, soaked to the skin. Millie and Hunter were lucky not to get doused.

The crowd watched as *Cardington R101*, the mightiest airship the world had ever seen, moved slowly over the field, her red and green running lights flashing. She wallowed into the darkness. Everyone began leaving the airfield. Soon, all roads to Bedford and the surrounding areas were choked with traffic and pedestrians.

Hunter dropped Millie at Bedford Station, where she caught the train to London and Croydon. On the train, the wheels reminded her of the last time she'd seen Hinchliffe waving goodbye. She had that same sinking feeling. That seemed a lifetime ago. She knew he'd be on the airship tonight. She also knew there'd be nothing he could do to save them. They were doomed.

Millie reached Croydon at about 9 o'clock, where she caught the last bus to the village. From there, she walked up the lane in the dark under her umbrella to her beloved cottage. She was greeted at the door by Kate, who rushed in and made her a cup of tea and rustled up some ham sandwiches.

"How did it go?" Kate asked, while Sinclair stood at her side. Chilled and damp, Millie sank into an armchair shaking her head wearily. Sinclair nodded, pursing his lips in resignation.

39

PASSAGE TO INDIA

Saturday, October 4, 1930.

After checking on the sleeping children and eating her sandwiches, Millie had a bath and stumbled into bed. She lay with her lantern glowing beside her. Despite her exhaustion, she had trouble sleeping. After a time, she began to doze. She dreamed of the airship battered by wind and rain, crossing London and weaving its way through the South Downs of Kent, toward the English coast.

*

Later, while Millie slept fitfully, *Cardington R101* was departing the English coast close to the Old Cliffe End Inn, between Hastings and Dungeness. As it sailed over at a strange crabbing angle, it was watched by revelers, sheltering under umbrellas in increasing winds. They waved their beer mugs up at the ship and cheered. *Cardington R101* trundled on into the darkness, over a raging sea, at eight-hundred feet.

*

The ghost of Captain Hinchliffe had been on the airship ever since everyone had gone aboard. He'd witnessed the weather conference in the chartroom. It'd been pointed out by the meteorologist that the weather *could* worsen; nonetheless, the decision was made to leave. Hinchliffe saw that this was much against his friend, Captain Irwin's will. He'd been bullied and shamed into it.

A test run was made around the town, 'a salute to Bedford' they'd called it. After getting airborne, there was no way they would've been able to land back at Cardington tower, the weather now much too severe. All they could do was press on. And that's just what they did. Hinchliffe was in great distress. It reminded him of his own foolish (or what seemed utterly foolish now), deadly Atlantic flight with Elsie. He paced around the ship. He saw how passengers were suffering with their nerves. Many were getting drunk, which he thought was probably as good a plan as any.

Maybe they all should drink themselves into oblivion!

They crossed London and then weaved their way through the Downs to the coast. He marveled at the skill of his good friend Johnny Johnston. He'd been glad to have him in the navigator's seat many a time—he was the best. As they crossed the English coastline and moved out over the black, raging water, Hinchliffe saw the look of dread on passengers' faces. Thomson himself was upbeat and completely confident—too confident. After enjoying a cigar in the smoking room with a number of others, and witnessing the sight of the French coast, he went to bed and wrote up his journal. He was jubilant. Hinchliffe leaned over his shoulder, reading his words:

His Majesty's Airship Cardington R101

Saturday October 4th, 1930.

A successful day. Airship standing up to gale admirably. Having crossed the English Channel, we are now heading toward Paris. Tomorrow, I anticipate enjoying sunshine over the Mediterranean. Today, we have put an end to all the naysayers. Success is within our grasp.

Hinchliffe then saw Thomson admiring the key ring and the postcards his valet had brought back from the souvenir vendor. He watched him happily slip the keyring into his dressing gown pocket. It was the red one.

Throughout the evening, Hinchliffe stayed close to his good friend, Sefton Brancker. He knew Brancker was terrified, he had been even before he'd arrived at the tower. But he'd gotten pretty sozzled and was feeling no pain. He was quite comical, with his monocle screwed tightly into his eye socket. Hinchliffe was glad he was just about paralytic when Lou Remington helped him into this cabin and laid him down on his bunk. The American was a good fellow. Hinchliffe liked him. It was a pity most of them would be dead before the night was over.

After crossing the French coast at St. Quentin, the airship struggled against what was now a full-fledged gale. The weather had become much worse, as Captain Irwin had worried it might. They were blown way off course toward the dreaded Beauvais Ridge—a place Irwin had been anxious to avoid. Hinchliffe paced around the ship, looking in on his friends. Brancker and Johnston were asleep in their cabins. Thomson was now also well away, snoring.

The ship came in low over Beauvais. Hinchliffe stood beside Captain Irwin and Commander Remington, gazing down at the city. It would have been a wonderful sight under normal circumstances, but not tonight. It was time to change the watch, but Irwin decided to remain in his place until they'd cleared Beauvais Ridge, then he'd hand over to the relief officers.

Hinchliffe left the control car and walked down to the crew's quarters, where he saw Binks still fast asleep in his bunk. His foreman was trying to wake him.

"Come on Joe, you should have been on watch by now! Bell's waiting for you," the foreman said, pushing a mug of cocoa at the bleary-eyed Binks.

"Oh bugger! I don't have time for that, Shorty. Bell's gonna be mad!"

"You'd better drink it, mate, or I'll be mad," the foreman warned.

Binks swallowed it down and sprinted out and along the catwalk to his engine car, followed by Hinchliffe. While lightning flashed, Binks slithered down the steel ladder, hanging on for his life and into his engine car. Bell gave him a dirty look.

"Well, thanks for coming Joe," Bell said, eyeing the wall clock. "Glad you could make it!"

Binks peered out the window and gasped. He'd seen something in a flash of lightning.

"What's the matter with you?" demanded Bell.

"I just saw a church steeple," Binks whimpered. "Only yards away!"

Bell pushed Binks aside, and looked out. "Silly sod. You're still asleep. I can't see anything."

Suddenly the ship dived, throwing Binks back against the engine. "Oh, bloody 'ell!"

"Don't panic Joe, it's only the storm," Bell assured him.

But then, above their heads, they heard the rumble of stampeding feet.

"Something's very wrong, Ginger. I'm *really* scared," Binks whimpered.

The ship leveled out, but as it did, they felt harmonic vibration, and then an awful creaking and groaning. Suddenly, the telegraph bell rang. They saw the indicator move to SLOW. This filled Binks with terror. "Oh, no! Now what?" he groaned. There were more pounding feet. "Oh, blimey!"

The ship dived again and both men were thrown backward a second time. Now, they heard Chief Coxswain 'Sky' Hunt's voice above in the crew's quarters. "We're down lads!"

"Oh, no, that's Mr. 'unt. We've had it now!" Binks sobbed.

Hinchliffe had stuck with these two characters all through this episode. Hinchliffe knew Binks could see him, when he showed himself. The time had come to help Binks and Bell. In mere moments, after the commotion above, and being suspended at a strange, almost vertical downward angle, the ship gently settled on the ground. But the feelings of relief for these two men were short-lived. They felt massive explosions start at the bow and work in their direction, toward the stern. All around them was suddenly ablaze.

Binks stared out the window from the center of this inferno at the muddy, wooded plateau. It was difficult to believe they were down— there'd been no jarring crash. They watched the rapidly disappearing airship cover being devoured by fire and the vast steel skeleton exposed in blinding light. Hinchliffe sensed their terror, although he couldn't feel their pain. Their faces and bodies were being blistered by the searing heat, especially their legs, where flames were licking up through floor.

"Safety first. What a *bleedin'* joke!" Bell shouted.

"Sweet Mother of Jesus, save us," Binks cried.

"We've got to get out. This thing's gonna blow any second," Bell hollered.

Hinchliffe knew they'd be done for if that starter engine petrol tank blew up. He stood near the doorway, enveloped in flames and smoke. Binks looked up and saw Hinchliffe. His eyes bulged out of his head.

"Don't move, Mr. Binks!" Hinchliffe yelled, putting up his hands.

Binks had no doubt Hinchliffe was there to help them. "Hey, hold on a sec, Ginger. Trust me on this," he shouted, putting a hand on Bell's chest. Bell frowned, but didn't move. A moment later, without warning, one of the ballast tanks above ruptured, sending a torrent of water cascading over them and their car. The flames were doused and the car cooled momentarily. The two men picked up their wet coats, and threw them over their heads.

"Come on, run for your lives," Hinchliffe shouted.

"Let's get out of here!" Binks screamed.

They climbed out onto the car's entry platform into intense heat and blinding fire, and jumped. They fell on their hands and knees into the mud, then dashed, slipping and sliding through smoke and steam to a safe distance, where they collapsed on the ground, badly burned, but alive.

"Thank you, dear merciful Lord God in Heaven!" Binks exclaimed. "And thank you, *Captain 'inchliffe!'*"

"I owe you one, Joe. I'm sorry I was mean to you about being late, mate!" Bell croaked. "But how did you know water would come down on us like that, eh?"

Binks laughed. "Captain 'inchliffe told me. It's a gift, Ginger."

"'Who is this Captain 'inchliffe?"

"Right now, mate, he's our *best friend*," Binks said, with a chuckle.

*

When the chief coxswain shouted, "We're down lads," it woke Millie from her slumbers. She heard it as clearly as if he'd been standing in her bedroom. Suddenly, the airship was foundering in front of her, in a steep dive. She watched as the bow gently kissed the ground. The great bulk seemed to be hardly moving. Millie saw the ship's nose cone plough a furrow in the ground well into the forest, which bordered the grassy terrain. She heard tree branches snapping off, clanking sheep bells, and wild bleating, in all the confusion.

Millie watched the airship gently settle down onto the plain with half its structure in the trees, and then gasped in horror as six million cubic feet of hydrogen erupted in a series of explosions. Flames lit up the French countryside for miles. She heard the cries of hapless souls on board, and could smell the foul, burning odors wafting across the fields. A hundred yards from the wreck, she saw the diminutive rabbit poacher sitting in shock, clinging to his terror-stricken prize. The eyes of both creatures seemed to protrude from their heads, so great was their dread.

The scene unfolded as if Millie were in a movie theater. Men emerged from the wreck, all of them blackened, burned, unrecognizable. They fell down on the ground in the mud and merciful rain, moaning. Soon, a column of lights came across the fields from a local village—rescuers, carrying lanterns, stretchers, ropes, spades, shovels and sheets.

Millie's vision faded. She sat up holding her head, trying to catch her breath. What could she do? Nothing. She lay back down, numb, for half an hour, until she'd recovered her composure. She got up, went to the kitchen and made tea. Presently, Kate joined her, telling her she couldn't sleep either. Then Sinclair came down. Millie told them what she'd seen. They took it seriously. They sat drinking tea for an hour in an unhappy state, and then returned to their beds to wait for morning. They'd listen to the news and find out what happened.

Sinclair was up before six and turned on the BBC for the 6 o'clock news. They listened again at seven, and at eight, and nine. There was no news of the airship. Not a word. The fact that there wasn't even a progress report, seemed ominous. If only she could contact Hunter. He'd know what was going on, Millie thought. She jumped in the car and went to the phone booth in the village and got through to his desk. He confirmed her worst fears.

"Millie, *Cardington R101* crashed in France on a hillside near Beauvais—just as you said it would," he said.

He'd been up all night monitoring foreign news outlets. They had a shortwave radio in the office, and knew about it almost as soon as it happened from French radio reports. He said they thought there were eight survivors. The *Sunday Express* printing presses had been stopped during the night, so they could write the story. They were putting out a late edition.

40

CAXTON HALL

L ord Inchcape sat perfectly still in Millie's ornate armchair, in which many other notables had sat before him. He wore a Harris Tweed jacket of gray tones, a white shirt and a black and blue tartan cravat. His attitude was different from the last time they'd spoken at Glenapp Castle.

"I have a confession. I must admit I didn't come here just to have my portrait painted," he said suddenly.

Millie put down her pallet and brushes.

"No, please, don't get me wrong. I want the painting. I'll pay you handsomely for it. But it wasn't my main reason, that's all."

"Why *did* you come?"

"First of all, I want to pay for Elsie's portrait. I was so very impressed—and it's given us all so much comfort."

"No—that was my gift to Jonathan."

"I also want you to know that, although our religion frowns on communication with the dead, I admire you very much for everything you've done."

Millie sneered with self-contempt. "I failed miserably."

"It may seem to you that you've not succeeded, but you have, in ways that you can't comprehend. You've been very brave."

"Elsie was very brave too, you know."

"Yes, I realize that now."

Lord Inchcape put his hand in his pocket and pulled out a small box. He handed it to Millie.

"I wanted you to have this," he said.

Millie opened it. It contained an ornate, gold crucifix on a chain. She cradled it in the palm of her hand.

"It was one of Elsie's. It's been in our family for centuries."

Millie was touched. "I'll treasure it. Thank you."

"There's something I ought to tell you, though I was sworn to secrecy at the time. But *that* doesn't matter now."

Millie frowned. "What is it?"

"Regarding the settlement: I was under enormous pressure from every quarter—you have *no* idea. Lord Thomson called me, urging me to make a settlement. He said you deserved the money and that your husband was a great pioneer. He said you'd made his life difficult—but he admired you. He'd followed your every move. Said you were one of the most courageous women he'd ever met."

Millie was incredulous. "My Goodness!"

Oh dear, poor Lord Thomson. I was so hard on that man.

"He wasn't such a bad old chap, was he? He said good things about Elsie too." At this, he dropped his head.

She remembered her thoughts of Thomson at the tower and all the qualities his aura conveyed. "No, he certainly wasn't. Misguided, that's all."

"There's something else," Inchcape said, putting his hand in his pocket again. Suddenly, he held up Hinchliffe's lucky black cat charm, swinging from side to side on its string of worry beads. Millie eyes widened in astonishment, as it swung in front of her face.

"I believe this belonged to your husband?" he said.

Millie sat in her bedroom at her writing table, his worry beads beside her. She'd decided to write a book. The title would be: *The Return of Captain Hinchliffe.* Her goal was to educate people about life after death. Hunter had introduced her to a publisher interested to look at a finished manuscript. He also said he'd gladly give her assistance. Millie stopped after writing a few sentences to reflect on the past eight years. She fingered the worry beads as she glanced out the window at the garden. The flowers that she and Hinchliffe had planted the year he met Elsie were finished for the season. Most of the leaves had fallen, creating a golden carpet. The climbing rose he'd planted below the pergola clung to the structure, leafless and without blooms.

There was a sound across the room and she turned toward it. Hinchliffe had materialized, holding a white rose. "They were beautiful this year, weren't they?" he said, referring to the climbing roses.

"I was just thinking that, and of you and our friends," Millie said.

"I know you were."

"Are they with you?"

"I've spent a lot of time with Bird, Johnny and old Branks. They've been in a bad state. They say they feel like murderers for killing all those boys. I've not seen Thomson yet. He has much to answer for. I would not want to be him. That burden will be heavy on his soul for some time."

Tears were welling up in Millie's eyes. "You've come for a *reason, haven't* you, Ray?"

"Yes, I have. I know you'll cope, Millie."

"Yes, I suppose, I will somehow."

"I've been happy that George Hunter has been so helpful. He's a bit rough around the edges, but he's got a good heart. He thinks the world of you, you know."

"I've been lucky to have him around. I must admit he's grown on me."

"I liked that American fellow. That was a nice portrait you did of him. I know you admired him."

"Yes, he was lovely," Millie said with a rueful smile. "He reminded me of *you*."

"Not as reckless—or as good-looking. But he's out of the picture now, Millie."

Millie nodded sadly. Hinchliffe laid the rose down on her manuscript and moved close to her. "I've loved you so much, Millie. I tried so hard. I was foolish—very foolish. I'm *truly, truly* sorry."

"Oh, Ray. I'll always love you, you know."

"It's time for you to live your life now, Millie," Hinchliffe said, tenderly kissing her forehead.

She sobbed quietly as he faded away. She picked up the rose and smelled its fragrance, closing her eyes.

Later that day, Millie went down to her studio and worked on the finishing touches of Hinchliffe's portrait. She'd never felt so completely alone. Over the weeks since the crash of *Cardington R101*, she'd felt the need to complete it, as though this was the right time— the end of a major chapter. Hinchliffe stood before his Sopwith Camel, dressed for flight in his leather greatcoat, pilot's cap and goggles pushed up over his forehead. She painted him with his black leather eye-patch—it gave him that proud, indomitable look—the stuff of the British Empire!

*

It was dark and it was cold when Millie arrived at Caxton Hall in a black Daimler, sent by the organizers to collect her from Pickwick Cottage. The Sinclairs traveled with her, leaving the children with a newly hired nanny. Despite the weather, there were throngs of people under the canopy awaiting Millie's arrival at the front steps of the building. Two festive Christmas trees, decorated with colored lights, stood each side of the entrance. An advertisement in a glass case announced coming events.

TONIGHT 8 pm

MRS. HINCHLIFFE SPEAKS

LIFE AFTER DEATH

Speed Graphics flashed as Millie elegantly eased herself out of the limousine onto the sidewalk. For a few moments she posed, beautifully dressed in black furs and a striking red cloche hat, her face radiant and perfectly made up. Photographers and reporters pushed forward excitedly around her, calling out questions.

"Mrs. Hinchliffe, what have you come to tell us this evening?"

"I am overjoyed! And tonight, I shall tell you why," Millie responded.

"Is it true you're writing a book ma'am?

"How do you feel about airships now?"

Millie closed eyes, pained. Her long lashes fluttered. "I'm very sad —and extremely bitter, as you can imagine. I suppose hard lessons have been learned by our government—at least we can only hope so!"

She made her way to the doors and was escorted along a corridor leading to the rear of the stage in the Great Hall. There was an excited buzz in the auditorium filled with mostly older ladies dressed in their

Sunday best. At last, the house lights were dimmed and a voice came over the speakers.

"Ladies and gentlemen, welcome to Caxton Hall. It gives us great pleasure to bring you here tonight a lady who needs no introduction, a person whom the British people have taken to their hearts. A lady who has for the past two years issued dire warnings—warnings from the grave. Mrs. Emilie Hinchliffe will speak to you about her experiences and the subject of life after death. Please welcome, *Mrs. Emilie Hinchliffe!*"

Enthusiastic applause erupted. All eyes watched the dark blue stage curtains in anticipation. And then, to everyone's delight, came the gentle strains of Beethoven's Moonlight Sonata. The Great Hall fell silent. The curtains slowly opened to reveal Millie, at a grand piano, dressed in cobalt blue, surrounded by her artwork, displayed on easels, each bathed in its own beam of light: The newly completed portrait of *Captain Hinchliffe* at center, *Elsie Mackay, The Endeavour, Sir Sefton Brancker, Major Herbert Scott, Mrs. East, Sir Arthur Conan Doyle, The Death of Freddie Marsh, The Last Straw, Death of R101 Near Paris, R101 & The Rabbit Poacher, The Mass Grave, Westminster Hall,* and *The Tomb at St. Mary's.* Millie had recently completed a portrait of *Lord Thomson of Cardington,* and it too, stood proudly with the rest.

When Millie had finished playing the first movement, she got up and came to the lectern amid cheers and more applause. She looked down into the front row seats into the faces of Mrs. East, George Hunter, the Sinclairs, Reverend Grey, Barney, the Blacksmith, Jonathan Mackay and Lord Inchcape. Also in that row were Joe Binks and Arthur Bell. The men in bowlers were noticeably absent. As applause died down, and people took their seats, Millie instinctively scanned the auditorium for Hinchliffe. She checked the end seat on the back row where he always sat. It was the only empty seat in the house. A wave of sadness washed over her and her heart almost stopped. He'd gone. She'd be on her own from now on. For solace, she put her hand to her neck touching Elsie's gold crucifix, preparing herself to begin. But before she did, she thought of Doyle. She'd miss him too. He'd been good to her—like a protective father. She remembered his words, and did as he'd instructed. She lifted her head high and spoke boldly to those at the back of the auditorium.

"Good evening, my name is Emilie Hinchliffe." More applause. "I've come here tonight to tell you my story," she gestured to the relevant subject of artwork as she spoke. "It's about an heiress, an aeroplane, a ghost and the mightiest airship the world has ever seen. I know you've read the story of what happened to me, and to my husband and to many of his friends just recently. Tonight, I'm going to tell you the *whole* story. During and after that terrible war, Ouija boards became an obsession. How could they not, with so many of our husbands, sons, fathers and brothers lost—not to mention our wonderful sisters, who went to nurse those very men at the Front in those fields of death, to comfort and to heal, and who were, themselves, killed. My husband always called them 'Angels of Mercy'. There wasn't a family that hadn't lost *someone*. ..."

*

After the crash of *Cardington R101* and the bodies had been removed, four items of note were found: a monocle, a red key ring marked *R101*, a stylish woman's shoe and a smoldering Persian carpet.

*

The next Spring, Hunter arrived at Pickwick Cottage in a van he'd borrowed. It was full of timber he'd bought from the local wood yard, along with tools, nails and white paint. He set about completing the picket fence Hinchliffe had started a long time ago. He was ably assisted by Sinclair and Joan.

*

The following year, a government report was issued after an extensive, well-managed inquiry. No blame was cast. The cause of the disaster was due to a loss of gas, the report stated, and not due to any structural failure. There was no criticism of Lord Thomson, the Air Ministry or the Royal Airship Works at Cardington. Nor was any fault found with the ship's captain, her officers or her crew.

*

In that same year, *Cardington R101's* sister ship, *Howden R100* constructed by Vickers, was carefully dismantled and systematically destroyed. It was announced by the Prime Minister, Ramsay MacDonald, that the British Airship Program had been terminated.

Millie's vision of the tomb in St. Mary's Churchyard, Cardington.
Photograph courtesy of Jane Harvey.
Artwork by Eddie Ankers.

WEATHER MAP OF NORTH ATLANTIC OCEAN
March 13, 1928.

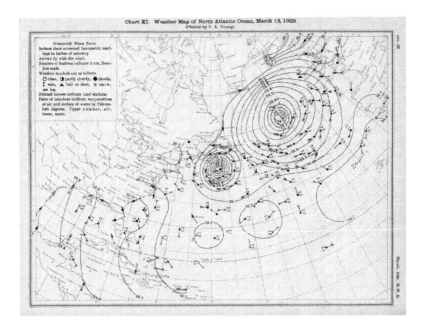

Reprinted by permission of American Meteorological Society

This weather map was current around noon. The low
pressure system moved toward the east during the flight of
Endeavour.

THE FLIGHT OF *ENDEAVOUR* MARCH 13, 1928

&

NORTH ATLANTIC CURRENTS

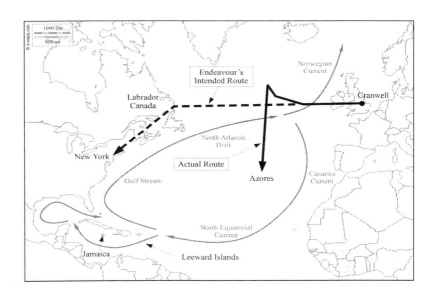

North Atlantic map courtesy of d-map.com.

Route and currents by John Taylor

AUTHOR'S NOTE

This is a work of fiction based on actual events. It is my hope that this novel piques the reader's interest in this dramatic era of aviation history, especially concerning the brave women aviators of that period—and there were many whose stories have been forgotten.

Some characters are based on real people, others are fictional. Some events in the novel took place, others did not. After some years of research, I took what I thought was the essence of the characters involved and built on those qualities for dramatic effect, with fictional characters woven into the story to take part and to witness events.

I took liberties for dramatic effect with information drawn from many books. Actual events on board during flights, as well as the dialogue throughout the novel is, of course, conjecture. However, much of the dialogue during the seances is true.

ACKNOWLEDGMENTS

Special thanks to my consulting editor at LCD Editing (lcdediting.com) who has put many years into this project.

I am also indebted to John Taylor, lighter-than-air flight test engineer and consultant and writer of *Principles of Aerostatics: The Theory of LTA Flight,* who conducted a technical review and spent many hours reading and critiquing this manuscript and offering a wealth of advice, not only regarding airships, but also on formatting and preparing this book for publication.

Artwork and book cover design by Anthony Close, Dartmouth, Great Britain.

BIBLIOGRAPHY AND SOURCES

Inspiration, information and facts were drawn from an array of books, newspapers, magazines and documents of the period, including:

The Return of Captain W.G.R. Hinchliffe D.F.C., A.F.C. Emilie Hinchliffe

The Airmen Who Would Not Die. John Fuller. G.P. Putnam's Sons, New York.

Report of the R101 Inquiry. Presented by the Secretary of State for Air to Parliament, March 1931.

Icarus Over the Humber. T.W. Jamison. Lampada Press.

To Ride the Storm. Sir Peter Masefield. William Kimber, London.

Millionth Chance. James Lessor. House of Stratus, Stratus Books Ltd., England.

Sefton Brancker. Norman Macmillan. William Heinemann Ltd., London.

The Tragedy of R101. E. F. Spanner. The Crypt House Press Ltd., London.

Daily Express March 17, 1928 newspaper article.

Daily Express March 22, 1928 newspaper article.

Daily Express August 1st, 1928 newspaper article.

AUTHOR'S BIOGRAPHY

David Dennington was born in Durham, England, and was raised in Brixton, a suburb of London. He graduated from Brixton School of Building and became an Associate of the Chartered Institute of Building. He traveled and worked in Dubai, the Bahamas, Bermuda and Florida where he worked as a construction manager. He now resides in Virginia with his wife.

For more information please visit the author's website

http://www.daviddennington.com

twitter @ddennington1

facebook

THE AIRSHIPMEN

A NOVEL

DAVID DENNINGTON

Some of the characters in *The Ghost of Captain Hinchliffe* also appear in *The Airshipmen*, an epic adventure, portraying the lives, sweat, tears and heartbreak of the men and women involved in building and flying the great airships of the Golden Age.

Available on line at Amazon worldwide and at retail booksellers.

PRAISE FOR THE AIRSHIPMEN

This is a big story, layered and cinematic, that I did not want to end. I could not imagine myself reading a book about airships, but it's much more than that - it's about blinding love, vaulting ambition, loyalty, greed, deception and the whole gamut of human frailty. It's about a wonderful group of people that I came to love - full of secrets and surprises. This book is hard to put down. **Edith Schorah, Editor, Palm Beach Co., Florida.**

A riveting story that plays out against the background of one of the most intriguing chapters in aviation history. David Dennington weaves a fascinating web of romance, courage, tragedy and shattered dreams and gives the reader a front row seat to eye-opening, high-stakes political battles on two continents. A real page turner with the constant feeling that something new and unexpected is about to unfold.
David Wright, former journalist with the Daily Mirror.

Hats off! A gripping story masterfully told, the book reverberates in the reader's mind long after it is over. The characters are believable and involving, complicated, rich and conflicted. The chronicle renders these historical characters in flesh and blood, their saga replete with concrete and exquisite details. This is a wonderful book—humane and filled with the love of the men for their wives and families while at the same time highly attuned to the highest levels of power and the effect that the decisions made at those echelons influence not only the course of human events on the grand scale, but the very humble small-scale lives of the men caught in the crossfire. It illuminates a fascinating period of recent history almost lost from view and it does justice to the complexities of the personalities of the people involved.
Steven Bauer, former Director of Creative Writing, Miami University, Oxford OH.

An impressively crafted multilayered novel, The Airshipmen is a fully absorbing read from beginning to end and clearly showcases author David Dennington as a gifted storyteller of the first order. A solidly entertaining novel, The Airshipmen is very highly recommended for community library General Fiction collections. **Midwest Book Review**

The Airshipmen is a very human story ... historical fiction based primarily in Britain in the 1920s and follows the sweeping passions and adventures of the airship industry... with main characters, Lou and Charlotte, both beautifully flawed characters. Lou is haunted by his experiences in The Great War, as well as the *R38* disaster, but his love for airships keeps drawing him into a high-risk career path. Charlotte had witnessed the *R38* disaster firsthand. She doesn't trust airships and longs for Lou to walk away from them ... an incredibly interesting fictionalized take on an important time in air travel ... recommended for fans of historical fiction with a touch of fantasy.
Portland Book Review

A very big novel in every way, unique, beautifully written and perfectly paced ... setting the scene so well ... the first of a true new genre ... weaving us around the events of the great *Airship R101* tragedy, the people and places we know well ... with wonderfully rich characters ... researched in immaculate detail. **Alastair Lawson, Vice Chairman, Airship Heritage Trust, Cardington, UK.**

Made in the USA
Lexington, KY
30 August 2017